Sapper is the pen name of Her  at the Naval Prison in Bodmin, Cornwall, where his father was Governor. He served in the Royal Engineers (popularly known as 'sappers') from 1907–19, being awarded the Military Cross during World War I.

He started writing in France, adopting a pen name because serving officers were not allowed to write under their own names. When his first stories, about life in the trenches, were published in 1919, they were an enormous success. But it was his first thriller, *Bulldog Drummond* (1920), that launched him as one of the most popular novelists of his generation. It had several amazingly successful sequels, including *The Black Gang*, *The Third Round* and *The Final Count*. Another great success was *Jim Maitland* (1923), featuring a footloose English sahib in foreign lands.

Sapper published nearly thirty books in total, and a vast public mourned his death when he died in 1937, at the early age of forty-eight. So popular was his 'Bulldog Drummond' series that his friend, the late Gerard Fairlie, wrote several Bulldog Drummond stories after his death under the same pen name.

CONTENTS

CHAPTER I

The Game Begins

Colonel Henry Talbot, CMG, DSO, pushed back his chair and rose from the dinner table. His wife had gone to the theatre, so that he was alone. And on that particular evening the fact caused him considerable relief. The lady of his bosom was no believer in the old tag that silence is golden.

He crossed the hall and entered his study. There he lit a cigar, and threw his long, spare form into an easy chair. From the dining-room came the faint tinkle of glass as the butler cleared the table: save for that and the ticking of a clock on the mantelpiece the flat was silent.

For perhaps ten minutes he sat motionless staring into the fire. Then he pulled a sheet of paper from his pocket and studied the contents thoughtfully, while a frown came on his forehead. And quite suddenly he spoke out loud.

"It *can't* be coincidence."

A coal fell into the grate, and as he bent over to replace it, the flames danced on his thin aquiline features.

"It *can't* be," he muttered.

The clock chimed nine, and as the final echo died away a bell shrilled out. Came a murmur of voices from the hall: then the butler opened the door.

"Captain Drummond and Mr Standish, sir."

Colonel Talbot rose, as the two men came into the room.

"Bring the coffee and port in here, Mallows," he said. "I take it you two fellows have had dinner?"

"We have, Colonel," said Drummond, coming over to the fire. "And we're very curious to know the reason of the royal command."

"I hope it wasn't inconvenient to either of you?" asked the colonel.

"Not a bit," answered Standish. "Not only are we curious, but we're hopeful."

The colonel laughed: then he grew serious again.

"You've seen the evening papers, I suppose."

"As a matter of fact I haven't," said Drummond. "Have you, Ronald?"

"I only got back to London at eight," cried Standish. "What's in 'em?"

There was a short pause: then Colonel Talbot spoke deliberately.

"Jimmy Latimer is dead."

"What!" The word burst simultaneously from both his listeners. "Jimmy – dead! How? When?"

"Put the tray on my desk, Mallows," said the colonel. "We'll help ourselves."

He waited until the butler had left the room: then standing with his back to the fire he studied the faces of the two men who were still staring at him incredulously.

"A month ago," he began, "Jimmy put in for leave. Well, you two know what our leave frequently covers, but in this case it was the genuine article. He was going to the South of France, and there was no question of work. I got a letter from him about a fortnight ago, saying he was having a damned good time, and that he'd made a spot of cash at Monte. He also implied that there was a pretty helping him to spend it.

"Last night, about ten o'clock, I got a call through here to my flat from Paris. Jimmy was at the other end. He told me he was on the biggest thing he'd ever handled – so big that he could hardly believe it himself. He was catching the eight-fifty-seven from the St Lazare Station and crossing via Newhaven. It arrives at Victoria at six o'clock in the morning, and he was coming direct to me here. Couldn't even wait till I got to the office.

"As you can imagine, I wondered a bit. Jimmy was not a man who went in off the deep end without a pretty good cause. So I ordered Mallows to have some breakfast ready, and to call me the instant Jimmy arrived. He never did: when the boat reached Newhaven he was dead in his cabin."

"Murdered?" asked Standish quietly.

"My first thought, naturally, when I heard the news," said the colonel. "Since then we've obtained all the information available. He got on board the boat at midnight, and had a whisky and soda at the bar. Then he turned in. He was, apparently, in perfect health and spirits, though the steward in the bar seems to have noticed that he kept on glancing towards the door while he was drinking. Ordinarily that is a piece of evidence which I should discount very considerably. It is the sort of thing that, with the best will in the world, a man might imagine *after* the event. But in this case he actually mentioned the fact to his assistant last night. So there must have been something in it. And the next thing that was heard of the poor old boy was when his cabin steward called him this morning. He was partially undressed in his bunk, and quite dead.

"When the boat berthed, the police were of course notified. Inspector Dorman, who is an officer of great ability, was in charge of the investigation, and very luckily he knew Jimmy and Jimmy's job. So the possibility of foul play at once occurred to him. But nothing that he could discover pointed to it. There was no sign of any wound, no trace of any weapon. His kit was, apparently, untouched: his money and watch were in the cubbyhole beside the bunk. In fact, everything seemed to indicate death from natural causes.

"But Dorman was not satisfied: there still remained poison. But since that would necessitate a post mortem, and it was clearly impossible to keep the passengers waiting while that was done, he sent one of his men up in the boat-train with instructions to get everybody's name and address. Meanwhile he had the body taken ashore, and got in touch with a doctor. Then he went on board again, and cross-examined everybody who could possibly throw any light on it.

"He drew blank. Save for the one piece of evidence of the bar steward which I have already told you, no one could tell him anything. One sailor thought he had seen someone leaving Jimmy's cabin at about one o'clock, but when pressed he was so vague as to be useless. And so finally Dorman gave it up, and taking all the kit out of the cabin, he sat down to await the doctor's report."

The colonel pitched the stub of his cigar into the fire. "Once again, blank. There was no trace of any poison whatsoever. The contents of the stomach were analysed: all the usual tests were done. Result – nothing. The doctor was prepared to swear that death was natural, though he admitted that every organ was in perfect condition."

"I was just going to say," remarked Drummond, "that I've seldom met anybody who seemed fitter than Jimmy."

"Precisely," said the colonel.

"What do you think yourself, sir?" asked Standish quietly.

"I'm not satisfied, Ronald. I know that the idea of poisons that leave no trace is novelist's gup: I admit that on the face of it the doctor must be right. And still I'm not satisfied. If what that barman said is the truth Jimmy was afraid of being followed. We know that he was on to something big: we know that his health was perfect. And yet he dies. It can't be coincidence, you fellows."

"If it is it's a very strange one," agreed Standish. "And if it isn't it must be murder. And if it was murder, the murderer was on board. Have you a copy of the list of the passengers?"

Colonel Talbot walked over to his desk and handed Standish a paper.

"As you will see," he remarked, "the boat was very empty. Most of the passengers were third class."

"It's not a particularly popular boat, I should imagine," said Drummond. "I mean I can't see anybody who hadn't got to, for economy or some other reason, crossing by that route."

"Precisely," remarked the colonel gravely, and the two men looked at him.

"Something bitten you, Colonel?" cried Drummond.

"Something so fantastic, Hugh, that I almost hesitate to mention it. But it was because what you have just said had struck me also that this wild idea occurred to me. Run your eye down the list of first class passengers – there are only eight – and see if one name doesn't strike you."

"Alexander: Purvis: Reid: Burton... Charles Burton. The millionaire bloke who throws parties in Park Lane... Is that what you mean?"

Colonel Talbot nodded.

"That is what I mean."

"But, damn it, Colonel, what on earth should he want to murder Jimmy for?"

"Not quite so fast, Hugh," said the other. "As I said, the idea may be fantastically wrong. But we've all heard of Charles Burton. We all know that even if he isn't a millionaire he's extremely well off. But who is Charles Burton?"

"I'll buy it," said Drummond.

"So would most people. Where does Charles Burton get his money from?"

"I gathered he was something in the City."

"Which covers a multitude of sins. But to cut the cackle, his name jumped at me out of that list. Why on earth should a man of his position and wealth choose one of the most uncomfortable Channel crossings to come over by?"

"It's a goodish step from that to murder," said Standish.

"Agreed, my dear fellow. But sitting in my office this afternoon, the question went on biting me. And at length I could stand it no longer. So I rang up the Sûreté in Paris, and asked them if they could find out in what hotel he was staying. Of course I knew he'd left, but that didn't matter. A short while after they got back to me to say that he had been staying at the Crillon, but had left for England last night. So I got through to the Crillon, where I discovered that Mr Charles Burton had intended to fly over today, but that he had suddenly changed his mind yesterday evening, and decided to go *via* Newhaven and Dieppe."

"Strange," said Standish thoughtfully. "But it's still a goodly step, Colonel."

"Again agreed. But having started I went on. And by dint of discreet enquiries one or two small but interesting facts came to light. For instance, I gathered that on his frequent journeys to the Continent, he *always* flies. He loathes trains. I further gathered, or rather failed to gather, from various men I rang up, what his business was. He has an office, and the nearest I could get to it was that he was something in the nature of a financial adviser, whatever that may be. No one seemed to know who he was or where he came from. It seems he just blossomed suddenly about two years ago. One day he was not: the next day he was. But the most interesting point of all was a casual remark I heard in the club this evening. His name cropped up and somebody said: 'I sometimes wonder if that man is English.' I docketed that for future reference."

"Look here, Colonel," cried Drummond. "Let's get this straight. You started off by saying your idea was fantastic, but unless I'm suffering from senile decay, you're playing with the theory that Jimmy was murdered by Charles Burton."

"You could not have expressed it better. *Playing* with the theory."

"And you want us to play too?"

"If you've got nothing better to do. I haven't a leg to stand on: I know that. But Jimmy, who was in possession of very important information, died. Travelling in the same boat was a man whose origin is, to say the least, not an open book. Further, a man who, if he did change his habitual method of transport, would surely choose the Golden Arrow. I remember what you two did," he continued, "when that Kalinsky affair was on, over Waldron's gas and Graham Caldwell's aeroplane. You were invaluable, and this *may* be a case of the same type. You both of you go everywhere in London: all I'm asking you to do is to – "

"Cultivate Mr Charles Burton," said Drummond with a grin.

"Exactly, Hugh. For if there is anything in my suspicions, I think you two, acting unofficially, are far more likely to get to the bottom of the matter – or at any rate to get on the trail – than I am through official channels."

"It's a date, Colonel," cried Standish. "But before we push off there are one or two points I want to get clear. In the letter you got from Jimmy a fortnight ago was there any hint he was on to something?"

"None at all."

"Have you heard from him since?"

"Not until he telephoned yesterday."

"So you don't know when he left the Riviera?"

"Not got the ghost of an idea. But we could find that out by wiring the hotel."

"Which was?"

"The Metropole at Cannes."

"I wish you would find out, Colonel. In your position you can do so more easily than we can, and it's information that may prove important."

"I'll wire or 'phone tomorrow, Ronald."

"Just one thing more. I assume some reliable person has gone through his kit and papers with a fine-tooth comb?"

"Dorman himself. There was nothing: nothing at all. But if our wild surmise is correct that is what one would have expected, isn't it? The murderer had plenty of time to examine all the kit himself."

"True," agreed Standish. "And yet a wary bird like poor old Jimmy has half a dozen tricks up his sleeve. Shaving soap: tooth paste…"

"I know Dorman. He's up to every trick himself. And if he says there's nothing there – then there is nothing."

"By the way," put in Drummond, "was Jimmy engaged?"

"Not that I've ever heard of."

"Who is his next of kin?"

"His father – Major John Latimer. Lives at his club – the Senior Army and Navy."

"A widower?"

"Yes. His wife died about three years ago." Drummond rose and stretched himself. "Well, Ronald, old son, it seems to me that we've been handed out what dope there is. Let us go and kiss dear Charles good night."

"One second, Hugh," said Standish. "I suppose you've got no idea, Colonel, what tree Jimmy was barking up?"

"Absolutely none. It may be a spy organisation: it may be a drug gang: it may be anything. But whatever it is, it's something big or Jimmy wouldn't have said so."

"No hint, of course, of the possibility of foul play will appear in the papers?"

"Good Heavens! no," cried Colonel Talbot. "No hint, in fact, that he was anything but an ordinary army officer with a job at the War Office."

He strolled into the hall with the two men.

"I'll let you know what I hear from Cannes," he said. "And you have my number here and at the office. Because I've got a sort of hunch, boys, that the less we actually see of one another in the near future the better. And my final word – watch your step."

A slight drizzle was falling as Drummond and Standish reached the street, and they hailed a passing taxi.

"United Sports Club," said Drummond. "We may as well get down to this over a pint, Ronald."

Standish lit a cigarette.

"A rum show," he remarked. "Damned rum. And the annoying part of it is that it's impossible to find out from Burton whether he had a good and perfectly genuine reason for crossing by that service. He may have had, and in that case the Chief's theory goes up in a cloud of steam. But if he didn't have – "

"In any event he'd manufacture one," Drummond cut in.

"If it wasn't true it might be possible to discover the fact. But the trouble is that it would immediately arouse all Burton's suspicions."

The taxi pulled up at the club, and they went inside. The smoking-room was practically empty, and drawing two easy chairs up to the fire they sat down.

"Let's pool resources, Hugh," said Standish. "What, if anything, do you know of Charles Burton?"

"I have seen him in all about six times," answered Drummond. "I accidentally trod on his foot at some ghastly cocktail party old Mary Wetherspoon threw at the Ritz, and we had a drink over the catastrophe. Save for that I don't think I've addressed three sentences to the man in my life. He seems a reasonable sort of individual though he ain't the type I'd choose to be shipwrecked on a desert island with."

"How did that remark about his not being English strike you?"

"It didn't – particularly. So far as I remember he speaks without the faintest trace of accent. In fact he must do, or the point would have occurred to me. But to be perfectly candid, Ronald, I do not feel that I know the man nearly well enough to form any opinion of him. He is the most casual of casual acquaintances."

"Have you ever been to his house in Park Lane?"

"Once – with some wench. Another cocktail party. I don't think I even spoke to him."

"But the flesh-pots of Egypt all right?"

"Very much so. Though the whole turnout rather gave one the impression that he had issued an ultimatum – 'Let there be furniture: rich, rare furniture. Let there be pictures: rich, rare pictures.'"

"Precisely the criticism I heard," said Standish. "And it rather confirms what the Chief was saying about one day he was not – the next day he was."

"Yes," agreed Drummond doubtfully. "But I don't see that it takes us much further. I can think of three or four men who have suddenly made money, and promptly bought a large house with instructions to furnish regardless of cost."

"Do you know when he bought that house?"

"The time I went there was about a year ago, and so far as I know he'd been in it several months then."

"So presumably he took it when he first blossomed out in the City."

"Presumably."

"It would be interesting to know his history before then."

"That, I take it, he would say was nobody's business."

"D'you see what I'm getting at, Hugh? If by some lucky speculation he made a packet in the City before he burst on society, it is one thing. If on the contrary he just arrived out of the blue, it is another. In the first event Talbot's question as to where he got his money is answered: in the second it isn't."

"It should be easy to find out," said Drummond.

"It doesn't seem as if the Chief has been able to do so, and he can ferret out information from a closed oyster. Of course, he's had a very short time. But I can't help feeling that our first line is Mr Charles Burton's past. Did he have a father who left him money? Did he make it himself, and if so where? Or..."

"Or what?" asked Drummond curiously.

"Has he been installed there for some purpose which at the moment is beyond us?"

"And Jimmy was on the track."

"Exactly. I believe that is what was at the bottom of the Chief's mind. And if so the sorest man in England was our Charles when his name was taken going up in the boat-train."

Hugh Drummond lay back in his chair and lit a cigarette.

"First line settled," he remarked. "But it is the second that contains the snags, I'm thinking. I hardly know the blighter: you, I gather, don't know him at all. How do we set about attaching ourselves to his person with a view to extracting his maidenly secrets? Charlie is going to smell a rodent of that size pretty damn' quick."

"Sufficient unto the day, old boy. It'll have to be worked through mutual friends. By the way, has he got any other house besides the one in Park Lane?"

"Ask me another. Not that I know of, but that means nothing."

Drummond sat up suddenly.

"An idea, by Jove! Algy. Algy Longworth. He knows Burton fairly well. Waiter! Go and telephone to Mr Longworth and tell him to come round to the club at once under pain of my severe displeasure.

"I remember now," he continued, as the waiter left the room. "Burton has got a house in the country somewhere. Algy went and stayed there last summer. Crowds of fairies: swimming-pool: peacocks in the grounds type of thing."

"However he got it the money is evidently there," said Standish dryly.

"Mr Longworth is coming round at once, sir."

The waiter paused by Drummond's chair.

"Good. Then repeat this dose and bring one for Mr Longworth. A drivelling idiot is our Algy," he went on as the man moved away, "but there is a certain shrewdness concealed behind that eyeglass of his which may prove useful."

"At any rate he gives us a point of contact with Burton," said Standish. "And that's all to the good."

Ten minutes later Algy Longworth arrived and Drummond swung round his chair.

"Come here, you pop-eyed excrescence. What the devil are you all dressed up like that for? And you've dribbled on your white waistcoat. You look awful."

"Thank you, my sweet one. Evening, Ronald."

The newcomer adjusted his eyeglass, and smiled benignly.

"Evening, Algy. Take a pew."

"You wish to confer with me – yes? To suck my brain on some deep point of international import? Gentlemen – if I may be permitted so to bastardise the word – I am at your service."

"Look here, Algy," said Drummond, "there *may* be a spot of bother in the air. Only may: we don't know yet. So this conversation is not to go beyond you. What do you know about Charles Burton?"

"Charles Burton!" Algy Longworth stared at him. "What's he been doing? Watering the Worcester sauce? As a matter of fact it's darned funny you should ask that, Hugh; I'm going to that place of his tonight. Hence the glad rags."

"What place? His house in Park Lane?"

"No; no. The Golden Boot."

"The new Club that's just opened? It's Burton behind it, is it?"

"Entirely. He found all the others so ghastly boring that he decided to have one run on his own lines. More than likely he'll be there himself. However, what is it you want to know about him?"

"Everything you can tell. What sort of a bloke is he?"

"He's all right. Throws a damned good party. Stinks of money. Clean about the house and all that kind of thing."

"D'you know where he got his money?"

"Haven't an earthly, old boy. Cornering lights for cats, or something of that sort, I suppose. Why?"

"Where is his house in the country?"

"West Sussex. Not far from Pulborough. I went and stayed there last July."

"I remember you telling me about it," said Drummond. "Algy, would you say he was English?"

Algy stared at him, his glass halfway to his mouth. "I've never really thought about it," he said at length. "I've always assumed he was, especially with that name. He speaks the language perfectly, but for that matter he speaks about six others equally well. I'd put it this way – he isn't obviously not English."

"That I know," said Drummond.

"And I should think Sir George would have satisfied himself on that point," continued Algy. "You know old Castledon – the most crashing bore in Europe?"

"His wife is the woman with a face like a cab horse, isn't she?"

"That's it. Well, Molly, their daughter, is an absolute fizzer. When you see the three of 'em together you feel that you require the mysteries of parenthood explained to you again. However,

Burton met Molly at some catch-'em-alive-'o dance in Ascot week, and as our society writers would say, paid her marked attention. So marked that Lady Castledon who was attending the parade as Molly's chaperon had a fit in a corner of the room, and was finally carried out neighing. She already heard the Burton doubloons jingling in the Castledon coffers, which by all accounts sadly need 'em."

"What's the girl's reaction?" asked Drummond.

"Definitely anti-click. After all, she's young: she's one of this year's brood of debs. But what I was getting at is, that though Sir George can clear a room quicker than an appeal for charity, he's a darned fine old boy. And he's not the sort of man who'd let his daughter marry merely for money, or get tied up with anyone he wasn't satisfied about."

Algy drained his glass.

"Look here, chaps," he said, "it seems to me I've done most of the turn up to date. Why this sudden interest in Charles Burton?"

"We've got your word you'll keep it to yourself, Algy?"

"Of course," was the quiet answer.

"Good. Then listen."

He did – in absolute silence – whilst they put him wise.

"Seems a bit flimsy," he remarked when they had finished. "Though I agree that it's not like Burton to cross *via* Newhaven."

"Of course it's flimsy," said Drummond. "There's not a shred of evidence to connect Burton with Jimmy's death. It's just a shot in the dark on the Chief's part. And if we find out nothing, no harm is done. On the other hand it is just possible we may discover that it was a bull's-eye."

"I must say that he's not a man I'd like to fall foul of," remarked Algy thoughtfully. "I don't think he'd show one much mercy. He sacked the first manager he put into the Golden Boot at a moment's notice for the most trivial offence. But murder is rather a tall order."

"My dear Algy," said Standish, "the tallness of the order is entirely dependent on the largeness of the stake. And if Jimmy was on to something really big…"

He shrugged his shoulders and lit a cigarette.

"Perhaps you're right," said Algy. "Well, boys, I'm afraid I haven't been of much assistance, but I really know very little about the fellow myself. Why don't you come round to the Golden Boot with me now?"

"Short coats all right?"

"Good Lord! yes. Though he insists on evening clothes. Of course, I can't guarantee that he'll be there, and even if he is I don't see that it will do any good. But you might stumble on something, and you're bound to find a lot of people there that you know."

"What about it, Ronald?" said Drummond. "It can't do any harm."

"It can't. But I don't think we'll both go, Hugh. If anything comes out of this show it would be well to have one completely unknown bloke on our side – unknown to Burton, I mean. Now he knows you and he knows Algy; he does not know me. So for the present, at any rate, we won't connect you and me. You toddle off with Algy; as he says, you might find out something. Let's meet here for lunch tomorrow, and I'll put out a few feelers in the City during the morning."

Drummond nodded.

"Sound idea. You've got a wench with you, I suppose, Algy?"

"I'm with a party. Why don't you join up too?"

"I'll see. It's one of these ordinary bottle places, I take it?"

"That's right. Same old stunt in rather better setting than usual – that's all. Night-night, Ronald."

CHAPTER 2

The Golden Boot

As Algy Longworth had said, it was the same old stunt. After a slight financial formality at the door, Drummond became a guest of the management for the evening with all the privileges appertaining to such an honoured position. Though unable to order a whisky and soda, he was allowed – nay, expected – to order a bottle. To consume one drink was a crime comparable to murdering the Archbishop of Canterbury: to consume the entire bottle was a great and meritorious action.

Accustomed, however, as he was to these interesting sidelights on our legal system he gave the necessary order, and then glanced round the room. Being only just midnight there were still many empty tables, though he saw several faces he recognised. It was a long, narrow building, and a band, in a fantastic red and green uniform, was playing at the far end. But the whole get-up of the place was, as Algy had said, distinctly better than usual.

Algy's party had not yet arrived, so they sat down at an empty table, near the microscopic dancing-floor, and Drummond ordered a kipper.

"I'll wait, old boy," said Algy, and at that moment a girl paused by their table.

"Hullo! darling." He scrambled to his feet. "You look absolutely ravishing. Hugh, you old stiff – this is Alice. Around her rotates the whole place: she is our sun, our moon, our stars. Without her we wilt: we die. Hugh: Alice."

"You blithering imbecile," said the girl with a particularly charming smile. "Are you his keeper, Hugh?"

Drummond grinned – that slow, lazy grin of his, which made so many people wonder why they had ever thought him ugly.

"Lions I have shot, Alice; tigers, even field mice; but there is a limit to my powers. When this palsied worm joins his unfortunate fellow guests will you come and kipper with me?"

"I'd love to," she answered simply, and with a nod moved on.

"I'm glad you did that, Hugh," said Algy. "She's an absolute topper, that girl. Name of Blackton. Father was a soldier."

"What's she doing this job for?"

"He lost all his money in some speculation. But you'll really like her. There's no nonsense about her, and she dances like an angel." He lowered his voice. "No sign of C B so far."

"The night is yet young," said Drummond. "And even if he does come I'm not likely to get anything out of him. It's more the atmosphere of this place that I want, and sidelights from other people."

"Alice might help you there," remarked Algy. "She's been here since it opened. Hullo! here come my crowd. So long, old boy, and don't forget if anything does emerge the bunch are in on it."

He drifted away and a smile twitched round Drummond's lips. How many times in the past had not the bunch been in on things? And they were all ready again if and when the necessity arose.

If and when... The smile had gone, and he was conscious of a curious sensation. Suddenly the room seemed strangely unreal: the band, the women, the hum of conversation faded and died. In its place was a deserted crossroads with the stench of death lying thick like a fetid pall. Against the darkening sky green pencil lines of light shot ceaselessly up, to turn into balls of fire as the flares lobbed softly into no-man's-land. In the distance the mutter of artillery: the sudden staccato burst of a machine-gun. And in the ditch close by, a motionless figure in khaki, with chalk white face and glazed staring eyes, that seemed to be mutely asking why its legs should be lying two yards away being gnawed by rats.

"A penny, Hugh."

With a start he glanced up: Alice was looking at him curiously.

"For the moment I thought of other things," he said quietly. "I was back across the water, Alice; back in the days of the madness. I almost seemed to be there in reality – it was so vivid. Funny, isn't it, the tricks one's mind plays?"

"You seemed to me, Hugh, to be staring into the future – not into the past." She sat down opposite him. "The world was on your shoulders and you found it heavy. This is the first time you've been here, isn't it?" she continued lightly.

"The future." He stared at her gravely. "I wonder. However, a truce to this serious mood. Yes, it is the first time I've been here: I've been up in Scotland since it opened. And as such places go it seems good to me. I gather that one Charles Burton is behind it?"

"Do you know the gentleman?" Her tone was non-committal, but he glanced at her quickly.

"Very slightly," he said. "You do, of course."

"Yes, I know him. He is in here most nights when he's in London."

"Do you like him?"

"My dear Hugh, girls in my position neither like nor dislike the great man. We exist by virtue of his tolerance."

Drummond studied her in silence.

"Now what precisely do you mean?" he enquired at length.

"Exactly what I say. Caesar holds the power of life or death. There is no appeal. If he says to me: 'Go' – I go. And lose my job. Which reminds me that you'll have to stand me a bottle of champagne for the good of the house. Sorry about it, but there you are."

Drummond beckoned to a waiter and glanced at the wine list.

"Number 35. Now tell me, Alice," he said when the man had gone, "do you like this job?"

"Beggars can't be choosers, can they? And since secretaries are a drug on the market what is a poor girl to do?"

"Does he expect you to – ?"

"Sleep with him?" She gave a short laugh. "So far, Hugh, I have not been honoured."

"And if you are?"

"I can think of nothing I should detest more. I hate the swine."

"Steady, my dear." For a moment he laid his hand on hers. "The 'swine' has just arrived. And I don't think you'll be honoured this evening at any rate."

A sudden silence had fallen on the Golden Boot. Head waiters, waiters, under-waiters were prostrating themselves at the door. And assuredly the woman who had entered with Charles Burton was sufficient cause. Tall, with a perfect figure, she stood for a moment regarding the room with an arrogance so superb, that its insolence was almost staggering. Her shimmering black velvet frock was skin-tight; she wore no jewels save one rope of magnificent pearls. Her eyes were blue and heavy-lidded; her mouth a scarlet streak. And on one finger there glittered a priceless ruby.

As if unconscious of the effect she had created she swept across the room behind the obsequious manager, whilst Charles Burton followed in leisurely fashion, stopping at different tables to speak to friends. At length he reached Drummond's and the eyes of the two men met.

"Surely…" began Burton doubtfully.

"We met at a cocktail party, Mr Burton," said Drummond with a smile. "I trod on your foot and nearly broke it. Drummond is my name."

"Of course, I remember perfectly. Ah! good evening, Miss Blackton." He gave the girl a perfunctory bow: then turned back to Drummond. "I don't think I've seen you here before."

"For the very good reason that it is the first time I've been. I've only just got back from the north."

"Shooting?"

"Yes. I was stalking in Sutherland."

"Well, now that you've been here once I hope you'll come again. It's my toy, you know."

With a nod he moved on, and Drummond watched him as he joined the woman. Then he became aware that a waiter was standing by him with a note.

"From the gentleman with the eyeglass, sir."

He opened it, and saw a few words scrawled in pencil.

Charlie B. He make whoopee. But what about poor
Molly C.

Drummond smiled and put the note in his pocket.

"From the idiot boy," he said. "Commenting on Mr Burton's girl friend."

"She's an extraordinarily striking woman," said Alice Blackton. "I wonder if he picked her up at Nice."

Drummond stared at her.

"Did you say Nice?"

"I did. He's just come back from the Riviera, you know."

"Has he indeed? That is rather interesting."

She raised her eyebrows.

"I'm glad you find it so. I'm afraid that Mr Burton's comings and goings leave me stone cold."

"Tell me, Alice, why do you hate him?"

"Hate is perhaps too strong a word," she said. "And yet I don't know. I think it's because I don't trust him a yard. I don't mean only over women, though that comes into it too. I wouldn't trust him over anything. He's completely and utterly unscrupulous."

"Are you speaking from definite knowledge, or is that merely your private opinion?"

"If by definite knowledge you mean do I know that he's ever robbed a church – then no. But you've only got to meet him in a subordinate capacity like I have, to get him taped."

She looked at Drummond curiously.

"You seem very interested in him, Hugh."

"I am," said Drummond frankly. "Though the last thing I want is that he should know it."

"You can be sure that I won't pass it on. Why are you so interested, or is it a secret?"

"I'm afraid it is, my dear. All I can tell you is that I'm very anxious to find out everything that I can about the gentleman. And though I can't say why, your little piece of information about his having been on the Riviera recently, is of the greatest value. Do you know how long he was there for?"

"I can tell you when he left England. It was exactly a fortnight ago, because he was in here the night before he flew over."

"I gather he always flies," said Drummond.

"He's got his own machine," remarked the girl. "And his own pilot."

"Did he go over in it this time?"

"I suppose so. He always does."

"Curiouser and curiouser," said Drummond. "I know," he went on with a smile, "that this must seem very mysterious to you. Really, it isn't a bit. But at the moment I just can't tell you what it is all about. Your father was a soldier, wasn't he?"

"He was. Though how did you know?"

21

"Algy told me. Now I can let you in to this much. It is the army that is interested in Mr Burton. I tell you that, because I'm going to ask you to do something for me."

"What?" said the girl.

"Keep an eye on him – that's all, and let me know anything about his movements that you can find out, however seemingly trivial."

"My dear man, I can't do much, I'm afraid."

"You never know," said Drummond quietly. "As I've already told you, that piece of information about Nice is most valuable. Another thing. Not only his movements, but also the people be brings here. Now would it be possible to discover the name of that woman?"

"Presumably he's signed her in, but whether under her real name or not is another matter. I can find out if you like."

"Do – like an angel."

"All right. I'll go and powder my nose."

A good wench, reflected Drummond as he watched her threading her way through the tables. Definitely an asset. And though probably ninety per cent of what she could pass on would be valueless, the remaining ten might not. Witness the matter of Nice. True that would certainly have come out in the course of time – Burton's visit there was clearly no secret. At the same time it was useful to have it presented free of charge, so to speak. But the really important thing was the installation in one of the enemy's camps of a reliable friend.

"OK, baby?"

Algy had strolled over to his table.

"Very much so, old boy. A damned nice girl."

"That's a bit of mother's ruin our Charlie has got with him."

"Alice is just trying to find out who she is. Algy – Burton was at Nice, while Jimmy was at Cannes."

Algy whistled.

"The devil he was. Have you told Alice anything about it?"

"No. Safer not to at present. She doesn't like him, Algy."

"None of the staff do, old lad. Alice – my life, my all – this revolting man hasn't been making love to you, has he?"

"Not so that you'd notice, Algy," laughed the girl, sitting down. "She is a Madame Tomesco, Hugh."

"It has a Roumanian flavour," said Drummond.

"And mark you, boys and girls, I could do with a bit of Roumanian flavouring myself," declared Algy. "I could do that woman a kindness: yes, I could. Well, *au revoir*, my sweets. If he plucks at his collar, Alice, it's either passion or indigestion, or possibly both. You have been warned."

"Quite, quite mad," said the girl. "But rather a dear. You must give me your address, Hugh, before you go, so that I can send along the doings."

He scribbled it down on a piece of paper and his telephone number.

"Be careful, my dear," he said gravely. "I have a feeling that if the gentleman got an inkling that you were spying on him he would not be amused. I'll go further. If there is anything in what we suspect you'd be in grave danger."

Her eyes opened wide.

"How perfectly thrilling! Promise you'll tell me sometime what it's all about?"

"Thumbs crossed. Waiter, let me have my bill. I've put my name on the whisky: keep it for me for next time."

"Come again soon, Hugh," said the girl.

"I sure will. Good night, dear. I really am infernally sleepy."

The rain had ceased when he got outside, and refusing a taxi he started to walk to his flat. Though the Golden Boot was much better ventilated than the average night club, it was a relief to breathe fresh air again. The streets were wet and glistening in the glare of the arc lights: the pavements almost deserted. Every now and then some wretched woman appeared from seemingly nowhere, and it was while he was fumbling in his pocket for some money for one of them that his uncanny sixth sense began to assert itself.

"Bless you! You're a toff," said the girl, but Drummond hardly heard her. He was staring back the way he had come. What was that man doing loitering about, some fifty yards away?

He walked on two or three hundred yards: then on the pretext of doing up his shoe he stopped. The man was still there; he was being followed. With a puzzled frown he strode on; how in the name of all that was marvellous could he have incurred anybody's suspicions?

He decided to make sure, and to do so he employed the old ruse. He swung round the corner from Piccadilly into Bond Street; then he stopped dead in his tracks. And ten seconds later the man shot round too, only to halt, in his turn, as he saw Drummond.

"Good evening," said Drummond affably. "You are not, if I may say so, very expert at your game. Possibly you haven't had much practice."

"I don't know what you're talking about," muttered the other, and Drummond studied him curiously. He looked about thirty, and was decently dressed. His voice was refined: he might have been a bank clerk.

"Why are you following me?" he asked quietly.

"I don't know what you mean. I'm not following you."

"Then why did you stop dead when you came round the corner and saw me? I fear that your powers of lying are about equivalent to your powers of tracking. Once again I wish to know why you are following me."

"I refuse to say," said the man.

"At any rate we advance," said Drummond. "You no longer deny the soft impeachment. But as it's confoundedly draughty here I suggest that we should stroll on together, chatting on this and that. And in case the point has escaped your notice, I will just remind you that I am a very much larger and more powerful man than you. And should the ghastly necessity of hitting you arise, it will probably be at least a week before you again take your morning Bengers."

"You dare to lay a hand on me," blustered the man, "and I'll..."

"Yes," said Drummond politely. "You'll what? Call the police? Come on, little man: I would hold converse with you."

With a grip of iron he took the man's right arm above the elbow, and turning back into Piccadilly he walked him along.

"Who is employing you?"

"I refuse to say. God! you'll break my arm."

"Quite possibly."

And at that moment a policeman came round Dover Street just in front of them.

"Officer," cried the man. "Help!"

For a moment Drummond's grip relaxed, and like a rabbit going down a bolt-hole the man was across the road and racing down St James's Street.

"What's all this, sir?" said the constable as Drummond began to laugh.

"A gentleman who has been following me, officer," he said. "I'm afraid I was rather hurting him."

"Oh! I see, sir."

The constable looked at him significantly and winked. Then with a cheery "Good night, sir," he resumed his beat.

But the smile soon faded from Drummond's face, and it was with a very grave expression that he walked on. He had only got down from Scotland that day, so under what conceivable circumstances could he be being followed? That it was added confirmation that the Chief was right was indubitable: it could not be anything else than the Jimmy Latimer affair. There was literally *nothing* else that it could be. But how had they got on to *him* – Drummond? That was what completely defeated him. For one brief moment the possibility of Alice Blackton being a wrong 'un crossed his mind: then he dismissed it as absurd. What could be her object? She had his address: she knew his name, so what purpose would it serve to have him followed home? But if it was not her who could it be?

He reached his house and produced his latch-key. The road was deserted: there was no sign of the man who had bolted so precipitately. But as he mixed himself a final night-cap he was still frowning thoughtfully. For he had suddenly realised that all the arguments that applied to Alice applied equally to Charles Burton. He, too, knew Drummond's name, and even if he did not know the address he could easily find it in the telephone directory. So again what was the object in having him followed? And the problem was still unsolved when he met Standish just before lunch next day.

"There can be only one solution, Hugh," said that worthy when Drummond had finished telling him. "They picked us up at the Chief's flat. It was he who was being watched, and anybody who went to see him."

He sipped his sherry thoughtfully.

"We ought to have been more careful," he went on. "However, the mischief is done now, so it can't be helped. You see we gave the club address to the taxi driver, which made it easy to follow us here. Then you were shadowed to the Golden Boot: I was almost certainly traced to my flat. As a matter of fact there was a loafer hanging about to open the door of the taxi who could easily have heard the address. And, finally, your friend tried to follow you home."

"But if Burton is at the bottom of it, why worry about me? You, I can understand, but he knows me."

"True, old boy," said Standish, "but he doesn't know, or didn't know then, that you were mixed up in the matter. Assuming for the moment that Burton is at the bottom of it, what happened, as I see it, is this. He issued orders for the

26

Chief's flat to be watched, and anything of interest to be reported to him today. So by this time he knows that I had an interview with the Colonel last night, and that a large man who left the Golden Boot in the early hours was also present at that interview. Which, I fear, points unerringly to you."

"There were a lot of people there, Ronald."

"Well, let's hope for the best. But we mustn't bank on it. We must play on the assumption that Burton knows we're both in the game."

"You are definitely converted to the Chief's theory."

"I am becoming more and more so. Would they have bothered to watch his flat if Jimmy's death had been a natural one? No; the cumulative effect of all this evidence, to my mind, is that Jimmy was murdered. And if he was murdered there is a strong probability that Burton had something to do with it."

"I hope to Heaven I've not put that girl in any danger," said Drummond in a worried voice.

"Drop her a line and tell her to watch her step."

"And this Tomesco woman means nothing in your life?"

"Not a thing. But a name is a matter of small moment."

"Did you find out anything this morning?" asked Drummond.

"Merely additional confirmation that there doesn't seem to be anything to find out. Which in itself is suspicious. He has an office in Fenchurch Street with a small staff. Frequently for days on end he is not there. He doesn't appear to have many clients, and nobody seems to know exactly what his business actually is. One line, apparently, consists of considerable speculation in foreign currencies."

A page boy came up with a letter on a salver.

"From the Chief," said Standish quietly. "Let's see what he's got to say."

He read the letter through; then handed it to Drummond.

DEAR RONALD [*it ran*],

I have been in touch with manager of the Metropole at Cannes. Jimmy died (?) on Wednesday night: he left the hotel most unexpectedly on the Tuesday and caught the Paris express. It came as a complete surprise to the manager as, only that very morning, he had booked his room for another week.

That was all I could get over the phone. Evidently something happened on Tuesday which caused this sudden change of plan. But there is another peculiar feature. He must have arrived in Paris early on Wednesday morning. Why did he not cross earlier, or fly over? What was he doing in Paris all that time? And if the matter was not so very urgent why didn't he wait till Thursday and cross in comfort?

I can't help thinking that one or both of you should go to Cannes, and see if you can pick up any threads there. Possibly also a few discreet enquiries at the Hotel Crillon might help.

Yours,

HENRY TALBOT.

PS. Am sending this from my club. I shall be here for the next hour.

"I agree," said Drummond. "And since we know we've been shadowed, the objection to our being seen together no longer exists. I suggest that we both go."

"OK by me," answered Standish. "Just one moment, old boy: I'm going to drop a line to the Chief. Then we'll discuss plans."

He went to a writing-desk, whilst Drummond lit a cigarette and ordered another glass of sherry. Undoubtedly the Chief was right: they were at a dead end here in London. And in Cannes they might stumble on something.

"Read what I've said, Hugh. I'll send it round by hand to his club."

> DEAR COLONEL,
> We will both go as you suggest. Do you know that Burton was in Nice while Jimmy was at Cannes?
> Your flat is being watched: we were both shadowed last night when we left you. Hugh caught his sportsman who admitted the fact. This looks to me to be strong confirmation of your theory that Jimmy was murdered.
> Have you a line on a Madame Tomesco? She was with Burton last night, and according to Hugh she knocked even the habitués of the Golden Boot – which is financed by Burton – quite flat.
>
> Yours sincerely,
> RONALD STANDISH.
> PS. The messenger will wait for an answer.

It came in five minutes, scribbled characteristically on the back of the note itself.

> Good. Was he, now? That's interesting.
> I'm not surprised. But if it continues *they* will be! Of course he was murdered.
> Afraid not. Will make enquiries.
> H T

"How shall we go?" said Standish as they sat down to lunch.

"Since there are no papers or *triptyques* required for France, I suggest we go by car," remarked Drummond. "It takes a little longer, I know, but once we're there it gives us much more freedom. Shall we do Paris before or after Cannes?"

"After," said Standish decidedly. "Let's begin at the beginning if we can, and work forward."

"And when shall we cross?"

"As soon as possible. What about the four-thirty service *via* Folkestone? The boat leaves at six-thirty. We can be alongside by a quarter to six."

"On our heads," said Drummond. "What's the distance from Boulogne to Cannes?"

"Seven hundred miles odd."

"We can do that tomorrow driving turn and turn about if we start early."

"Right. All settled. And I for one, old boy, am taking a gun."

"You stagger me," grinned Drummond, as he inspected the Stilton. "Personally, I think a piece of this would be just as efficacious."

CHAPTER 3

Midnight Interview

The lounge in the Metropole was full of middle-aged women knitting incomprehensible garments when they arrived there at ten o'clock the following night.

"What a galaxy!" muttered Drummond. "I wonder why Jimmy stopped here."

"I shouldn't think he was in much," laughed Standish.

They were standing by the concierge's desk registering. The management had been enchanted to give them rooms on the third floor facing the sea, and as they signed their names, the manager himself approached with the air of a high priest.

"You are staying long, gentlemen?" he enquired.

"Probably three or four days," said Standish.

The manager sighed. Extras were his life, and these two Englishmen did not look of the type who made a small bottle of *vin ordinaire* last a week, like most of his visitors.

"I wonder if we could have a little private talk in your office," continued Standish. "Perhaps you will join us in a bottle of wine, and we could have it sent in there."

"But certainly," cried the Frenchman. "*Henri! La carte des vins. Messieurs; vous permettez? Une bouteille de dix neuf, et trois verres. Au bureau.* Follow me, gentlemen."

He led the way along a passage, and opening a frosted glass door, he gave a brief order to a girl who was immersed in a vast ledger. She left the room, and, having sat down at his desk, the manager waved Drummond and Standish to two chairs.

"Now, gentlemen. What can I do for you?"

"You have recently had staying here, m'sieur," said Standish, "an English officer called Latimer – Major Latimer."

The Frenchman nodded.

"I had guessed, gentlemen, that that was your business. Only yesterday I was on the telephone to London about him."

"You know, of course, that he is dead."

"Dead!" The manager sat up with an amazed jerk. "Dead! *Ce n'est pas possible.* How did he die?"

"We can rely on your discretion, m'sieur?"

A superb gesture indicated that they could.

"Major Latimer was found dead in his cabin in the Dieppe–Newhaven boat on Wednesday night. And we are not quite sure what caused his death. On the face of it, it appears to have been natural, but he was a singularly healthy man. We know that he was in possession of certain information which he was bringing back to England, and we are very anxious to find out what that information was. Now, in view of what you said over the telephone to London we cannot help thinking that his abrupt departure from this hotel has some vital bearing on the case. What we, therefore, would like to find out is what Major Latimer's movements were on Tuesday last, after he had renewed his room for another week. Because it seems clear that it must have been then, that whatever it was took place."

The waiter paused in the act of pouring out the wine.

"*Pardon, m'sieu. Vous dites mardi? M'sieur le majeur a accompagné Madame Pélain en auto. Ils sont sortis à onze heures.*"

"Merci, Henri."

He dismissed the man, and himself handed the wine to his guests.

"Gentlemen," he cried, "I go – how do you say it – wool gathering. One must be of a discretion, *naturellement*, but since the poor fellow is dead one may be permitted to speak. As you will understand, most things in an hotel like this come to my ear sooner or later, and it would not be an exaggeration to say that the major and Madame Pélain saw much of each other during his stay here. He seemed to prefer her company to that of the other charming ladies whom you saw in the lounge as you passed through."

His mouth twitched behind his moustache, and with one accord Drummond and Standish burst out laughing.

"Precisely, messieurs," continued the manager, laughing himself. "In fact, though perhaps I should not say it, if Madame had not been here, I fear your poor friend would not have remained. It was reported to me by Henri that at dinner the first night he did nothing but call ceaselessly upon the good God to deliver him."

"Do we understand," said Standish, "that Madame Pélain is still in your hotel?"

"*Mais oui, m'sieu*. It is for that I say I go wool gathering. For it is she who can tell you far more than I. But almost certainly will she be at the casino now. It will be a great shock to her. I will swear that she has no idea that he is dead."

He lit a cigarette and looked curiously at the two men.

"Is it permitted to ask, gentlemen, what it is that you think has happened? Is it that you fear he was the victim of foul play?"

"You have struck it, m'sieur," said Drummond. "We think it more than possible that he was murdered."

"*Mon Dieu! c'est terrible.*"

"But please keep that to yourself," said Standish. "All that has appeared in the papers is that he died in his sleep on board the boat. Have you any idea when Madame is likely to return?"

The manager shrugged his shoulders.

"*À minuit, peut-être.* You would wish to talk to her tonight?"

"The sooner the better, Hugh, don't you think?"

"Certainly. Unless she is too tired. Tell me, m'sieur, of what – er – type is Madame?"

"*Très chic: très élégante.*"

"Is there a Monsieur Pélain?"

"I understand Monsieur Pélain resides in Paris," said the manager diplomatically.

"And you think we can rely on anything she may tell us?"

Once again the manager shrugged his shoulders.

"If I knew enough about women, m'sieur, to be able to tell that concerning any member of their sex, I would be President of France. She has a sitting-room: if she consents to receive you – as I am sure she will – you must judge for yourselves. You are not, are you, from Scotland Yard?"

"No. We are just two friends of Major Latimer's."

"And what would you wish me to tell Madame? That he is dead?"

"No," said Standish decidedly. "Just that we are two friends. And please impress upon her that if she is at all tired we would much prefer to wait till tomorrow morning."

A telephone rang on the desk, and the manager picked up the receiver.

"*Certainement, Madame. Tout de suite.* Madame has returned," he went on as be replaced the instrument. "She orders Evian. I will go to her at once and enquire if she will receive you."

"A nice little man," said Drummond as the door closed behind him. "Very helpful and obliging."

"I wonder if we'll get anything out of this woman," remarked Standish thoughtfully. "I shall be interested to see her reaction when she hears that Jimmy is dead. Who's going to do the talking – you or I?"

"You do it," said Drummond. "You're better at it than I am."

The door opened and the manager returned.

"Madame will receive you, gentlemen. I have told her nothing save that you are two friends of Major Latimer. Will you come this way? Her rooms are on the same floor as yours."

The lounge was deserted as they crossed it to go to the lift, and Drummond glanced at his watch. It was just half-past eleven, and he was beginning to wish that the interview had been postponed till the following morning. They had started from Boulogne at five o'clock, and though each of them had had an occasional doze while the other drove, he was feeling distinctly weary. At the same time he was conscious of a little tingle of excitement: would they find out anything worth while, or would they draw blank?

The manager knocked at the door, and a woman's voice called "*Entrez.*"

Madame Pélain was standing by a table in the centre of the room, with the fingers of one hand lightly resting on it. She had not yet removed her cloak, which was open, revealing her evening frock underneath. Her hair was dark and beautifully coiffured: her nails were red though not outrageously so. Attractive, decided Drummond: more attractive than pretty. But, emphatically, a charming woman to look at.

As the manager introduced the two men she gave each of them a keen searching glance: then sinking gracefully into an easy chair she lit a cigarette.

"Do smoke," she said. "Monsieur Lidet tells me that you are friends of Major Latimer."

Her voice was musical: her English almost devoid of accent.

"That is our excuse, Madame," said Standish, "for intruding on you at this hour."

With a murmured apology the manager left the room, and she leaned forward in her chair.

"You have a message for me from him?" she asked.

"I fear, Madame," answered Standish gravely, "that you must prepare yourself for a shock. Jimmy Latimer is dead."

She sat staring at him speechlessly, her cigarette half-way to her lips. And it was obvious to both men that the news had come as a complete shock to her.

"Dead," she stammered at length. "*Mais c'est incroyable.* How did he die, m'sieur?"

Briefly Standish told her and she listened in silence. And when he had finished she still did not speak: she sat in a sort of frozen immobility with her eyes on the carpet. At length she drew a deep breath.

"I wonder," she whispered.

"Yes, Madame?" said Standish quietly.

"You think poor Jimmy was murdered?"

"I think nothing, Madame. But something must have happened on Tuesday to make him change his plans so suddenly, and since you were with him all that day we think you might know what that something was."

For a space she stared at them without speaking.

"How am I to know that you are what you profess to be?" she said at length. "How can I be sure that you are Major Latimer's friends?"

"I fear, Madame," said Standish frankly, "that you can only take our word for it."

Once again she studied them thoughtfully: then, rising, she began to pace up and down the room.

"I'll trust you," she said suddenly: "I will tell you all I know, though I fear it is not very much. On Tuesday Jimmy and I lunched Chez Paquay, a restaurant on the Corniche road between here and St Raphael. Our table was laid in a covered balcony with no window. Almost was it a room from which the window had been removed, with a red brick wall along the side that faced the sea. Another table was laid, but it was empty, and so we had the place to ourselves.

"Suddenly there came a gust of wind. The dust outside swirled in eddies: we gripped the tablecloth to save it blowing away, for it was fierce, that gust. And even as it died away two sheets of paper blew in and settled on the floor. Quite casually Jimmy bent down and picked them up. He glanced at them, and in an instant, m'sieurs, his face changed. To my amazement he crammed them in his pocket, and, even as he did so, we heard footsteps rushing down the stairs.

"'Not a word,' said Jimmy to me.

"The glass door was flung open, and a man dashed in.

"'Pardon,' he cried, 'but have you seen two pieces of paper? They blew out of my bedroom window in the wind and fluttered in here.'

"Jimmy made a pretence of helping him to look.

"'I'm afraid they must have fluttered out again,' he said. 'What sort of size were they?'

"'The size of a piece of note-paper,' answered the man, and he was staring hard at Jimmy. 'And they did not flutter out again.'

"'Then they must still be here,' said Jimmy indifferently.

"He sat down and poured me out some more wine, whilst the man stood hovering by the other table in a state of the most obvious indecision. He was, of course, in a quandary. It was clear to me that the papers were important, otherwise Jimmy would not have acted as he had: it was clear also that the man was convinced that they had not blown away. But what was he to do? Twice he made a step forward as if to speak: twice he drew back. And then he made up his mind.

"'As a mere matter of form, sir,' he said, 'I wonder if you would mind turning out your pockets? The papers are of the utmost importance, and –'

"'What the devil do you mean, sir,' remarked Jimmy, slowly getting up. 'Your suggestion is the most monstrous piece of impertinence I have ever heard. Emphatically I will *not* turn out my pockets. Why, damn it, it's tantamount to accusing me of having taken your two confounded pieces of paper! Get to hell out of it.'

"And then the lobster arrived, and Jimmy resumed his seat, the picture of righteous indignation, while the man, with one last vindictive look at both of us, left the room.

"'Jimmy,' I said, when we were once more alone, 'that was very naughty of you. Why have you stolen the poor man's papers?'

"He looked at me, and I had never seen him so serious.

"'I've only had one fleeting glimpse at them,' he said, 'and I don't propose to do more than that here. But that glimpse was enough to make me wish I could steal all his other papers as well.'

"And it was then, m'sieurs, he told me that he was in your Secret Service, and not, as I had thought, just an army officer *en permission*."

"Just one moment, Madame," said Standish. "This man – was he English?"

"No. He spoke it well, but with a strong accent."

"I see. Please go on, Madame, you are interesting us profoundly."

"We finished our lunch," she continued, "but Jimmy was *distrait*. All the time I could see that he was itching to be gone so that he could examine the papers at his leisure. But he was far too clever to appear to be in a hurry.

"'When one comes,' he said, 'to a restaurant where the food is as famous as here, one takes one's time. It is over little things like that, that mistakes are made. And mistakes in my trade are apt to be dangerous.'

"So we had our coffee and liqueurs, and it was while we were drinking them that the man again came in, this time with a woman of most striking appearance. They took the other table, so that I had ample opportunity to study her. She was tall, slender, and very made-up, with an expression of insolent arrogance. But her expression did not ring true. It was a pose, a mask. The woman was bourgeoise.

"They talked in French, but again that was not their native language. The man's was better than his English: the woman's very good. But they were neither of them French. I tried to listen, but could hear nothing of any interest. Just banalities on food and wine and the beauty of the coast.

"When our bill was brought, the man came over to our table. I saw Jimmy stiffen, but this time it was only to apologise for his apparent rudeness. He again stressed the importance of the papers as his excuse, and there the matter ended, except that as we got into the car escorted by the *patron* Jimmy enquired their name. It was Pilofsky."

Madame Pélain paused and took a sip of Evian water. "On the way back," she continued, "we examined the papers. The first was covered with writing in a foreign language which Jimmy told me was Russian. It was numbered three, and was evidently one of a series. I couldn't read a word of it, and was more interested in the second which, at any rate, was intelligible. It was a map of England and Scotland in outline. Jimmy said it was what you would give to children to fill in the counties. On it were a large number of red dots: I should say thirty or forty. In some places they were closely grouped together: in others they were scattered. And against each dot was a number.

"These numbers varied considerably. The lowest I saw was 50, the highest 2,500. But you will understand, m'sieurs, that it was difficult to read in the jolting car. However, one thing I did notice. It was in your manufacturing districts that the dots were close together, whereas in the agricultural areas they were few and far between.

"I asked Jimmy what he made of it, and he shrugged his shoulders.

"'When I get back to the hotel,' he said, 'I'll try and make a rough translation of this other document. I know a certain amount of Russian, and I may be able to get the gist of it.'

"He left me the instant we got back, and went to his room, whilst I awaited him here. One hour passed, two – and then he came."

Once again she paused and the two men craned forward eagerly.

"M'sieurs," she said deliberately, "I have never seen anyone in such a state of suppressed excitement. He was like a man in a fever: he paced up and down the room like a maniac.

"'God!' he exclaimed again and again, 'if only I could get the rest of those papers.'

"At length he calmed down a little, and threw himself into a chair.

"'A plot,' he said, 'the like of which out-Vernes Jules Verne himself. And I'm only on the fringe of it. Or is it the wild fantasy of a diseased brain?'

"Once more he began pacing up and down, talking half to himself.

"'It's possible... Given the organisation it's possible... And the will to carry it through... Listen, Marie, I have made a rough translation of that paper. I cannot tell even you what it is; the whole thing is too gigantic – too incredible. It might put you in peril yourself. But I must leave for Paris tonight, and then return to England.'

"Naturally," she continued, "I was very disappointed, but I made no effort to dissuade him. To do so would have been wrong, for with a man duty must always come first. But I went with him to the station to see him off. And as he was stowing his baggage in the sleeper I happened to look along the train. Getting into another coach were the Pilofskys; there was no mistaking that woman even at a distance. So I told Jimmy, and his face became grave.

"'I wonder if that means he still suspects me,' he said.

"'I don't see how he can,' I answered, though I was wondering the same thing myself.

"And then just as the train was starting, he leant out of the window.

"If by any chance something happens to me,' he said, 'will you remember one thing? Sealed fruit tins.'"

"Sealed how much?" ejaculated Drummond incredulously.

"Sealed fruit tins," she repeated. "M'sieur, I was as amazed as you. I stared at him with my mouth open, almost wondering if he'd taken leave of his senses. And then the train steamed out, and I returned here. Which is all, messieurs, that I can tell you." She sighed. "Poor Jimmy!"

For a space there was silence, whilst Drummond stared at Standish, and Standish stared at Drummond. The same thought was in both their minds: was the woman trying to pull their legs? All the first part of her story had the genuine ring of truth: but the climax was so utterly bizarre, so apparently fatuous that it had acted like a douche of cold water.

"You have no idea what he meant by this strange remark, Madame?" said Standish after a while.

"*Mais non, m'sieu*," she cried. "It was as incomprehensible to me then as it is to you now."

"There was no little joke that had arisen between you during your acquaintanceship that could account for it," he persisted.

"Monsieur Standish," she said with a certain *hauteur*, "is this the moment I would choose to mention little jokes?"

"I apologise, Madame. But you will, I am sure, agree that the remark seems so meaningless that I was trying to exhaust the possibilities of there being some commonplace explanation. But if there is none then it is quite certain that the words have a definite significance. And what that significance is, it must be our job to find out."

Madame Pélain lit a cigarette.

"Both of you are also in the Secret Service?" she asked quietly.

"Something of the sort," admitted Standish with a smile.

"Then you realise that it is tantamount to signing your death-warrant if you proceed."

"Our death-warrants have been signed so often in the past, Madame," said Drummond cheerfully, "that we keep carbon copies to save trouble. As a matter of interest, however, why are you so very pessimistic?"

She looked at him gravely.

"If it was worthwhile murdering one man because he was in possession of certain information, it is worth while murdering two. And the fact that in reality you have not got that information won't help you, if it becomes known that you have met me. So far as the other side is concerned, they have no idea what Jimmy told me. He might have told me everything, and I might have passed it on to you."

"That is true, Madame," agreed Standish. "What alarms me, however, far more than that, is the possibility that you may be in danger."

She shrugged her shoulders.

"Fortunately, m'sieur, I am a fatalist. I don't know if you have been out East; if so you will understand. *Tid apa.* Nothing matters. Jimmy was a dear; I liked him immensely. And if I can do anything to bring his murderer to book, you can count on me."

"Good for you, Madame," cried Drummond approvingly. "At the same time, speaking on behalf of all my sex, please be careful."

She flashed him a swift smile.

"*Merci, m'sieu,*" she murmured. "*Vous êtes gentil.* But what," she continued, becoming practical again, "do you propose to do now?"

"That requires a little thought," said Standish. "At the moment, it doesn't seem to me that there is much more to be found out here."

"I suppose, Madame," put in Drummond suddenly, "that you have never met a man called Charles Burton on the Riviera? He was staying at Nice recently."

She shook her head.

"I do not recall the name," she said. "Burton: no. Do you know at what hotel he put up?"

"I have no idea," answered Drummond. "Though one should have no difficulty in finding that out. He is a gentleman of great wealth, who would certainly stop at one of the best."

"Is he involved in this matter?"

"We do not know," said Drummond. "We think that possibly he may be. He was at Nice while Jimmy was here."

"Jimmy never mentioned him to me."

"There was no reason why he should. I doubt if he even knew the man. Well, Ronald," he went on, "I think we have kept Madame up quite long enough. What about a spot of bed?"

The two men rose.

"One minute before you go," she said. "With regard to this Mr Burton. There is a man in Nice – an Englishman – who has made it his headquarters for years. He is a strange character; very intelligent; very cultured; very cosmopolitan. But if anybody can give you information about any well-known visitor, he can. His name is Humphrey Gasdon, and he lives at the Negresco. If you like you can easily meet him."

"It must be done with great discretion, Madame," said Standish. "The last thing we want is even a hint that Charles Burton is anything but what he professes to be."

"But why should there be any hint? Go, tomorrow, and lunch at the Negresco. Humphrey is invariably in the bar before lunch. Equally invariably does he talk to all and sundry whom he meets there. Mention that you come from this hotel in the most casual manner, and he will almost certainly ask if you know me…"

"Which we don't, Madame," cut in Standish. "Don't forget that. So far as is humanly possible we wish to keep you out of this. Tomorrow we meet as strangers."

He paused suddenly, staring at Drummond.

"What is it, Hugh?"

Moving with the silence of a cat, Drummond was crossing towards the door that led to Madame Pélain's bedroom. Crouched double, he flung it open, and even as he did so, there came the sound of the door leading into the corridor being closed.

He darted across the room, and opened it. The corridor was empty, but just opposite the splash of water proclaimed that someone was turning on a late bath.

He returned to the sitting-room and his face was grave.

"Too late for that pretence, Ronald," he said. "Someone has been listening."

"Their espionage system is certainly efficient," remarked Standish after a pause, watching Drummond who had gone to the sitting-room door and was peering out.

"Still running the water," he said. "This complicates matters," he continued, coming back into the room.

"It's obviously a guest or an employé of the hotel," said Standish thoughtfully. "Have you noticed anyone particularly these last two or three days, Madame?"

She shook her head.

"Because it is clearly you who are being watched. The same as in London, Hugh. They got on to us there through the Chief: they've got on to us here through Madame."

"But, m'sieur," she cried, "have you no inkling at all as to who 'they' are?"

"Not the faintest, Madame," he answered. "But they are thorough in their methods, to put it mildly."

"In any case it simplifies one thing," she said quietly. "Since they know you have met me I shall come with you openly to

Nice tomorrow for lunch. I do not like being spied upon from my bedroom."

She rose and held out her hand.

"Good night, messieurs. You must assuredly be tired after your long run."

With a nod and a charming smile she dismissed them, and for a moment or two they stood talking in low tones outside her door. The bath was still occupied and Drummond eyed the door longingly.

"I would greatly like to see the occupant," he muttered.

"So would I," agreed Standish. "What do you make of her, Hugh?"

"Genuine," said Drummond promptly. "I believe every word she said. I hope to Heaven she's in no danger."

"She is sure to lock her door," answered Standish. "Anyway, old boy, I'm practically asleep as it is. We'll make discreet enquiries from Monsieur Lidet tomorrow, and see if we can get a line on the listener. Night-night."

He opened his door, and Drummond went on to his own room, where he unpacked his bag. Then he undressed and got into bed, to find that all desire for sleep had left him. Light was streaming into his room through a frosted glass window over the door, and he grew more and more wide awake. And then the light went out: save for a faint glimmer from a street lamp outside, the room was in darkness.

From across the road came the low murmur of the sea: except for that the night was silent as the tomb. Occasionally the leaves of an acacia tree outside his window rustled in a fitful eddy of wind, and once a belated motor passed the hotel at speed. Cannes slept: at length he began to feel drowsy himself.

Suddenly he sat up in bed: a dim, flickering light was illuminating the glass above the door. It moved jerkily, increasing in power: then it died away again, and in a flash Drummond was putting on his dressing-gown. Somebody was moving in the passage outside carrying a torch or a candle.

He crossed to the door, and with infinite care he opened it and peered out. And what he saw made him draw in his breath sharply. Some way along the corridor a circle of light was shining on a keyhole – a keyhole into which a hand was inserting a key. And the keyhole was that of Madame Pélain's bedroom.

Not for an instant did he hesitate. The possibility of his appearance on the scene proving embarrassing he dismissed as absurd: if Madame was entertaining anyone she would hardly expect him to pick the lock. And so it transpired that the owner of the hand, though blissfully unconscious of the fact, had behind him, two seconds later, a foe more dangerous far than anything he had ever imagined in his wildest dreams.

At length the key turned, and inch by inch the hand pushed the door open. Then the torch illuminated the bed, and there came a sigh of relief. Madame, breathing a trifle heavily, was fast asleep.

The torch moved forward: still she did not stir, even when it halted by the bed. And then things happened quickly. For the hand that had held the key now held a stiletto, and even as it was raised to strike, a scream like a rabbit caught by a stoat, came from its owner's throat.

The dagger and torch dropped from nerveless fingers and still Madame slept. Came a crack and a howl of agony, and the room was flooded with light. And the owner of the hand, the arm of which was now broken, stared fascinated at the terror which had come on him out of the night – a terror which had just been joined by a companion.

"I heard the commotion, Hugh," said Standish. "What's the trouble?"

"Attempted murder," answered Drummond, picking up an empty tumbler from beside the bed and sniffing it. "Drugged," he said laconically.

"Who is this little swine?"

"The would-be murderer. I've just broken his arm. Well, you rat, who and what are you?"

The man scowled and said nothing.

"Ring the bell, Ronald," said Drummond. "Presumably there's a night porter about. We must get Lidet up."

At length a sleepy-eyed individual came padding along the corridor in carpet slippers, and he was promptly despatched to rouse the manager. Fortunately no one else seemed to have been awakened by the noise, and when Monsieur Lidet arrived a few minutes later he found the two Englishmen leaning up against the door smoking.

"I fear, monsieur," said Drummond, with a smile, "that we are rather stormy petrels."

"But what has happened?" cried the little man.

"That engaging feller over there endeavoured to murder Madame Pélain, having previously drugged her, with the stiletto you see on the floor."

"Murder Madame," stammered the manager. "But it is Louis – one of the floor waiters."

"Nice pleasant manners he's got," said Drummond. "Very suitable for bringing one's breakfast."

"You vile scoundrel," cried Monsieur Lidet in a frenzy. "Have you nothing to say?"

"I should think he's got a lot," remarked Drummond. "But he doesn't seem to want to say it."

"Villain, dastardly villain." The manager was almost beside himself with rage. "What did you want to murder Madame for?"

The man shook his head sullenly, and then a groan burst from his lips.

"I broke his arm for him," explained Drummond. "Well, m'sieur, I suggest that you send for the police. Perhaps they will loosen his tongue. And since Madame may wake at any moment, I suggest also that we await their arrival somewhere else. It might embarrass her to find cohorts of men in the room." They went down to the lounge, where he turned to the waiter. "And if you try to bolt, you scum, I'll break your other arm."

But there was no fight left in the would-be murderer; he sat dejectedly in a chair with his eyes fixed on the ground awaiting the gendarmes.

"What do you make of it, Ronald?" said Drummond in a low voice.

"It's clear that the motive was not robbery," answered Standish. "Having drugged her, there was no need to murder her if that was the case. I'm inclined to think, old boy, that it was an attempt to kill two birds with one stone."

"You mean – "

"I mean that if Madame Pélain had been found dead when she was called tomorrow morning, you and I would have been in a very awkward position. We were the last people to be with her: our arrival at the hotel and our whole interview with her was unusual. And I think we should have found ourselves very seriously inconvenienced by enquiries."

"I'm afraid we still shall," said Drummond.

"Not if we can persuade Lidet to keep his mouth shut. There is no doubt, of course, that it was Louis you heard in her bedroom, and there is no doubt that it is our arrival here and our interview with her that has caused the whole thing. But I don't see why we should tell the police all that – at any rate, at present."

"He may speak." Drummond jerked his thumb at the waiter.

"On the other hand he may not. If, as seems fairly obvious, we are up against some powerful organisation, he may be frightened to tell the truth. Here is Lidet."

"The police are coming at once," said the manager as he joined them. "It is a terrible thing this, gentlemen."

"It might have been very much worse, m'sieur," answered Standish. "Thanks to Captain Drummond no harm has actually been done. Which brings me to a request I am going to make to you. Had Madame Pélain been murdered it would, of course, have been impossible to keep back anything. But since she is unharmed I am going to ask you not to mention what we told you last night about Major Latimer."

"You think there is a connection between the two things?"

"Undoubtedly. Otherwise the coincidence would be too incredible. We are moving in deep waters, M'sieur Lidet: how deep neither Captain Drummond nor I have at present any idea. But it will seriously hinder our enquiries if what we have told you is made public."

The manager looked doubtful.

"But is it fair to Madame?"

"Let us leave that until Madame can answer the question herself," suggested Standish.

"What then will you say?"

"The truth – so far as it goes. That Captain Drummond being wakeful, heard a sound in the corridor and looked out of his room. He saw Madame's door being opened, and fearing foul play he dashed along just in time to avert a brutal crime. Believe me, m'sieur," he continued earnestly, "there is much at stake. We are only on the fringe of things at the moment, and it is vital that we should remain free to carry on our investigations. As I said to Captain Drummond, I am sure that one object of the attempted crime was to incriminate us. Had it succeeded he and I would have been in a nasty hole. And that is why I don't want a word said which will enlarge the scope of the police enquiry. Let it remain what it appears to be on the surface – an inexplicable attempt at murder."

"Very good, gentlemen," said the manager. "I will do as you ask. But only on the condition that Madame, when she recovers from the effect of the drug, must be consulted."

"Certainly," answered Standish. "I quite agree with you. And now," he continued to Drummond as the manager went forward to greet the police who had just arrived, "all we can hope for is that that little worm of a waiter keeps his mouth shut."

Which was precisely what he did do. No amount of cross-questioning – an art at which the French police are adept – had the smallest effect. He maintained an air of sullen silence, which even threats could not shake. And at length he was removed in custody by the two gendarmes, while the sergeant remained behind at the hotel to make a search through his belongings. This, too, proved abortive: nothing of the smallest interest was discovered. In fact the only information of any value came from the head waiter who had been fetched from his bed. According to him the man, Louis Fromac, was a good and reliable waiter in every way: he would have to be so in order to be promoted to a floor, which was always regarded as a prize. But, though he never talked of such things in the hotel, he spent most of his leisure in a small inn, situated in the old part of the town, which was the headquarters of a revolutionary club. So far as he knew the members did no harm: they drank much wine and talked interminably.

"I, too, know that club," said the sergeant. "It is the head-quarters of the Communists in Cannes." He shrugged his shoulders. "They shout at one another without waiting for an answer, and think they are rebuilding the world. No, gentlemen, the more I think of it the more do I believe that this is one of those strange sex crimes of which one hears from time to time. It is more a matter for a doctor than for the police. But I will return tomorrow morning when Madame is recovered, and see if perchance she can throw any light on his motive."

He bowed to the three men, and left the hotel.

"His theory suits us, Hugh," said Standish as they walked up the stairs. "And the one thing we've got to do is to get Madame's ear before the worthy sergeant does his stuff."

"Anything in this Communist business?" remarked Drummond thoughtfully.

"It seems to me to be the one ray in the darkness," said Standish. "Though what the links are between Charles Burton, millionaire, and Louis Fromac, waiter, is a bit obscure."

"Think so, Ronald? I don't. The links are two sleepy Englishmen, one of whom, at any rate, is now going to bed. Night-night."

CHAPTER 4

Fair Warning

Their luck was in next day. It seemed to Drummond that his head had only touched the pillow when he was awakened by a waiter with a note. It was from Madame Pélain.

"Please come to my sitting-room at once."

The sun was pouring in at the window as he shaved rapidly, and then scrambled into his clothes. And as he stepped into the corridor he ran into Standish evidently bound on the same errand.

Madame was in a peignoir, and though pale she was completely self-possessed.

"There is no time to lose," she began at once. "The sergeant of police is waiting below to see me. I have heard what has happened from Monsieur Lidet: I have heard, Captain Drummond, that I owe you my life. But the immediate point is, what am I to say to the sergeant? Lidet has told me the line you took up last night: is that what you want me to stick to?"

"It is, Madame," said Standish promptly. The telephone jangled on the table, and she picked up the receiver.

"*En cinq minutes,*" she said.

"You wish me to profess complete ignorance as to the reason of this waiter's action?"

"Please, Madame."

"It was, of course, connected with Jimmy's death and our interview last night."

"I see no other possibility," said Standish. "But with all due deference to the worthy sergeant, I think we are more likely to progress if he knows nothing about it."

"Very good, messieurs. I will do as you say. It will be well now if you return to your rooms. We must not let the sergeant think that we have been arranging things. Come back in half an hour."

They bowed and left her.

"A worthwhile ally, Ronald," said Drummond. "I liked that prompt, unquestioning acquiescence. Come and bite a roll in my room."

Standish poured himself out a cup of coffee and strolled over to the window.

"Worthwhile she may be, old boy," he agreed, "but it complicates matters. I don't quite know what we're going to do about her. There are other Louis Fromacs, and next time you may not be awake."

"You think they'll have another dip at her?"

"We dare not risk them not doing so. Though everything depends, of course, on the motive behind the attempt on her life. If it was merely to involve us with the police, and keep us tied by the heels here for some days, then she would be safe the instant we leave Cannes. But if there was any question of revenge in the matter, or if they have decided that she knows too much, she won't be safe wherever we are."

"If it was a question of her knowing too much, why did they wait to strike? They could have doped her two nights ago."

"That's perfectly true." Standish lit a cigarette. "And yet there is a certain Machiavellian cunning in getting at us through her which I should have said was a bit above a waiter's form."

"But, my dear fellow, Fromac is very small beer. He was only carrying out instructions."

"When did he get 'em? No one knew we were coming here till we arrived."

"Not you and I personally, I grant you. But they must have guessed that *somebody* would arrive here to pump the lady. At any rate they took precautions in case anybody did come. If they were wrong, and no one came, then she was safe. There was no point in murdering her unnecessarily. What is more," continued Drummond, "it seems to me that there is no object in murdering her at all now. So far as they know we two are in possession of all the dope, so that getting her out of the way is merely bolting the stable door after the horse has hopped it. It's you and I, old son, who will have to watch our step."

"That's nothing new," said Standish with a grin. "I wonder who this man Gasdon is she wants us to meet," he went on thoughtfully.

"What I wonder a darned sight more," remarked Drummond, "is what poor old Jimmy meant by sealed fruit tins."

There came a knock at the door, and Monsieur Lidet entered.

"None the worse, I trust, gentlemen," he asked solicitously, "for your disturbed night?"

"Not a bit, thank you," answered Drummond.

"Since the matter was bound to come out, I have let it be understood that the whole thing was an attempt on Madame's jewels," continued the manager. "It is as good a story as any other and it will satisfy the visitors. By the way, the sergeant is interrogating Madame now."

"We have already seen Madame," said Standish. "She has agreed to follow our suggestion as to what she tells him."

"Then the condition I made is fulfilled, gentlemen. And as for me, my lips are sealed. But I confess to an overwhelming curiosity."

"Which I can assure you we would gratify if we knew the answer ourselves," said Standish frankly. "But we are every bit as much in the dark as you are. There is, perhaps, one thing you could do for us," he added as an afterthought. "A Mr Charles Burton was stopping at Nice about a week or ten days ago. Could you find out at what hotel he was staying and when he left? He is a man of considerable wealth, and so it would probably be one of the biggest."

"I will do so at once," cried Monsieur Lidet. "I have below the *listes des etrangers* of the past month."

He bustled out of the room, and a few moments later the telephone rang. Drummond answered it.

"Thank you, m'sieur," he said when the voice ceased. "That is just what we wanted to know."

He replaced the receiver.

"Burton stayed at the Ruhl for the inside of a fortnight," he said. "He left last Friday."

"Before the Pilofsky episode at Chez Paquay."

"Exactly. Before that episode. It is, therefore, clear that Burton's departure was quite unconnected with Jimmy getting those papers."

"So that if Burton murdered him it was because of what he learned from Pilofsky."

"Undoubtedly," said Drummond. "Pilofsky followed Jimmy to Paris, and there told Burton what had happened. My hat! old man, those papers must have been important. Remember Pilofsky had no proof that Jimmy had got them. And yet the bare chance of his having them was enough for murder."

"Jimmy's sudden change of plan was suspicious. Pilofsky would have had no difficulty in tracing him to this hotel. He could have made enquiries from the driver of the car the instant he first suspected anything at Chez Paquay. Then it was easy money to discover that Jimmy, after taking on his room that very morning, had suddenly decided to leave. And a bloke who's running round with a delightful woman like Madame Pélain doesn't do that without a mighty good reason."

Once again the telephone rang: this time it was the lady herself to say that the police had gone and that she would like to see them.

"First and foremost," she said as they entered her sitting-room, "I want to thank you, Captain Drummond, for what you did."

"It was nothing, Madame," said Drummond lightly. "The astounding piece of luck was that I happened to be awake, in view of how infernally sleepy I'd felt a bit earlier on."

"Even so, *mon ami*, not everyone would have troubled to get out of bed in the middle of the night as you did. However," she added with a smile, "it is not difficult to see that you are the type of man who would loathe any further allusion to the subject."

"You're quite right there, Madame," laughed Standish. "He might even blush."

"And so," she continued, "let's come to the next point. What do we do now?"

The laugh faded: Standish looked at her gravely.

"Madame," he said, "there is no good in beating about the bush. Last night's events prove conclusively that we are up against a powerful and dangerous organisation. What that organisation is it is Captain Drummond's and my job to try and find out. With you, however, it is a different matter altogether. You have become mixed up in it by a sheer accident, and to be perfectly frank I do not see that you can help us any more. You have told us all you know, and it merely means that you are running an unnecessary risk by remaining here."

"What then do you suggest that I should do?" she asked quietly.

"Disappear, at any rate temporarily," answered Standish. "Go on a motor tour; anything you like. It will be necessary for us to remain here for a day or two over this Fromac affair, but then we shall be returning to England ourselves. And I know that we shall both feel easier in our minds if we know you are safe."

"What about Humphrey Gasdon?" she asked.

"The main object in meeting him has gone," said Standish. "We have found out from Lidet about Charles Burton. He left the Ruhl in Nice last Friday. From there he went to Paris."

"Nevertheless," she said thoughtfully, "I would like you to meet Humphrey. I have a feeling, Mr Standish, that he can help you. As I told you last night he is a strange man, with an almost uncanny knowledge of all sorts of strange things."

"Well, Madame," remarked Standish, "from what you said there should be no difficulty in making his acquaintance at the bar."

"None. For all that, I think I will come too. Stop, please," she said with a smile as Standish started to protest. "Your solicitude for my safety is very sweet and I appreciate it. But I am not going to run away from here because a miserable waiter tries to stab me. And that being the case I, personally, shall lunch with Humphrey today. I want his opinion on this strange attempt on my life. You and Captain Drummond must, of course, please yourselves. But should you happen to be in the bar of the Negresco at twelve o'clock today we could doubtless all lunch together."

"We capitulate, Madame," laughed Standish. "So may we have the pleasure of taking you over?"

"*Enchanté, m'sieu.* I will be in the lounge at eleven-thirty."

"What about a leg-stretcher?" said Drummond as they went down the stairs, but Standish shook his head.

"Not for me, old boy. Developments in this affair are so rapid that a full report to the Chief is indicated."

"Perhaps you're right," said Drummond. "Thank God! no one can read my writing, so get to it, my trusty old comrade."

He strolled through the open door and across the promenade. The sea was at its bluest, and for a while he stood, with eyes half closed, accustoming himself to the glare. To the right behind the Casino lay the harbour full of yachts of all sizes, and after a time he sauntered in that direction. How often, he reflected savagely, must Jimmy have taken the same stroll!

By the door of the Casino he paused: should he go in and have a look at the papers? He decided he would and, after getting the *Continental Daily Mail* from the reading-room, he threw himself into an easy chair by the big window in the bar.

The place was almost empty, and beckoning to the barman he ordered some beer. And it was while he was consuming it, resignedly – in Drummond's estimation, French beer was an outrage on public decency, and a probable cause of civil riot – that he noticed two men standing by the door in earnest conversation. And suddenly one of them glanced at him, only to look away immediately on catching his eye.

A faint smile twitched round his lips: some more developments for Standish. Then from behind his paper he waited the next move.

It came shortly. One man left the place; the other having given an order to the barman, came over to the window and took the easy chair next to his.

"Captain Drummond, I believe," he began without any preamble.

"Your belief is correct," said Drummond. "Though I fear you have the advantage of me."

"My name is quite immaterial," remarked the stranger, lighting a cigarette. "From what happened at the hotel last night I gather that you are a man of prompt action. Am I right?"

Drummond stared at him thoughtfully.

"Let us proceed on that assumption," he said.

"Good. I am going to suggest a very prompt action to you now."

Drummond raised his eyebrows.

"Very kind of you," he drawled. "I am agog with excitement."

"It is," continued the man calmly, "that you quit this place, and go on quitting. That you disappear entirely from the haunts of men, you and your friend – and hide yourselves, where not even your wife, if you have one, can find you."

"Splendid," cried Drummond, pouring out some more beer. "May I ask why you suggest those somewhat drastic manoeuvres?"

"For the simple reason that if you don't do what I say you will be killed as surely as night follows day. You laugh, but I can assure you, Captain Drummond, that it is no laughing matter. I myself am running a grave risk in talking to you. But I disapprove of life being taken unless it is unavoidable. And so I am warning you: disappear. For you have no more chance of escaping, if you continue on your present line, than a moth has of coming alive out of a killing-bottle."

"My dear fellow, your solicitude for my safety is as touching as your simile is apt. What, precisely, may I ask, *is* my present line?"

"You are out here in connection with the death of Major Latimer," answered the man quietly. "Further enquiries on that subject can only result in your own. So if you take my advice you will beat it while the going is good."

The man drained his glass and rose to his feet.

"I can assure you," he went on, "that I am not exaggerating. I am speaking honest, unvarnished truth. You are meddling in things of the magnitude of which even I have only a hazy idea. And if you go on doing so you will die with the utmost certainty. Good morning."

"It would be a much better one if this beer wasn't so foul," said Drummond. "However, I'm much obliged to you for our entertaining little chat."

He watched the man till he was out of sight: then he beckoned to the bar-tender.

"Have you any idea who that gentleman was?" he asked.

"None at all, sir," said the barman. "I've never seen him before."

Drummond lit a cigarette, and lay back in his chair. That the man had been in earnest he had no doubt. The quiet way in which he had spoken, the complete absence of any truculence or threats, proved that. And the calm assurance with which he had mentioned Jimmy Latimer showed that he had reliable inside information.

It was very decent of the man, reflected Drummond. What he had said about the risk he ran himself was in all probability correct. And he had done it for an absolute stranger. The point to be decided, however, was what notice, if any, should be taken of the warning.

All through his long and troublous career, there was one mistake Drummond had never committed: he had never underestimated his opponents. And the extreme efficiency of the staff work on the other side, in this case, showed that it was doubly important not to do so now. The difficulty lay in the fact that neither Standish nor he knew who those opponents were, whereas they themselves were marked down. As things stood at the moment, the dice were heavily loaded against them. Moreover, he failed to see how that state of affairs could be rectified unless they actually did what the stranger had recommended – disappear.

Suddenly he saw Standish strolling along the road outside, and knocking on the window he beckoned him in.

"I've had a little chat since I left you, Ronald," he said. "With a stranger of kindly disposition."

Standish listened in silence, though his face became more and more grave.

"It's not the threat of death that I mind," he said when Drummond had finished. "We're used to that. It's the infernal quickness of their information bureau."

"Have you got that letter off to the Chief?"

"Yes. But I'll send along a postscript about this. In any event one thing is now absolutely *proved*. Jimmy was murdered."

"That's so." Drummond glanced at his watch. "What about this lunch?"

"I'm still for going. It won't compromise Madame Pélain more than she is compromised already, and the whole thing is so incredibly obscure that any chance of a ray of light ought not to be missed. But we'd better watch our step with the gentleman."

"You bet your life," said Drummond. "Let's get the bus."

They walked in silence through the drifting crowd of loiterers, each busy with his own thoughts. It was a perfect Riviera day, and the sun had brought the antiques from their lairs in droves. Vendors of tinted spectacles proffered their wares hopefully: it seemed impossible that there could be anything dark and sinister under the surface. And when they brought the car round to the hotel to find Madame Pélain waiting for them, completely surrounded by the knitting brigade, it seemed more impossible still. Nothing more nerve-shattering than a dropped stitch could ever happen in such an atmosphere.

She seemed in no way surprised when Drummond told her of his encounter in the Casino. But her reaction to it was very definite.

"It is what you must both do, my friends. I have been thinking things over since I saw you. When you leave Cannes you must vanish into thin air. If, as we think, big things are afoot, you must become the hunters and not the hunted. It is they who must be in ignorance of where you are going to strike: not the other way round, as it is at the moment."

"There is a lot in what you say, Madame," said Standish. "And my own inclination would be to get away at once. The trouble is the police formalities over last night."

"I think," she said, "that I can probably arrange matters over that. For I, too, have come to the conclusion that Cannes is not the only place in the world. And if I announce my intention of not pressing the charge against the wretched man, there should not be much bother."

She smiled slightly.

"Our police are very amenable at times."

"I am glad you have decided that," remarked Drummond. "We shall both feel easier in our minds. And even though I think that as soon as we have gone you will be safe, don't relax your guard, Madame. I am beginning to have a very healthy respect for these gentlemen, whoever they may be."

They swung into the Promenade des Anglais and a few minutes later pulled up outside the Negresco.

"Now let us see if we are in luck," she said, as they entered the hotel. "We are; the man himself."

A tall, hatchet-faced man was standing by the concierge's desk glancing through a bundle of letters. On one cheek was the scar of an old wound, and his hands were the hands of a man on whose face such a mark would cause no surprise. His hair was greying: his age, the early fifties. And both Drummond and Standish, than whom no better judges of a man existed, metaphorically put their thumbs up.

"Good morning, Humphrey."

With a start he looked up.

"Marie!" he cried, and bending over kissed her hand – an action which only one Englishman in a hundred can do without looking a fool. "This is delightful. You will join me in an aperitif?"

"Humphrey, I want you to meet two friends of mine – Captain Drummond and Mr Standish."

"Delighted. Let us become further acquainted in the bar. My mail seems more unbelievably dull than usual. And now" – when they were settled in a corner – "tell me what fortunate chance has brought you here?"

"Easily told," she laughed. "The fact that Captain Drummond couldn't sleep last night."

"I fear I may seem dense," he said with a smile, "but I think you must admit that your remark requires a little elucidation."

He listened in silence, and when she had finished, he lit a cigarette thoughtfully.

"I congratulate you, Captain Drummond," he said at length. "Though you hardly look the sort of bloke with whom congratulations cut much ice. What a very remarkable story!"

"Can you throw any light on the darkness, Humphrey?" And then she gave a sudden exclamation. "Look, Captain Drummond," she whispered. "Just coming into the bar now. Madame Pilofsky."

Drummond glanced up, and as quickly looked away again.

"Pilofsky," he muttered. "Ronald, it's Madame Tomesco."

"Pilofsky!" drawled Humphrey Gasdon, as she went back into the hall. "Tomesco! A rose by any name, etc. What seems more to the point, however, than the name, is the rose itself."

"Do you know the lady?" asked Drummond.

"By sight – well."

"Who is she?"

"The mistress of one of the most dangerous men in Europe – Menalin."

"Good God!" cried Standish. "The Russian financier."

"Is he Russian? Who knows? He is cosmopolitan. He knows no country: he cares for no country. He cares for nothing in this world save himself. And he is mad."

"Mad!" echoed Standish.

"Not in the sense of a man who thinks he is a poached egg and calls for toast to sit down on. But in an infinitely more dangerous way. He is the world's supreme megalomaniac, and the main driving passion of his life is his hatred of Britain and things British – a sentiment which he does not share alone."

"Now, Humphrey." Madame Pélain shook an admonitory finger at him.

"It's no good doing that, Marie. I know you think I've got a bee in my bonnet over it, but I know also that you know I'm right."

"You think as a nation we are disliked?" said Standish.

"My dear sir, we always have been. But in days gone by we were, at any rate, feared and respected. Now we are neither. How the devil can we expect to be when our armed strength might just cope with a three years' defensive war against Guatemala?"

"A slight exaggeration," smiled Standish.

"But with a very nasty element of truth in it. To me, living abroad, the thing is simply unbelievable as it is to every intelligent foreigner. *Quem Deus vult perdere, prius dementat.* One or two men at home have the courage to proclaim the truth; but the vast majority don't care."

"You've got the League of Nations, Humphrey," said Madame Pélain.

"League of Fiddlesticks, my dear," he answered. "If that damned hot air factory was anything resembling what it set out to be originally, there would be something in what you say. But we're not dealing with what might have been: we're dealing with reality. And it is my considered opinion that as it stands the League of Nations is the greatest menace to peace that exists in the world today. It is the sand into which, ostrich-like, England has stuffed her great fat head, and believing it to be a safeguard against future war has proceeded to disarm. Sorry," he continued with a short laugh, "but it makes me hot under the collar. Look, you people, on this picture and on that."

From his pocket-book he extracted two cuttings.

"If I may, I will read them to you. Here is the first:

"BROADCAST TO SIX MILLION.

"Six million Hitler boys and girls listened to this new version of the creed broadcast by all German stations from Leipzig, where a harvest festival of the Hitler Youth Organisation was celebrated (reported Reuter yesterday):

"'I believe in the community of all Germans, in a life of service to this community: I believe in the revelation of the God-given creative force, in pure blood shed in war and peace by the sons of the community of the German people buried in the earth, hallowed by it, resurrected and living in all for whom the sacrifice was made.

"'I believe in an eternal life of this shed and resurrected blood on earth in all who acknowledge the means of this sacrifice and are prepared to bow themselves down. Therefore, I believe in an eternal God, in an eternal Germany, and in an eternal life.'

"And here is the other:

"BISHOP CONDEMNS PACIFISTS.

"The Bishop of Sussex strongly disapproves of the Oxford Union's decision that 'in no circumstances will its members fight for King and country.'

"More power to his Grace's elbow! But does he really imagine his disapproval will make 'em fight? Not on your life. They'll be lining the streets hopefully throwing red, red flowers at the great, blond, fascinating brutes as they march in."

He replaced the two cuttings in his pocket.

"Comment is unnecessary. You may not like the first, but, by Heaven above, it doesn't produce a strong desire to vomit like the second."

"Mr Gasdon," said Standish, who had been whispering to Drummond, "it seems fairly obvious that you are, so to speak, one of the boys. And so with Drummond's approval, I am going to take you fully into our confidence. Madame Pélain has not told you everything. So if you can spare half an hour I would like to put you wise. Only I must have your word that you won't pass it on."

"You have it," said Gasdon briefly.

65

He listened with half-closed eyes as Standish told him the whole story, omitting nothing. And on its conclusion he lay back in his chair.

"How extraordinarily interesting," he remarked. "Let us get one or two things straight. It is, of course, obvious that the Madame Pilofsky of Chez Paquay would recognise you, Marie. What about the Madame Tomesco of the Golden Boot? Would she recognise you, Captain Drummond?"

"Hard to say," said Drummond. "She had no cause to look at me that night, and my back was towards her. But I wouldn't bank on it."

"And this Charles Burton. Is he a dark swarthy man?"

"The very reverse."

"Then he can't be Menalin under an assumed name. But since he was in the company of Menalin's mistress, it seems probable the two men know each other. And that throws a pretty sinister light on Mr Charles Burton. Surely our police – for, whatever I may have said about our country as a whole, they are still the finest in the world – surely, they can get a line on him."

"Don't forget," said Standish, "that it was only on Jimmy Latimer's death that the gentleman came into the limelight at all. And, but for Colonel Talbot's long shot, he wouldn't have done so even then."

"That's true," agreed Gasdon.

"And now that we know, from what you've told us, that he wants watching, he will certainly be watched."

"You say, Marie, that Major Latimer was greatly excited by the contents of the papers," said Gasdon.

"Very excited indeed. Gigantic; incredible; those were the words he used."

"And he was a man on whose judgment you would rely?"

"Emphatically," said Standish.

"I wonder if it's possible that they're going to have a dip at us before our so-called rearmament takes place."

"Who?" cried Standish.

Gasdon shrugged his shoulders.

"France hates us, and only the fact that she is terrified of Germany prevents her showing it. Italy frankly detests us, and small blame to her. Germany is an armed camp. Russia – well, Russia is a problem."

"Not the Communist bogey, surely," said Drummond.

"Are you quite sure it is such a bogey?" asked Gasdon quietly. "What about France recently, and Belgium? And Spain? They're fanatics, you know, and fanatics are dangerous men. Moreover they've always looked on us and our empire as the principal stronghold of all that they're up against."

"Jimmy said, given the organisation, it is possible," said Madame Pélain. "And the will to carry it through."

"Both could come from Menalin," remarked Gasdon. "Mark you, I don't say I'm right, but clearly it is something very much out of the ordinary, and Menalin is mixed up in it. And since Latimer was hurrying home it seems probable that England is involved."

"The idea seems almost fantastic," said Standish thoughtfully.

Gasdon gave a short laugh.

"Why? Fantastic perhaps when judged by the standards of even ten years ago. But is it fantastic now? We've got the biggest orchard in the world to rob, and one of the smallest forces to defend it with. We should, of course, regard it as a distinctly caddish action on the aggressor's part, and in the intervals of talking about the old school tie we should ask Honduras to apply sanctions. Damn it, man! When will our people begin to understand that because we don't want to go to war with anyone, having got all we want already, it doesn't follow that other nations feel the same about us. Lead me to alcohol; I get heated."

He beckoned to a waiter.

"What are those immortal lines of Sir William Watson?" he continued.

"Time and the ocean, and some fostering star,
In high cabal have made us what we are.

"Would he – *could* he – have written that today? At the present moment our fostering star is 'the voice that breathed o'er Eden': the ocean is as much use as a sick headache compared with the air, and in the next war we shan't have any time. However, I've been talking out of my turn. A desire for food is upon me. You will, I hope, all lunch with me, and we will forget such trifling matters in the joys of the chef's excellent *bouillabaisse.*"

CHAPTER 5

Gloves Off

Throughout the meal they discussed the matter from every angle, and the more Drummond and Standish saw of Humphrey Gasdon the more did they like him. From casual remarks he made it was evident that he had travelled not only widely but intelligently. Moreover he knew people as well as places, which was what was wanted in their present investigation. And towards the end of lunch his audience was more than half converted.

"There are two main questions to be answered," was his argument. "First – is it worthwhile? To that my answer is – yes, if it can be done rapidly; no, if it can't. Another war, such as the last one, dragging on for four years, would be sheer madness. But will it drag on for four years? Will there be time for us laboriously to build up our fighting forces after it has begun? We have it on the authority of Ludendorff himself that next time there will be no declaration of war beforehand. Which brings us to the other main point. Is it possible to knock us out in the first few weeks? That obviously only the experts can answer. But one does not require to be an expert to see that if it *is* possible, it may be worthwhile trying."

"Out-Vernes Jules Verne," said Standish half to himself. "I wonder if you're right, Gasdon."

"Lord knows!" The other drained his *fin champagne*. "But I'm certainly coming over to England with you to see. That is if we ever get there," he added with a laugh.

"As bad as that, you think?" said Drummond.

Gasdon nodded.

"It is clear from what happened to you, Marie, that the Reds are mixed up in it. Which means rather more over here than, at present, it does in England. There, up to date, they've stopped short of murder. Here it's a common occurrence. And really it's not surprising. When you remember that the casualty list for the first four years of the USSR was one million, eight hundred thousand dead, a few more thousand don't cut much ice."

"Is that really so?" cried Drummond.

"Certainly it is so. There it was the direct doing of the big men: here, as last night, it is an isolated job delegated by someone at the top to a local branch which obeys blindly. Do you remember the case of that White general in Paris who was reputed to have disappeared? Disappear my foot! He was murdered in broad daylight. An ambulance drove up behind him as he was strolling along, and the man beside the driver shot him from point-blank range with a gun fitted with a silencer. Before anybody had realised what had happened they had thrown the body inside and were off. That's how *he* disappeared. Another case I know of was that of the editor of a very anti-Red paper. He was reputed to have died of a heart attack when drinking an aperitif at his favourite café. He certainly had a heart attack, but it was brought on by having his drink poisoned. One man engaged him in conversation, his accomplice slipped the stuff into his glass. No, no, friends: do not, I beg of you, be under any delusions. As I say it has not got so far as that in England yet, but it is only a question of time. They've got all the necessary organisation there. And when you are dealing with a fanatic who is prepared to sacrifice his own life, if need be, provided he gets yours, and who, in addition, knows you while you don't know him, the thing becomes a little difficult."

Standish lit a cigarette: then, with his elbows on the table, he leaned forward.

"Let us work on the assumption, Gasdon, that you are right. What is to be our plan of campaign? First of all, who is on the marked list on our side? Drummond and I, naturally; Madame; and since we've lunched with you I'm afraid you must join the happy band."

"Don't let that give you indigestion," said Gasdon with a grin.

"Is there anyone else?"

"Not over here," said Drummond. "But in England there's the Chief."

"Right. Add him in. Now, exactly what do we want to do, and how do we propose to do it?"

"First part easy," answered Drummond. "Get over to England."

"And miss out Paris?"

"I think so," said Drummond. "Now that we *know* what we do I see no object in going there. What more is there to find out in France? It doesn't matter *how* Burton got on Jimmy's tracks; all that matters is that he did. Our job is to reverse proceedings and get on to Burton. He's the key to the situation."

"Make it so," said Standish. "And now, Madame, the next point is your charming self. What are you going to do?"

"I beg of you, Mr Standish, not to worry about me. Concentrate entirely on your own plans."

"My dear Marie, that is impossible," said Gasdon seriously. "It is essential that we should feel that you are safe. And I do most solemnly assure you that the danger is very real."

"Well, what do you suggest, Humphrey?"

"Have you any friends with a villa near here?"

"Yes; at Mentone."

"Excellent. Now it is most unlikely that you were followed here. Since all your kit is still at the Metropole, they will assume that you are returning there. My suggestion, therefore, is this. That you let me drive you to your friend's villa direct from here. I am fairly adept at the game, and I think I can spot at once if we are followed. From there you will telephone to Monsieur Lidet, but you will not give your address even to him. You will say that you will be returning in a week or a fortnight to the hotel, and give instructions for your room to be left intact. To your friends you can say as much or as little of the truth as you like. What necessaries you require your friend can obtain for you, but you yourself will lie low in the villa. Should the police make further enquiries with regard to last night, instruct Lidet to say that you are ill, and that he does not know where you are."

For a while she sat in silence, then: "You think that is best?"

"We all do, Madame," said Drummond.

"Very well, *mes amis*: I will do it. And you – what of you?"

"I would not presume to suggest a plan to you two fellows," said Gasdon. "But if you take my most earnest advice you, too, will not return to the Metropole."

"I've been thinking the same thing myself," remarked Standish. "I am certainly prepared to sacrifice my kit, such as it is."

"Same here," said Drummond. "And we can post a five-hundred-franc note to Lidet from somewhere en route. Were you serious when you said you were coming over to England, Gasdon?"

"Perfectly. If you have no objections I would like to come with you. Otherwise I will travel alone."

Drummond glanced at Standish, who nodded.

"Of course we have no objections," he said. "And it will certainly be easy to see on the run north if we are being followed."

"I'm afraid, Drummond, that your kit is not the only thing you'll have to sacrifice temporarily," said Gasdon. "What is the object in following us? Just as Latimer's goal was England, they'll know that yours is. And when you don't return to the hotel, they'll warn every port, if they haven't done so already, to watch out, not for you, but for your car. They're not the sort of people who would neglect such an obvious precaution as taking its number. And on the chance of your going to Paris they'll have spies at the Porte d'Italie, and the Porte de la Gare. No, old boy, I'm afraid you'll have to leave her in *la belle France* for the time. At some such place as Orléans. You see," he went on, "what Standish said is perfectly correct. They got you taped in Cannes through Madame. But if you, or rather we, now vanish into space they must lose the trail unless we throw the car at their heads. Their spies at Boulogne or Calais don't know us personally."

"Quite right," agreed Standish. "The man speaks sense. Well, I suggest, Gasdon, that the sooner we get on with it the better. Madame, I am not going to say an obvious goodbye. In case there is anybody watching us it's better that he should think we are just parting after lunch. But may I thank you from the bottom of my heart for all that you have done and told us."

"It was nothing," she said sadly, "if it has helped to revenge Jimmy. Goodbye; goodbye, Captain Drummond. I won't thank *you* again."

"And we will wait for you here, Gasdon," said Standish.

"Right. Sit in the bar, and keep your backs to the wall."

They sauntered across the room – a typical lunch party breaking up. And in the hall they paused.

"So we dine together tonight, Madame," said Drummond. "I will see that Monsieur Lidet excels himself."

"And after that the Casino," she cried. "*Au revoir.*"

"A damned plucky little woman," said Standish as they walked into the bar.

73

"And I hope a fortunate remark of mine," said Drummond. "Did you see the gentleman in the hall who half rose as we left the dining-room, and then sat down again?"

"No, I didn't."

"He was behind you, but I marked him down. Strikes me, old boy, that their staff work is marvellous, but that the actual performers are not so good."

"Full marks, I think, to Mr Humphrey Gasdon."

"Yes. Definitely good value. And a bloke of decided views. I wonder if he's right about this Communist stunt."

"He's right over one thing," said Standish. "They've got the necessary organisation in the country. That I know for a certainty: factory cells, street cells, the necessary instructors, street newspapers. All of which is well known to the police. But taking it by and large, they have so far failed to make much headway. Our fellows in the main have too much common sense, I suppose. Hullo! Here's the girlfriend once again. I wonder who the lucky boy is this time."

Madame Tomesco, *alias* Pilofsky, had entered the bar accompanied by a man.

"Dark and swarthy," muttered Drummond. "Perhaps it's Menalin himself."

As the two passed their table the lady's escort paused slightly and gave them each a cool and deliberate stare from under a pair of bushy eyebrows. He was clean-shaven with the high cheek-bones of the Slav. His nose was thick; his mouth both sensual and cruel. Not a very big man, yet he gave the impression of great physical strength. And there was a sort of feline grace in his walk as he followed the woman.

"Menalin for a fiver," said Standish. "And seemingly interested in our unworthy selves. I don't know that I want him as a pet. What do you want, Johnny?"

A small page with a newspaper on a salver had come up to the table.

"*Vous avez commandé ze* Daily Express, *m'sieu*?" said the boy.

"I have not commanded it," answered Standish. "Nevertheless I should hate to disappoint you, laddie."

He took the paper, and started fumbling in his pocket for a coin. And suddenly he stiffened: his eye had caught one of the headlines. He instantly recovered himself, tossed a coin on to the salver and put the paper on the table.

"Show no interest, Hugh," he said quietly. "We are being watched. They've got the Chief."

"My God!" muttered Drummond under his breath. "Let's see."

Standish spread out the paper, and to all outward appearances two bored men bent forward to read it. And from a few tables away came a woman's low laugh...

MURDER OF ARMY OFFICER.
AMAZING CRIME IN BROAD DAYLIGHT.
COLONEL HENRY TALBOT SHOT IN
HYDE PARK.

One of the most sensational crimes of modern times of a nature recalling the dastardly murder of the late Field-Marshal Sir Henry Wilson, took place yesterday afternoon in Hyde Park.

Colonel Henry Talbot, CMG, DSO, a highly-placed officer at the War Office, left Whitehall rather earlier than usual and started to walk home to his flat in Orme Square. This was his invariable custom if the weather was fine. His route was always the same; up Constitution Hill, into Hyde Park, and thence to Lancaster Gate.

It would appear that the unfortunate officer paused on the outskirts of a crowd gathered round one of the inevitable orators near Marble Arch. Suddenly he was seen to fall to the ground. At first those near him thought he was ill, when, to their horror, they perceived blood flowing from his head.

A constable was on the spot immediately, and it was obvious at once that the Colonel had been brutally murdered. He had been shot through the head from behind at point-blank range.

That such a thing could happen in broad daylight, in such a place, is well-nigh inconceivable. No shot was heard, but this, of course, would be accounted for by the use of a silencer. None of the people in the vicinity had seen or heard anything suspicious, though one man – Mr John Herbert, of Islington – said that he thought he had noticed two men getting hurriedly into a waiting taxi just after Colonel Talbot fell to the ground. But he had paid no attention and could give no description of them.

What happened seems clear. The deceased officer, whose habit of walking home was evidently known to the murderer, must have been followed from his office. The man or men had a taxi in readiness behind them. When Colonel Talbot paused on the edge of the crowd they seized their opportunity to commit their atrocious crime, trusting to the shifting listeners to make a safe get-away. And this, unfortunately, they seem to have done.

The crime is an inexplicable one. So far as is known Colonel Talbot had no enemies. His military record was a brilliant one. He served throughout the Egyptian campaign and the South African War, in the latter of which he was awarded the DSO for conspicuous gallantry at Magersfontein. In the Great War he was twice wounded, receiving the CMG and being five times mentioned in despatches.

He leaves a widow and one son, Captain Edward Talbot, who is at present serving at Aldershot with his regiment, the Royal West Sussex.

And once again came the low mocking laugh of a woman...

It failed conspicuously if, by it, she hoped to make them display any emotion: she was dealing with far too old hands for that. But inwardly both men were raging with anger. That she and the man with her were responsible for the paper being brought to them was a trifle: it was the filthy murder of one of the finest men in England, and a great friend into the bargain, that got them.

Particularly Drummond. Similar though they were in many ways there was a streak of the primitive in him that Standish lacked. And though both of them had liked Jimmy Latimer, the murder of Colonel Talbot seemed more personal. He was their Chief whom they were actually serving under at the time.

One thing, however, it emphasised – the power of the organisation they were up against. Murder in the Park in broad daylight was not a matter to be undertaken lightly. It showed an almost incredible disregard for ordinary values. As Gasdon had said, England was not France: London was not Paris.

"It would seem," said Drummond quietly, "that when we get back to England there will be several scores to settle."

"When," remarked Standish with a short laugh. "We've been in many tight corners before, old boy, but we've never been in such danger as we are at the present moment seated in this bar. There is an efficient ruthlessness about our opponents that I find most refreshing. And it piles proof upon proof that the issue is big."

"You're right there, by Jove!" Drummond's jaw was sticking out. "So much the better. For after this" – he tapped the paper – "it's war to the knife. No quarter given and none asked."

"That'll be grand when we're in a position to give it," said Standish grimly. "Just at the moment I'm afraid the mouse has to be rather tight before he says it to the cat. Everything depends on whether we can do a get-away from here. And it's not going to be so easy as those swine found it at Marble Arch."

The bar gradually filled, but of Gasdon there was no sign. Menalin – if it was Menalin – and the woman had gone shortly after the episode of the paper, but they neither of them felt any the easier for that. They were marked men, and they knew it. There was not the remotest chance of their leaving the hotel unnoticed.

At last they saw Gasdon coming towards them, and he looked worried.

"Madame Pélain is safe," he said as he sat down. "I am tolerably certain we were not followed. But she rang up Lidet while I was there. And the police have been round asking for you two, over last night's effort. At my instigation she said you were both returning to the Metropole for dinner, but that she did not know where you were at the moment. Now it is essential that you should not go back. There will be delays: possibly engineered delays…"

"Not possibly, but certainly," said Standish. "Read that."

"Good God!" said Gasdon as he put the paper down.

"Worse still," continued Standish, and told him of the woman and her companion.

"That's Menalin right enough," said Gasdon. "And he'll fix the police. You'll be kept there hanging about till there is a suitable opportunity to murder you."

"The only chance," said Drummond, "is to walk calmly out of the hotel as if we were going back to Cannes – all three of us. We can talk as we go for the benefit of anyone in the hall. And it is just possible that if they think we are going to Cannes they will not bother to follow us."

"I doubt it." Gasdon shook his head. "But it's the only thing to try. And at once. If that was Menalin, and from your description I'm sure it was, it is more than likely that he will put a call through to the police to say you're here. And if that happens you're done. Come on. We've got to make plans as we go."

They rose and strolled into the hall, and a man studying some travel brochures drew slightly nearer.

"Let's go back to the Metropole now and order the dinner," said Drummond. "Though personally I would sooner feed at the Reserve at Beaulieu."

"Too far afterwards, old boy," objected Gasdon. "It's only a step to the Casino from the Metropole."

"All right, have it your own way," said Drummond languidly. "*En voiture.*"

They sauntered outside, three care-free Englishmen, and got into the car. And the brochure studier sauntered also, at the same time giving the faintest perceptible nod to two men in a low-bodied, powerful racing car whose bonnet was almost touching the tail of Drummond's car.

"Actual performers are poor," drawled Drummond.

"That nod was quite unnecessary and settles things. We have equerries in attendance."

He was fumbling in the cubby-hole in front of him as he spoke.

"Stupid of me, Ronald," he cried. "I never put a lashing on that luggage grid. Do you remember how it rattled like hell?"

"Hardly could hear yourself speak, old boy," agreed Standish, lighting a cigarette, and watching Drummond out of the corner of his eye as he got out of the car.

The brochure studier had disappeared: the light was failing, and Gasdon was fidgeting.

"What the devil does it matter about the luggage grid?" he muttered. "Every second is precious."

"My dear Gasdon," said Standish quietly, "you can take it from me that there is generally a reason for everything that Drummond does. In due course you will find that out for yourself – perhaps sooner than you think. There was no squeak in the luggage grid."

Gasdon's lips twitched into a grin.

"I'm beginning to like you two blokes," he remarked. "You're going to wake me up. I was getting fat and lazy."

"Lucky they were so close to us," said Drummond, getting back into the car. "And now, my loved ones, hey – nonnie – no, for the great open spaces."

"What on earth have you been doing?" asked Gasdon curiously as Drummond let in the clutch.

"Adjusting my maiden's helps," answered Drummond. "Never known to fail. Entirely my own invention. If the little pretty wants to escape with boy friend from parents in attendant car so that she may dally awhile in leafy glades, she puts one of these under the front wheel of said parents' car after lunch. The most infallible puncture producer of this or any other age. I am never without 'em."

Gasdon was shaking helplessly as he looked at the maiden's help. It consisted of a very sharp three-inch nail which, instead of possessing the usual head, was fitted with a small triangular stand so that the nail would stand upright in the road.

"Placed so that the point of the nail just touches the tyre," explained Drummond, "and it's through Pop's reinforced Dunlop before the old boy has begun to digest the salmon mayonnaise. What's happened to our escort?"

"They're about a hundred yards behind us," said Standish. "Yes…yes…OK, boy. They're pulling up. They're out. By Jove! they've got two punctures. Both front wheels…"

"Excellent," remarked Drummond calmly. "And they have only one spare. It would, I feel, be vulgar to wave. Now what's the plan: to Cannes or not to Cannes?"

"I think not," said Gasdon, grown serious again. "We could, of course, go by the Rue d'Antibes, miss the hotel, and head for Brignoles. But if they do warn the police to stop the car that route will be watched for an absolute certainty. And we've got to run the gauntlet of every gendarme between here and Cannes.

Our best hope is Grasse. Swing right-handed when we get to Cagnes golf course."

"Your slightest word is law, dear boy," said Drummond. "You know this country a deuced sight better than we do, so we are in your hands. The car, I am glad to say, is fast."

"Very fast," agreed Gasdon. "The trouble is that there is something which is a damned sight faster – the telephone. Drummond, we've got to abandon car mighty soon, I'm afraid. I know of a by-road by which we can skirt round Grasse, but after that the trouble begins. We get up into the mountains, and roads are few and far between."

"What do you suggest?" asked Drummond. "As I said, you know the geography."

"We've got to concentrate, chaps, on getting out of France. Now let us assume the worst. When it is discovered that we have bolted, the first thing the police will do is to issue a general warning to look out for the car. Therefore, as we have already agreed, the car must be abandoned, though possibly it might be safe to drive through tonight."

"I doubt it," said Standish, "but go on."

"What is the next thing the police will do? They know our names, and when no information of the car comes to hand, they will assume we have taken to the railway. Which is what, incidentally, I suggest we should do at the earliest possible moment. And here comes the vital difference between our cases. Whatever Menalin and Co. may think of me, the police don't want me. You two are all that count in their young lives. And so I propose that we separate. I'll go to Paris and cross to England in the ordinary way, but what are you going to do? Let's work it out. Every railway frontier will be watched for you two by name. It is just possible, and it seems to me to be your only hope, that the road frontiers will be watched for by car."

"My God!" cried Drummond, "you don't suggest we should walk across France, do you?"

Gasdon laughed.

"Not quite. I suggest that we should all make for the Grenoble line. That I should go to Paris, and that you should make for Geneva. Go to Aix-les-Bains. There hire a car and drive to Evian on the Lake Geneva, where you can pick up one of the steamers. And once you've done that you're in the straight run home."

"It sounds feasible," said Standish. "The only drawback to my mind is that if we are caught, such a very elaborate scheme makes us look infernally guilty."

"You'll have to chance that," answered Gasdon. "Don't forget you can always tell the police the real reason for what you've done."

"That's so. Just now, however, the pressing need is the immediate future. It is almost dark, and, I take it, that's Grasse in front of us."

"Go slow," said Gasdon. "Here is the turning to the left. It's a bad road, but we can skirt the town and come out beyond it on the Digne road. Then we're safe as far as Castellane."

"Thank the Lord you know the old terrain," laughed Drummond. "What a fun, boys, what a fun! But could little Hugh do with a pint? The answer, jolly old speaker, is in the affirmative."

"It is definitely a sound idea, Gasdon," said Standish after they had driven in silence for some time. "If we can make Switzerland, we're on velvet. Through Germany to either the Hook or Ostend."

"Just so," said Gasdon. "And before we separate we'll agree where we meet in England."

"Sure bill," cried Standish. "But since you will certainly be there first, get in touch at once with Lawson – Major Lawson – at the War House, and tell him the whole story."

Once more silence fell. By now it was quite dark, and the road was rising rapidly, though the car made light of the gradient. Mile after mile fell away behind them, and soon the lights of Castellane appeared ahead. And it was then that Drummond had a brain-storm.

"What's wrong with you taking the car on, Gasdon?" he exclaimed. "As you said, the police don't want *you*. Standish and I will get out now and walk to the town. It goes to my heart to leave her in some wretched little garage here. If the police should stop you, you are merely driving the car to Paris at my request, and we are still, as far as you know, on the Riviera."

He stopped the car and lit a cigarette.

"If the police don't stop you, you might even take her on to Boulogne," he continued. "But if you think that's unwise park her in some good garage in Paris."

"I'm not sure you're not right," said Gasdon. "It might help to throw 'em still off the scent. What do you think, Standish?"

"I think it's a good idea. Where's our nearest station?"

"Hire a car and make for Sisteron. It's about sixty miles. And now about England. Where do we meet?"

"Keep in touch with Lawson. We'll get at you through him."

"Right. Well, so long, chaps. And good luck."

"Little did I think, old boy," said Drummond resignedly as the lights of the car vanished round a bend, "that I should ever be marooned amongst the virgin snows in the middle of the night. Come on, I could do with a spot of solids."

Ten minutes' walk brought them to the bridge over the river Verdon, that marks the entrance to the town; another five and they were in the main square. And there with a gendarme on each side, stood the car.

Matters had evidently reached a deadlock. One gendarme was scratching his head, the other was sucking a pencil. And Gasdon, a picture of outraged innocence, was haranguing them from the driver's seat in fluent French.

"It is monstrous," he cried. "It is of an imbecility incredible. Is it the car that is required for these formalities at Cannes? The owner, my great friend, knowing he must await the police investigation, lends me his car to go to Paris. Is not that sufficient proof, you fatheads, that he is still there? If he had wished to go himself, would he not have been in the car? And in any case, why should he go? He was not accused of anything. It is merely a question of his evidence."

"Our instructions are that there are three men in the car." The pencil sucker had produced his notebook. "Le Capitaine Drummond: M'sieur Standish and M'sieur Gasdon. And the M'sieur Gasdon has a scar on his face."

"Name of a name," cried Gasdon. "Regard the scar. Obtained, *mon brave*, at Fricourt. I am Monsieur Gasdon, and when I left Nice le Capitaine Drummond and Monsieur Standish were with me in the car. But I dropped them near Cagnes."

"At what house, m'sieur?" demanded the gendarme.

"The house of a lady friend." Gasdon dug the pencil sucker in the ribs, and they all laughed. "And now since you are both satisfied that neither of them are in the car, I must get on."

He let in the clutch and drove off, and after a while the two gendarmes went indoors. Assuredly very peculiar: if three men were reported to be in the car, it was obviously most irregular that there should only be one. And, as they disappeared the two onlookers did likewise in the opposite direction.

"They lose no time," said Standish gravely. "And I have my doubts if Gasdon gets through."

"Which makes it the more imperative that we should," answered Drummond. "There's a garage on the other side of the road. Let's see if we can raise a car."

They could – an incredibly ancient Renault. And three hours later they bumped into Sisteron. The first part of their journey was over.

"And now, old boy," said Drummond as they paid off the car, "we separate. It gives us two chances instead of one. Make for the Hotel les Bergues at Geneva."

CHAPTER 6

Drummond Alone

During the season Evian-les-Bains is a charming spot. On the high ground behind the town there are tennis courts and golf links set in delightful surroundings, for those who will to use. A tiny harbour filled with gaily coloured boats abuts the casino: beautiful women and brave men lounge gracefully over their "five o'clock". That is during the season.

Out of the season Evian-les-Bains resembles a town of the dead. The links are shut; holland covers encase the casino furniture. The beautiful women have departed long since; the inhabitants appear to have fallen into a coma. And it was out of the season when Drummond, paying off his taxi on the outskirts of the town, proceeded to enter it on foot.

The time was midday, and the boat, so he had discovered from the concierge at Aix, arrived at two-thirty. Which left him two and a half hours to put through, and made him regret that he had left his hotel quite so early. Not that he hankered after Evian in gala mood, but because, if the police were on the lookout, he was so much more conspicuous in the deserted streets.

Strolling towards the harbour he espied a sports shop, in the window of which some rucksacks were hanging. And it struck him that it might help to account for his presence if he pretended to be on a walking tour. So he purchased one, and a long stick with an embossed handle. A hunting horn he refused: likewise a little green hat with feathers in it. To overdo a part is bad art...

Leaving the shop he walked on towards the lake. And then, finding a small café within sight of the landing-stage, he entered and enquired about lunch. It seemed that an omelette and a bottle of wine was all that Madame could run to, so he ordered it and lit a cigarette.

Since the morning before he had practically not seen Standish. They had travelled in the same train from Sisteron to Aix, but in different compartments, whilst at Aix they had stayed at different hotels. And now Drummond began wondering where he was. The two-thirty was the only boat he could catch, since the service was greatly curtailed as soon as the summer tourist season ceased.

Slowly the time went by, until suddenly Madame pointed over the lake.

"*Voilà, m'sieu: le bateau.*"

The paddle boat had just heaved in sight coming from St Gingolph, and he frowned a little. Standish was cutting it fine. Faint human stirrings in the square outside began to manifest themselves: evidently this was the event of the day. He could hear the thresh of the paddles now, so, paying his bill, he rose to go. And at that moment a car drove up with Standish inside.

From the doorway Drummond watched. The engines of the boat were in reverse: cables fore and aft were being flung ashore. And then he saw them. Advancing majestically towards the shore end of the gangway were two gendarmes in gorgeous uniforms. Moreover it appeared that they wished to see Standish's passport.

Drummond's eyes narrowed: rapid thought was necessary. They were stopping Standish in spite of his indignant protestations. And if they stopped Standish they would also stop him. Madame was adjuring him to hurry if he wished to catch the boat, but he only smiled at her and came back into the café. It would not do to arouse her suspicions in any way, so he told her that he had decided to continue walking, and ordered another bottle of wine. From outside came again the sound of paddle wheels: the boat was leaving. And in a few minutes peace once more reigned in Evian.

Convinced by now that the large Englishman was more than usually mad, Madame had retired into some inner fastness, leaving Drummond alone in the café. What was the best thing to do? Any attempt to rescue Standish or even to communicate with him would be madness. The police were merely doing their duty, and the only result would be that he would be stopped as well.

Equally would it be madness to wait on with the idea of catching the boat on the following day: the police would still be on the lookout. In fact any idea of leaving France by Evian must be abandoned. Where, then, could he go?

A map was hanging on the wall, and he rose and studied it. There, just across the water – so near and yet so far – lay Lausanne and safety. Should he wait for darkness, steal one of the boats in the harbour, and row across the lake? But after a few moments' reflection he dismissed the idea as too dangerous. The police headquarters were too close: the risk of being seen or heard too great. So the only alternative was to cross the frontier by land.

To the east lay St Gingolph only about twelve miles away. But to reach that he had to cross the square in front of the police station, and moreover do so fairly soon. For it had dawned on him that this café was not too safe. The gendarmes, exhausted by their labours, might decide to recuperate their strength with alcohol at any moment, and the café was very handy.

So there was only one course open. He would strike westward towards Geneva and cross at Hermance. That they would be on the lookout for him there, was obvious, but the same thing applied to every *douane*. So the only thing was to hope for the best when he got there.

He slipped into the street, and heaved a sigh of relief when he was out of sight of the police station. He had twenty-five miles to cover, and the prospect of walking did not amuse him. On the other hand if he hired a car and arrived in broad daylight, the attempt was foredoomed to failure.

He strode along thinking things over, and wishing that he knew the country he would have to negotiate when he came to the frontier. For it had soon occurred to him that by far the best, if not the only, chance of getting through would be to cross between *douanes*. That would entail leaving the road before he got to the frontier: skirting round the village and rejoining the road again farther on when he was safe in Switzerland. What difficulties there would be he had no idea: as a performance it was a new one on him. But he assumed that in peace time any system of patrols between posts would be of a very perfunctory nature.

And so, when it came to the point, it proved to be. Save for falling into a wet ditch the whole thing passed off without incident. As soon as the lights of the *douane* showed up in the distance he struck off left-handed across the fields. Once a dog began barking furiously, but, except for that, the night was still. Hardly a light was showing; the whole countryside was asleep. And at 11.41 p.m. Drummond stepped back on to the road with France a kilometre behind him. In the distance glittered the lights of Geneva: a far more welcome sight, however, was a faint chink filtering through the wooden shutters of an inn just ahead. A room was available, and ten minutes later Drummond, having taken off his shoes and coat, was fast asleep.

It was past ten when he awoke next morning and the sun was streaming in through the window. So at peace with the world, and no longer feeling that at any moment he might feel a gendarme's hand on his shoulder, he drank two large cups of coffee. Then, having hired a taxi, he drove into Geneva over the Pont de Mont Blanc.

It was his first visit to the Hotel les Bergues and the concierge eyed him a little doubtfully. With a certain amount of excuse let it be admitted: Hugh Drummond's general appearance was not such as is generally to be observed in that hotel. He wanted a shave, and his shoes still bore record to yesterday's walk. But at that moment an exquisite individual came sauntering down the stairs, who paused, stared, then with a cry of amazement held out his hand.

"What in the name of all that's fortunate are you doing here, old boy? And why this strange garb with rucksacks and things?"

"Hullo! potato face," said Drummond. "Glad to see you. I didn't know any of you blokes ever got up before midday."

The Honourable James Tagley grinned amiably. A younger son of old Lord Storrington, he had drifted peacefully into the Foreign Office, where he remained a monument of beauty and a joy for ever.

"We do every second Friday," he remarked. "But joking apart, Hugh, what does bring you here?"

"A desire to study Swiss architecture first-hand," said Drummond with a smile.

"Are you up to some of your games?" demanded the Honourable James.

"My dear potato face, I don't understand you. I am now a respectable member of society."

"You're a damned old liar," said the other. "I say, what a shocking thing that was – those swines murdering Talbot."

"You're right," agreed Drummond. "Any inside information come through to this centre of gossip?"

"No. But the motive must have been political."

Drummond raised his eyebrows.

"I shouldn't have said that he was much mixed up in politics. However, doubtless you know best, James. Tell me; how stands the international barometer?"

The other lowered his voice.

"Officially, old boy, set fair. Unofficially – not quite so good. There are vague mutterings and signs and portents."

"Are you allowed to tell?"

"The devil of it is that there's nothing to tell. Nothing definite, that's to say. But in some ways, you know, this place is as sensitive as the Stock Exchange. Whispers go round in the most incredible fashion, and when you've been here some time it's amazing how quickly you become aware of them. There's something in the air, Hugh: there has been for some time."

"What sort of thing?"

"I don't know: I can't tell you."

"Do you mean there's a possibility of war?"

"My dear fellow, that possibility is always there – League of Nations, or no League of Nations. But I don't mean war this time. It's something else, and" – his voice sank to a whisper – "we are involved."

Drummond lit a cigarette.

"You interest me profoundly, James," he remarked.

"Mind you, Hugh," said Tagley, "this is not to go beyond you. Good morning, sir."

A well-known figure in English public life nodded as he passed through the hall.

"Do you want a lift?" he called out.

"Thank you, sir. I must go, Hugh. Shall I see you at lunch?"

"Perhaps, potato face. I don't know."

For a moment or two Drummond stood motionless as Tagley hurried after the great man to a waiting car. Then he turned to the concierge.

"I want a call to London," he said. "How long will it take?"

"It depends, sir. But if you will give me the number I will get through for you. It would be well to remain at hand. Sometimes one connects almost at once."

Taking a pencil Drummond wrote down Ginger Lawson's number at the War Office. Then he sat down on a chair nearby. So James Tagley confirmed the fact that something was in the wind. ... Strange – very strange...

"God!" he muttered to himself. "If only Latimer had put those papers in an envelope and posted them in Paris!"

For perhaps ten minutes he sat there, idly watching the people as they passed in and out of the hotel. Every nationality: every colour... Every nationality, that is to say, except three... What a farce: what a roaring farce...

Suddenly he saw the concierge approaching him.

"M'sieur's call to London."

He entered the box and picked up the receiver.

"Hullo! Ginger: that you?"

With remarkable clearness he heard Lawson's voice from the other end.

"Drummond speaking from Geneva."

"Geneva! What on earth are you doing there?"

"Too long to tell you now, Ginger. I'm writing you a full report this morning, but it will be two or three days before I'm back. For reasons I can't go into at the moment I'm not going through France. I shall either fly from Brussels or cross via Ostend or the Hook."

"Postpone it for a day or two, old boy," came Lawson's voice. "It's providential you're in Switzerland. Do you know young Cranmer – Archie Cranmer?"

"Vaguely. He's with you, isn't he?"

"That's right. But he's new on the game. At the moment he is in Territet at the Grand Hotel. Will you go over and get in touch with him? I'll wire him to expect you."

"All right, Ginger. It's urgent, is it? Because I want to get back to England as soon as possible."

"It is urgent, Hugh. It concerns the Chief's murder. And I'd feel easier if you were helping Archie."

" 'Nough said, Ginger. I'll get off my report to you, and then go straight to Territet. By the way you have Ronald's from Cannes, haven't you?"

"Yes. I recognised the writing and opened it. We are keeping an eye on the gentleman he mentions from here. Is Ronald with you?"

"No. I'll explain everything in my report. So long, Ginger."

He rang off, and having paid for the call he wandered upstairs in search of the writing-room. It was the part of the job that he disliked most, but he dared not bank on the fact that Standish would get another report off from France. And so for an hour he toiled laboriously: then with a sigh of relief he addressed the envelope and slipped it in his pocket. A shave; a drink; Territet – that was the programme as he proposed it. And that was the programme as he carried it out.

He arrived at Territet at three o'clock, having lunched at Lausanne Station, and went straight to the Grand Hotel. And the first person he saw sitting in the glassed-in verandah was Archie Cranmer.

"How are you, young feller!" he said. "I don't know if you remember me. My name is Drummond."

"Of course I do," answered Cranmer getting up. "But it almost seemed as if you expected to find me here."

"I did," laughed Drummond. "I've come over from Geneva especially to see you at Ginger Lawson's request. Have you had a wire from him?"

"No."

"It'll come. And in the meantime let's hear all about it."

Cranmer shook his head.

"Very sorry, Drummond. I'm sure it's all right, but..."

And once again he shook his head deliberately.

"Good for you," said Drummond with a grin. "I was only trying you out. In our game, Cranmer, a man ought not to trust his own mother. However, I don't think we'll have long to wait.

This page boy has the appearance of one who bringeth news. A telegram, my lad? There's the gentleman."

Cranmer opened it; then with a smile passed it over to Drummond.

Work with Hugh Drummond. – LAWSON.

"So that's that," he said. "Sorry if I seemed suspicious, but your appearance was rather unexpected. How much do you know already?"

"Merely that you are here in connection with the Chief's murder," answered Drummond.

"I see. Then I'd better begin at the beginning. You remember, don't you, that he always used to walk to and from the office?"

Drummond nodded.

"On the morning of his murder it so happened that for some reason or other he did not walk, but took a taxi. Incidentally both Lawson and I are convinced that if he had walked they'd have got him then. However, that is beside the point. The instant he reached the office he sent for both of us."

"'I had a visitor last night,' he began. 'At my flat. A peculiar card.'

"You remember that funny sort of clipped way he had of talking.

"'Yes,' he went on, 'a very peculiar card. At first I thought he wasn't all there. Mallows showed him into the study, and he kept looking round as if he expected a trap. Little, short, dark man with a whacking great moustache. Obviously not English though he spoke it quite well.

"'It transpired that he kept a barber's shop down Elephant and Castle way, which he ran under the name of Timpson. Further, that he was naturalised.

"'I always believe,' continued the Chief, 'in letting a man tell his story in his own way, but after a bit I got a trifle bored.

"' "Get down to it, Mr Timpson," I said. "I assume you haven't come here merely to tell me you cut hair."

"'He leaned forward impressively.

"' "Colonel," he said, "I have very valuable information for you."

"' "Good," I answered. "Fire ahead."

"Then one got his real character in his cunning, greedy eyes.

"'How much is it worth?'

"'That,' I said, 'depends entirely on what it is. If it really is valuable you won't have any cause for complaint.'

"'Very good. I will trust you. Now you will understand, sir, that many foreigners come to my shop, as well as English. And frequently I overhear their conversations. This afternoon there came two. They were speaking French, but it was not the French of Frenchmen. And as I listened to what they said I realised what they were. They were Swiss. After a while they were joined by two Englishmen, and they all talked together in low tones. Much of what they said I could not hear, but one or two things I did catch.'

"The little man's voice sank to a blood-curdling whisper.

"'And one of them was your name often repeated.'

"Apparently," continued Cranmer, "the Chief sat up at this. Why four scallywags should be discussing him in a cheap barber's shop was not easy to follow. He pressed this man Timpson as to how he knew it was him, since Talbot was not a particularly uncommon name. Answer was that Orme Square had been mentioned, which seemed fairly conclusive, and the Chief waited for more. He soon got it. The two Englishmen were known to Timpson as thoroughly dangerous characters, though he knew nothing about the Swiss. And it, therefore, seemed obvious that the conversation was not likely to have concerned a presentation of plate to the Chief.

"'Not that that worries me in the slightest,' he went on. 'In the ordinary course of events I should take no notice at all. But coming so soon after Jimmy's death I have notified the Yard, and I expect to hear from them at any moment. Why I've sent for you two fellows concerns the one other item of interest that Mr Timpson gave me. It's an address which he heard the Swiss mention two or three times: Villa Bon Ciel, Veytaux.'

"'Where's Veytaux?' asked Ginger.

"'Just what I wanted to know myself,' said the Chief. 'It's apparently a sort of continuation of Montreux and Territet going towards Chillon Castle. And that's where you two boys are bound for. A nice holiday in beautiful Switzerland.'

"At that moment the telephone rang, and the Chief answered it. And when he put down the receiver his face was grave.

"'Mr Timpson has not yet returned to his shop,' he said. 'His bed has not been slept in. I very much fear that he has more than earned the fiver I gave him.'

"'You think they've got him?' said Ginger.

"'My flat was probably being watched?' he said. 'Of course he may have gone on the binge and is sleeping it off, but...'

"The shrug of his shoulders was eloquent; it was obvious what he thought. And then for a time he sat there drumming on the desk with his fingers.

"'I don't like it,' he said at length. 'There's something going on I can't understand. Anyway you two had better keep your eyes skinned before, during, and after your visit to Veytaux.'

"With that he dismissed us, and it was the last time I saw him alive. Those swine got him, as you know, when he was walking home that afternoon."

"What of this man Timpson?" asked Drummond after a pause.

"There was no trace of him up to the time I left. You see, the Chief's death altered things. Ginger had to stop on in London, so I came over here alone."

"Quite," said Drummond absently. "Quite. When did you get here?"

"Early this morning by the Orient express."

"Have you done anything as yet?"

"I took a walk towards Chillon Castle, and located the villa."

"Good," said Drummond. "What sort of a place is it?"

"An ordinary sort of shanty standing way back up the hill, overlooking the lake. It's got a glassed-in verandah much like this one, only very much smaller, of course."

"Any other houses near it?"

"Nothing, I should say, within a hundred yards."

"How close did you get to it?"

"I didn't. I saw it from the main road down below. That's this one that goes past the hotel."

"And what were you proposing to do next?"

"To tell the truth, Drummond," said Cranmer with an apologetic laugh, "I wasn't quite sure *what* to do next."

"I don't wonder. The problem is not a very easy one."

"I thought I might make enquiries of the concierge as to who lives there."

Drummond shook his head.

"Certainly not that. In a place of this sort things get round in an incredibly short time. And if it came out that two Englishmen were interesting themselves in the owner of the Bon Ciel the pitch is queered at once. No, my boy; nothing so direct as that. You didn't get near enough to find out if the owner kept a dog?"

Cranmer shook his head.

"In any event it would probably have been inside the house," he said.

"Not of necessity," said Drummond. "A lot of these people here keep a dog on a long chain, simply as a watchdog. Then they don't have to pay a licence. However, we can but find out. Got any rubber-soled shoes?"

"No."

"Nor have I. Now look here, Cranmer, we'll split this job to start with. I will go down the town and buy two pairs of rubber shoes – your size looks about the same as mine. You will get hold of a telephone book, remembering that under no circumstances must you let the concierge know why you want it. You will then go laboriously down the list on the chance of finding that the villa is on the phone. If it is we shall get the name of the owner, though not of necessity the present tenant. It may help; it may not. Then when I return we will both take a walk past the villa to ensure that we can find it tonight."

"And tonight?"

"We will take another walk," said Drummond with a grin. "And then we will be guided by circumstances."

"Good Lord!" cried the other, "you don't intend to break in, do you?"

Drummond's grin grew more pronounced.

"Let us call it a tour of investigation," he remarked. "Get busy with the telephone book."

He left Cranmer settling down to his monotonous task, and walking down to the station stood waiting for a tram. On the opposite side of the lake rose the mountains of Haute Savoie culminating in the giant Dent du Midi, golden crested in the westering sun. A thin wisp of fog lay like a serpent against the dark massif, and in the distance the same steamer that Standish had missed the day before was pursuing its lawful occasions.

A tram came grinding to a standstill and he boarded it. Facing him, two very English old ladies were discussing church affairs with interest: he gathered that all was not going as it should do with regard to the approaching sale of work. And just for a second a faint smile twitched round his lips. They were so *very* earnest about it, and the ever-amazing contrasts that go to form this thing called life tickled his sense of humour.

He found a shoe shop without difficulty, and made his purchases. Then, strolling through the empty market-place, he started to walk back to the hotel along the lake front. Gulls, shrieking discordantly, rose from the railings as he approached, only to resume their perches when he had gone by. And at one corner a man of unbelievable antiquity, who was fishing with the longest rod Drummond had ever seen, had just landed a fish nearly two inches long.

He arrived back in the hotel, and told the concierge to have the parcel sent up to his room. Then he went through to the bar to find Cranmer who held up his thumbs as soon as he saw him.

"Luck's in up to a point," he said. "The house belongs to a man called Maier, but since Maier is about as common here as Smith is in England it doesn't seem to help us much."

"Still, it's something," answered Drummond. "Your shoes are in my room."

"I'll get 'em after dinner," said Cranmer. "Shall we do a spot of scouting now?"

Drummond nodded, and Cranmer rose.

"We go out by the other door," he went on. "My hat's in the hall."

In silence the two men strode along the main street until they came to a road branching off left-handed and leading up into the hills. Below them, about half a mile away, sombre and grim, Chillon Castle jutted out into the lake, whilst above it, far off in the distance, the peaks of the Dent du Midi had turned to purple.

There was a nip in the air, and they walked briskly. At first the houses were continuous, small ones of the working-man type. But shortly they ceased, and scattered villas took their place – villas which were approached by drives of varying length.

"There it is," said Cranmer. "The next one on the right."

"Good," cried Drummond. "Don't pause; we'll walk straight past."

It stood about thirty yards back from the road and below it. Though obviously inhabited there was no sign of any inmates. Nor was there any indication of a dog. An upstair window was open, and the curtains were stirring in the faint breeze. And as they passed a light was suddenly switched on in the room, and a man leant out. His back was to the light, so that all they could see was the silhouette of a broad-shouldered figure. Then he disappeared.

They walked on another hundred yards when Drummond stopped.

"About turn," he said. "There's nothing more to be found out now. Let's go back to the pub. Two things, old boy, which may help us. There's undergrowth on each side of the drive, and from the road one can see into the upstair window. Let us hope that the night may bring us luck."

"Probably bring us jug," laughed Cranmer. "However, the Swiss are a humane race. I don't suppose they torture their prisoners."

The bar had filled up when they returned, and having ordered two drinks they stood by it. In an adjoining room four people were playing bridge, and in one corner of the bar itself a large cosmopolitan party was drinking cocktails. They were talking French, but some were obviously Germans, and the remainder Americans.

"You see the very tall gentleman facing you, sir," said the barman in an undertone to Drummond. "That is your consul here – M'sieur Lénod."

"The devil it is," murmured Drummond. "He is a Swiss?"

"*Mais oui, m'sieu*. But he has spent much of his time in England. He speaks it perfectly."

"Thank you," said Drummond and turned to Cranmer. "I wonder if he could help us over Maier," he went on in a low voice.

"No harm in trying," answered the other. "By Jove! he's coming over here."

It was true: Monsieur Lénod was crossing to the bar to give an order.

"Excuse me, m'sieur," said Drummond when he had finished his instructions, "but I understand you are the British consul here."

"That is so," returned the tall man.

"I wonder if I could have a few minutes' conversation with you this evening?"

"If you wish to see me on business," said Monsieur Lénod, "you will find me at my office tomorrow morning."

"I'm afraid tomorrow morning will be too late," said Drummond. "I should esteem it a very great favour if you could waive professional etiquette on this occasion. I can assure you that it is very important."

"Under those circumstances, gentlemen, I will join you as soon as I can get away from my party."

With a courteous bow he moved back to his table, and Drummond turned to Cranmer.

"It may come to nothing," he said, "but as you say, it's worth trying. There's a vacant table over there. Let's go and sit down."

Ten minutes later the consul joined them.

"Well, gentlemen," he remarked. "What can I do for you?"

"In the first place," said Drummond, "we had better introduce ourselves. My name is Drummond, Captain Drummond, and this is Cranmer. We are over here, M'sieur Lénod, in connection with the murder of Colonel Talbot in Hyde Park, which you have doubtless read about in the papers."

The consul raised his eyebrows.

"Police?" he murmured.

"No, not police. Shall we say – Secret Service!"

Drummond paused for a moment and lit a cigarette.

"It has come to our knowledge," he continued, "that there is a certain villa in Veytaux which is in some way connected with the crime. In what way we don't know, but this villa was mentioned by men who are believed to be implicated in the murder."

"And the name of it?" asked the consul.

"The Bon Ciel."

The consul nodded thoughtfully.

"Monsieur Carl Maier," he said. "Well, gentlemen, I am not altogether surprised. Why he should be concerned in the murder of Colonel Talbot is completely beyond me, but if anybody here *is* concerned in it he would be the man I should pick on."

"So you know something about Maier," remarked Drummond quietly.

"Quite a lot. To begin with – though this is hardly relevant to the present matter – his villa was one of the centres of espionage during the war. As you can imagine all this shore of the lake was a happy hunting-ground for spies, who could enter the country from Germany, and find France just across the water. And though we could never prove it and, in fact, could do nothing even if we did prove it, Maier's villa was one of their principal rendezvous."

"What sort of a man is he?" asked Drummond.

"He is a German Swiss, born not far from Basle. His age is about sixty. By profession he is a clockmaker, though he has long given up actual work. He is, however, extremely clever with his fingers, at any form of mechanical contrivance. It is his hobby – messing about with springs and cogged wheels. So much for one aspect of the man."

The consul paused as if to weigh his words, and the others did not interrupt him.

"Now for another and possibly more important one," continued Monsieur Lénod. "In his early days he was a red hot revolutionary – practically an anarchist. I gather that he has mellowed somewhat with advancing years, but up till long after the war he was a fanatical extremist. Incidentally, Captain Drummond, the actual chair in which you are sitting is the one in which Lenin sat – night after night – before he went to Russia, and I have often seen Maier in here talking to him."

"How very interesting," said Drummond.

"But once again hardly relevant," said the consul with a smile. "However, I really don't know that I can tell you any more about him. I must say I would be interested to know how he can possibly be mixed up in that Hyde Park affair."

"So would we, M'sieur Lénod," remarked Drummond dryly. "By the way, is he married?"

"He was, but his wife died some years ago."

"Does he live alone?"

"Yes. Though sometimes a married daughter comes to stay with him, I believe."

"Has he any servants?"

The consul put down his glass.

"Captain Drummond," he said quietly, "may I ask the purport of your last few questions?"

Drummond's eyes twinkled.

"Officially or unofficially, M'sieur Lénod?"

"Well – I'm not in my office."

"A very good answer," laughed Drummond. "But even a better one is what the Governor of North Carolina said to the Governor of South Carolina."

He beckoned to the barman.

"M'sieur Lénod," he said quietly, "we are infinitely obliged to you for what you have told us. But I think in view of your position here it would be better if we now discussed the prospects of winter sport."

The consul gave a little chuckle.

"Perhaps you're right," he murmured. "Er – with reference to your last question – one old woman and she's deaf."

"Our friend the consul was very helpful," remarked Drummond ten minutes later, as they watched the tall figure passing through the swing doors. "Only one old woman, my boy, and she's deaf."

Cranmer looked a bit uneasy.

"You know, it's all right for you," he said. "You're a blinking civilian. Don't forget I'm a H'army H'orficer. Do you really intend to break in?"

Drummond lit a cigarette thoughtfully.

"I take your meaning, Cranmer," he answered. "And I can assure you, my dear fellow, that civilian or no civilian, I don't intend to spend the next few months sampling Swiss prison diet. But there can be no drawing back now. The whole matter has gone far beyond us and our little affairs. And if there's the slightest chance of our finding even the smallest ray of light in that villa it's our obvious duty to go there."

"And you think there is a chance?"

"Most certainly. Once again, you see, we come up against a man of pronounced red tendencies."

"Don't forget that I'm still very much in the dark," said Cranmer.

"I'll put you wise over dinner," remarked Drummond glancing at his watch. "And then we'll have to put through time till about midnight. It won't be safe to leave before."

"Won't it look rather peculiar – our sneaking out of here in rubber shoes?"

"We'll have to chance that, unless..."

He turned to the barman.

"Is there any haunt of vice in this delightful town?" he asked. "A night club, or something really dashing like that?"

"There's the Kursaal, sir. They have classical concerts there."

Drummond's face paled.

"No, no. Nothing quite so immoral as that. I mean some place where my friend and I could go in safety after dinner tonight."

"There's the Perroquet, sir. They dance there."

"That sounds more our form, Cranmer. The Perroquet. Delightful. We will repair to this sink of iniquity and have a look at the pretties. And with us," he continued in a lower voice, "we will take my rucksac *mit* rubber shoes complete, into which we will change just before reaching the villa. It is goot – yes?"

Cranmer grinned.

"You seem in devilish high spirits," he said. "You're used to little escapades of this sort: I'm not. And by the time it comes to midnight they won't need any castanets in the Perroquet band: I'll lend 'em my knees."

Drummond roared with laughter.

"Let's go and have some food," he cried. "You'll take to it like a duck does to water. And fortunately for us there's no moon."

CHAPTER 7

Death at the Villa

It was just after midnight when they once again approached the villa Bon Ciel. During their walk from the Perroquet they had hardly met a soul; Montreux is not a late town. One or two belated cars had passed them, and once, in the distance, under the light of a lamp they had seen the stocky form of a policeman.

The night was dark and overcast. Not a star was showing, and there was a damp, raw feeling in the air. But the conditions, though unpleasant, were perfect for their purpose, and Drummond whistled cheerfully under his breath as they left the main road and started to climb.

Two hundred yards from the villa they changed their shoes, and hid the rucksack under a bush. Then they stole forward towards a shaft of light which lay across the road, and which proved that someone was still up in Monsieur Maier's household. From far away came the ceaseless murmur of a mountain stream; otherwise the night was silent.

At length they reached the line of light, and paused under cover of some shrubs to reconnoitre. It came from the room in which they had seen the man that afternoon – a bright bar of yellow shining out underneath the blind which had not been quite pulled down.

The window was open, and the blind was moving gently in the faint night breeze. But from where they were standing it was impossible to see right into the room. They were too low down, and Drummond was just on the point of hoisting Cranmer upon his shoulders when a shadow appeared on the blind. It was that of a man standing with his hands in his pockets close to the window; they could actually see a strip of his legs through the chink.

They crouched down waiting and after a few seconds the shadow moved across the window and vanished.

"Our friend is evidently awake," whispered Drummond. "I fear, old boy, our vigil may be a long one."

"What do you propose to do?" muttered Cranmer. "Wait till he goes to bed, and then sample one of the downstair windows."

Slowly, interminably the time passed, but there was no sign of the light being put out. Nor was there any further reappearance of the shadow. And at length Drummond stooped down.

"Get your knees on my shoulders," he whispered, "and hold on to my hands. And for the love of Mike don't fall off in the bushes, or we're stung."

He straightened up, and a moment later heard Cranmer's whispered – "All right."

"What did you see?" he muttered as he put him down.

"He's sprawling over the table asleep," said Cranmer.

"Hell!" answered Drummond. "That's a nuisance. We'll have to chance it – that's all."

And even as he spoke came the sound of the front door opening, and footsteps on the gravel.

"Still as death," he breathed in Cranmer's ear. "If he comes this way I'll deal with him."

The gate opened, and a man came out on to the road not three yards from where they were standing. He paused to shut the gate quietly: then he strode off away from them in the direction of Montreux.

"Thank the Lord for that," said Drummond. "It would have complicated things if I'd had to dot him one. Get up on my shoulders again and see if that other bloke is still asleep."

"Yes."

From above his head came Cranmer's monosyllable.

"Good. Then we'll chance it now, before the other bird has time to return. Let's try the front door."

Cautiously Drummond pushed open the gate, and, followed by Cranmer crept towards the house. From above them came the tapping of the blind against the window sill as it oscillated to and fro. And once their shadows, distorted eerily, were flung on the bushes from the headlights of a car on the main road below.

They reached the door and Drummond flashed his torch on it.

"In luck," he whispered. "Not a Yale."

He turned the handle, and a moment later they were both standing in the hall. The house was absolutely silent: even the sound of the stream had ceased. But to Cranmer it seemed as if the beating of his heart must be audible in Montreux. His hands were shaking: his mouth felt curiously dry. And he started like a frightened colt as Drummond laid a hand on his arm.

"Steady, old boy," muttered Drummond with a little chuckle. "Just follow me, and don't make a noise."

Once again the beam of the torch explored the darkness: in front of them were the stairs. And almost before Cranmer had moved he heard an impatient whisper from the landing above, though of Drummond's movement there had been no sound.

"Come on, Cranmer: there's no time to lose."

The stairs bent round at right angles, and as he joined his leader they could both see the light shining under the door of the occupied room.

Step by step they mounted till they reached the top. And there Drummond bent down and peered through the keyhole.

"I don't like it, Cranmer," he said quietly as he straightened up. "I can't quite see, but no man has ever slept in that position. Be prepared for something."

He turned the handle, and gently pushed open the door. And Cranmer, standing behind him, heard his breath come in a sharp hiss, and saw his body stiffen. Then he peered over his shoulder, and felt violently sick.

Seated at the desk, which was more like a working bench, was a man whose head had literally been battered in. His injuries could only have been caused by an attack of well-nigh inconceivable ferocity. The blood which had formed a great pool on the table had welled over and was dripping sluggishly on to the wooden floor. One hand hung limply down: the other, still clutching a small hammer, was on the bench. And in the dead man's eyes there seemed to linger an expression of mortal terror.

"For God's sake – let's go," said a voice and Cranmer realised it was his own.

Once more he felt that firm, reassuring pressure on his arms: once again he heard that quiet voice.

"Steady, old boy. The poor devil's not a pretty sight, but we've got to go through with it. Stand here by the door, and don't under any circumstances let your shadow fall on the blind."

Crouching down, Drummond moved over to the body, while Cranmer, still feeling faint and sick, watched him, fascinated. Watched him as he went swiftly through the dead man's pockets: watched him glancing through the letters he found. Saw him open drawer after drawer of a cupboard that stood against the wall, and rummage through their contents: saw him pause and stand motionless as he stared at the last one.

For a moment what was in it conveyed nothing to Drummond: then, like a blinding flash there came back to his memory those last cryptic words of Jimmy Latimer to Madame Pélain as the train steamed out of Cannes Station. "Sealed fruit tins."

And there in the drawer were two fruit tins. True, they were not sealed: they had been opened, and their contents had been removed. In fact they were just two empty tins, and only by the pictures of fruit on the paper wrapper that was pasted round each of them was it possible to know what their contents had been.

Thoughtfully Drummond picked one up and examined it. It stood about four inches high; the diameter was approximately the same. The label proclaimed that it had contained Fancy Quality Fruit Salad, prepared by a firm called Petworth, who had packed it in their own orchard factory in Gloucestershire.

He looked inside: nothing. And then a peculiar point struck him. Under ordinary circumstances when a top is removed with a tin-opener, the resulting cut has ragged edges. But in the tin which he held in his hand the top edge was perfectly smooth. And when he looked at it more closely he could plainly see in places the marks of a file. Why had the owner of the tin taken the trouble to do such a thing?

He put it back and picked up the other one. And at once things became more interesting. To outward appearances the two tins were identical, but the interior revealed a striking difference. Soldered into the side, about an inch below the top, were three tiny metal cubes, each the size of a small die. Their positions formed the corners of an equilateral triangle.

For a long while he stared at them trying to think what possible object they could fulfil. In view of the fact that the dead man's hobby had been playing about with springs and things, he might have assumed that the tin was the outer case for some patent model he was inventing. But Jimmy's remark could not be ignored, so that that simple solution would not hold water.

He looked at the outside more carefully: no sign of the soldering appeared there. And a moment's reflection told him that even if any mark had shown on the metal, the paper wrapper would have concealed it.

He glanced up: Cranmer was standing beside him looking curiously at the tin.

"I told you about Jimmy's remark," said Drummond. "What's your reaction to this? You see the edge has been carefully filed down where the opener has been used."

"As a matter of fact," said Cranmer, "you don't use an ordinary opener with this brand. I happen to know, because I had to open one the other night. They have a key with a slot at the end into which you put a tongue of the metal fastening. Then you roll the key round and round…"

"I know," interrupted Drummond. "Still that doesn't explain those studs."

"It does not," agreed Cranmer. "My God! what's that?"

Both men stood rigid: the gate had shut and steps could be heard on the gravel. Worse still – voices.

"Quick," snapped Drummond. "Out on the landing and into some other room."

Like a flash they were through the door, closing it after them. And as they were on the landing, the newcomers entered the hall below.

"I tell you it's all right," came a guttural voice with a pronounced accent. "The woman is stone deaf. Almost as deaf" – he laughed harshly – "as he is."

Like shadows Drummond and Cranmer faded into a bedroom opposite as the footsteps came up the stairs.

"It is absurd," said another voice, "returning here at all. You have all that matters. Mother of Mercy!" The voice rose to a scream.

Cautiously Drummond opened the door a little and peered out. Two men were standing in the room they had just left. One was a big fellow; the other was short and rather fat. And it was he who was covering his face with his hands, as if to shut out the dreadful thing at the desk.

"Squeamish," sneered the big man. "When a man gets hit with a coal hammer he doesn't generally look as if he'd died of old age. Now then..."

The words died away, and Drummond saw him take a spring forward. And then there came from the room a flood of the most fearful blasphemy.

"It's gone, I tell you," cried the big man when he could again speak coherently. "It's gone."

"It can't have gone," said his companion in a trembling voice. "You must have made a mistake."

"I tell you, it's gone," snarled the other. "Here is the one without the studs, but the other is gone. Moreover" – into his voice there crept a note of fear – "this drawer was shut. He shut it himself."

"Well, assuredly, he could not have opened it again. Let us go. For God's sake, let us go. You have all that really matters in your pocket."

"How did that drawer come open?"

The big man came into sight again and stood staring at his trembling companion.

"I know it was shut," he went on. "When he became foolish he got up and he shut it. I can see him doing it now. He crossed and he shut it: then he returned to the chair and laughed at me."

"It is a little thing anyway whether it was open or shut. Let us go."

"But it is not a little thing that the tin has gone, you fool. Tins do not walk on their own. *He* could not have touched it. *So who has?*"

"Who, indeed?" whispered Drummond, and Cranmer could feel his grin of pure joy. "Put the tin on the bed, old boy: we'll each want both our hands shortly. I'll take the big 'un."

Again he peered out: the fat man was speaking in a quavering voice.

"What does it matter? If we are found here all is lost. It means prison."

"Shut up, you cur." His companion regarded him with contempt. "You haven't got the nerves of a louse. Don't you realise that someone has been here since I left?"

"All the more reason for us to go at once."

"It couldn't have been the police or they would still have been here."

"No. But whoever it was may inform the police."

The big man continued as if the other had not spoken.

"Yes. They'd still have been here. Now why should this unknown visitor take such an apparently useless thing as that tin? Answer me that."

But the fat man was beyond speech: rivers of perspiration were pouring down his face which he was endeavouring to mop up with a shaking hand.

"Is there any other number in Montreux? Speak, you worm!"

"Not that I know of," stuttered the fat man.

"Then it's an enemy... An enemy who knows... Come on...we'll go."

"Our cue," muttered Drummond, flinging open the door.

His appearance was so utterly unexpected that for a moment or two the big man stood staring dumbfounded across the passage. Which was unwise on his part. He had a fleeting vision of a man as big as himself materialising from nowhere: then something that seemed like a steam hammer hit him on the jaw. He crashed over backwards and his head hit the edge of the bench with a crack like the impact of two billiard balls. And it was perhaps poetic justice that, as he lay unconscious on the floor, a little rivulet of the blood of the man he had murdered welled over and splashed on his face.

"So much for you," grunted Drummond and turned to a corner from which a series of squeaks were issuing, reminiscent of a rabbit caught by a stoat. They came from the little fat man who was on his knees in prayer before Cranmer.

At any other time Drummond would have laughed – the sight was so ludicrous. But speed was the order of the day, and his quick eye had spotted a length of rope in some lumber behind the door.

"Bring him here, Cranmer," he said curtly. "Put him in that chair. Gag him with his own handkerchief... No, no. In his mouth, man, and knot it behind his head. Like a snaffle on a horse. That's right... Now his legs; there's some more rope over there."

They worked in silence, and the result was creditable to all concerned. It would have been hard to imagine a more scientifically trussed and gagged gentleman than the one who gazed at them fearfully from the chair.

"Go through his pockets, old boy," said Drummond. "I'll tackle the other."

He crossed to the unconscious man and felt his pulse; it was beating evenly and steadily. Fortunate; it would have complicated matters if he had killed him. Then he ran over him with skilled hands, and at once found a prize.

In one pocket was a piece of mechanism that looked like the inside of a clock. For a moment or two he studied it; evidently this was what had been alluded to as "all that really matters". He put it on the bench and continued his search. Two private letters; a pocket book which he went through; some money.

"Found anything on yours?" he asked.

"Not a thing," said Cranmer.

"Then we'll hop it. Get the tin."

And with one last look at the room – at the little fat man whose terrified eyes were roving incessantly; at the dead man whose terrified eyes were fixed and staring; at the unconscious man sprawling on the floor – Drummond shut the door. And a few minutes later with sighs of relief they felt the night breeze cool on their faces, and heard from afar off the ceaseless murmur of the mountain stream.

"I suppose I shall wake up in a moment," said Cranmer as they retrieved the rucksack and changed their shoes.

Drummond gave a short laugh.

"It's been a bit hectic for a first try out," he agreed. "But you did very well, my lad – very well indeed. Now everything depends on Monsieur Lénod."

Cranmer glanced at him.

"How do you make that out?"

"When the deaf servant wakes up tomorrow morning, it will not be long before she enters that room. Then the fat will be in the fire. By ten o'clock it will be all over the place. And after our conversation with Lénod tonight it would, under ordinary circumstances, be his bounden duty to tell the police."

"I hadn't thought of that. What do you propose to do about it?"

"Persuade him that the circumstances are *not* ordinary. It's our only hope. If he tells the police, the delay will be interminable. And we can't afford delay, Cranmer. We've *got* to get back to England at the first possible moment."

"The fat little man may squeal."

"He may. On the other hand fear of vengeance may prevent him. Anyway we've got to chance that. He doesn't know who we are, which is the main point."

They turned into the hotel, where a sleepy night porter wished them good night.

"Come into my room for a moment," said Drummond. "I want to look at this machine a little more closely."

He took it and the fruit tin out of the rucksack, and placed them on the table. And the object of the studs inside the tin at once became obvious. For the diameter of the machine was such that it would just slip inside the tin and then come to rest on the studs.

"So far so good," remarked Drummond. "But what the deuce happens next?"

Cranmer yawned.

"Ask me another," he said. "What feels like happening next to me is going to bed."

"Then you push off, old boy. If I can square Lénod I'll want you to fly from Zurich tomorrow. And you'll have to take this machine with you. The tin doesn't matter; we can get dozens in England."

"And what will you do?"

"Go *via* Basle through Germany, and probably fly from Brussels."

Cranmer yawned again.

"Well – I'll hit the hay. Good night."

"Night-night," said Drummond absently, and the last Cranmer saw of him as he closed the door was peering earnestly into the bowels of the machine.

Sick with weariness Archie Cranmer stumbled into his room, and almost before his head touched the pillow he was asleep. And it seemed to him only the next moment that he was awakened by someone shaking his shoulder.

The daylight was streaming into the room as he opened his eyes to find Drummond standing beside the bed.

"I've been to the consul," said that worthy, "and may Heaven be praised the man's a sportsman. When he'd got over his very natural wrath at being dragged from his bed at such an ungodly hour, he listened to what I had to say. I told him the whole story from A to Z; pointed out to him that if we'd had anything to do with the murder we should hardly have talked to him as we did last night; and finally appealed to his patriotism. And though he's a Swiss there's no doubt about that latter commodity. However, to cut a long story short, he has agreed to forget our conversation here last night."

"Stout feller," said Cranmer.

"If the fat man spills the beans sufficiently for us to be identified Lénod, of course, can do nothing. But if we are detained here he has agreed to see personally that that machine gets back to London, even if he has to take it himself, and to tell Ginger Lawson what happened last night. So that side of it is settled, so far as anything can be settled in this affair."

Cranmer jumped out of bed and began to shave.

"Do you want to borrow my razor?" he asked with a glance at Drummond's chin.

"No, old boy, I don't," said Drummond with a grin. "I have long had a fancy to see what I should look like with a beard. And I think it may prove useful in England."

"When do we start?"

"I've been looking up trains, and there seems a good one at eleven-fifteen. Part of it goes to Zurich and part to Basle. If we can get that I think we're safe."

And suddenly Drummond began to laugh.

"It seems funny, after my long career of singing in the village choir, that the only two occasions on which I've been really frightened of the police, are the two when I *haven't* done anything."

CHAPTER 8

Algy Intervenes

Algy Longworth was singing in his bath. It was not a pleasant sound, but his servant, though a little white about the gills was hardened to it, and continued to lay the breakfast. He even survived the sudden appearance of his master clad only in a bath towel, and proceeded to hand him his letters.

"We are in voice this morning, Marsh, are we not?" remarked Algy glancing through them. "Which, my trusty varlet, is surprising, because beneath this outer husk conditions are poor – very poor. Marsh, I could do with a horse's neck."

"Very good, sir. How much brandy?"

"Just as you take it yourself, Marsh. Or is it your considered opinion that half a pint of champagne would meet the case better?"

"I prefer it myself, sir. I find a horse's neck a trifle sweet at this hour of the morning."

"Spoken like a man. Champagne let it be. What are we doing today, Marsh?"

"Your engagement book states, sir, that you are lunching at the Ritz with a tow-haired filly – name unknown, and slightly knock-kneed."

"Impossible, Marsh. Impossible. How could a man of my exalted moral standing know anything about her knees. I wonder who the deuce she can be."

"That, sir, I fear is beyond me. The entry was made two or three days ago, after an evening you spent at the Golden Boot."

"I was there last night, Marsh. Tell me, old friend of my youth," he went on, lighting a cigarette, "have you noticed anything particularly attractive about me lately? Have I recently developed some hitherto latent charm of manner which endears me to the world at large?"

"I have noticed no change, sir."

"Last night, for instance, Marsh, I became conscious of an air of solicitude about my goings and comings, so to speak, which touched me greatly, but at the same time a little surprised me. Maiden and men concerned themselves with my poor affairs in a way which, I confess, astonished me. It removed, I am glad to say, any lingering doubts that I was one of the people aimed at in those delightful advertisements of 'What she said' and 'What she really thought.' But apart from that, Marsh, there was, as I say, an interest displayed in me which I really cannot account for."

His servant crossed to the window and glanced out.

"I wonder if it's part of the same things, sir. This flat is being watched."

"Watched! Are you sure?"

"Absolutely, sir. There's the bloke on the other side now. Same man who was here for a time yesterday."

"Come away from the window."

Algy Longworth sat down at the table, and his eyes had suddenly grown thoughtful.

"When did we last hear from Captain Drummond, Marsh?"

"He rang you up from his club, sir, about eight days ago. I took the message, and you went round to see him."

"And I rang him up two days after that and found he'd gone to France. It's funny, Marsh, all this. Mr Burton was asking me about him the night before last. He, too, seems to have become popular. Ring up his house, and find out if he's back in London."

"No, sir," said Marsh returning a few moments later. "He has not come back. I took the liberty, sir, of asking his man Denny if anyone was watching his house. He had not noticed it up to date, but he is going to keep a look-out in future."

"Good. I'm inclined to think, Marsh, that we may be finding ourselves on the warpath once again. And if so I must go into training. No more late nights: no more knock-kneed dames. Hullo! who's that?"

The front door bell had rung.

"Get me a dressing-gown, and go and see. And don't forget, the cautionary period has started."

"Very good, sir."

Came a murmur of voices from outside, and then suddenly a well-known laugh.

"It's all right, Marsh. I'm glad you didn't recognise me."

"Good Lord!" cried Algy, going to the door. "Talk of the devil! My dear old boy – what a magnificent make-up! I wouldn't have known you myself."

Hugh Drummond was standing in the hall, though only by his voice would anyone have known him. A master of disguise at any time, on this occasion he had excelled himself. A four-days' growth of beard adorned his chin: a greasy cap was pulled down over one eye. And by some extraordinary method he had managed to alter his actual features: slightly, but enough to deceive anyone. Round his neck was knotted a coloured handkerchief in place of a collar: his clothes were in keeping with his cap. And in his hand be carried a carpet-bag of plumber's tools which he put down on the floor.

"How are you, Algy?" he cried. "I'm just going to get through to Ginger Lawson and then I want a drink."

He dialled the machine, whilst Algy Longworth went back to get dressed. And when he returned to his sitting-room it was to find Drummond sitting in an easy chair with his face buried in a tankard of ale.

"What's the great idea?" he demanded.

"Are you all ready for the road, Algy?"

"Sure thing," said the other.

"Because we'll want all the boys. Something damned funny is on foot, old lad. You know I went over to France?"

"Yes."

"Well, I'll just tell you briefly what happened in that delectable country. You'd better make a few notes, because I'll want you to tell the others."

Algy Longworth listened in silence, except for putting in an occasional question.

"And you slipped out of Switzerland all right," he said, as Drummond paused for more beer.

"No difficulty there. Young Cranmer flew from Zurich and has duly arrived. I went through Germany and caught the afternoon boat yesterday from Ostend. Strong men shrank from me, appalled at the sight of my beard, but that couldn't be helped. And having suitably disguised myself this morning the game begins on this side."

He put down his tankard and his eyes were grim.

"They've been scoring, Algy, in a way that must cease. First, Jimmy Latimer: then the Chief. And from what Ginger Lawson said over the phone neither Ronald nor Gasdon have rung him up. Which means that they are still detained in France – if not worse."

Algy Longworth shouted for his servant.

"Clear these things away, Marsh. Look here, are you *absolutely* sure about that man outside?"

"Absolutely, sir."

"Rather a jolt, Hugh. This flat is being watched."

"The devil it is," said Drummond. "That's a nuisance."

"And last night at the Golden Boot several people were infernally inquisitive about you and me."

"Was Burton there?"

"Not last night. But little Alice Blackton told me that the day after you went there he tried to pump her about you."

"I know they've got me taped all right. And they're on to you because of me."

"You're sure you weren't spotted at Dover?"

"My dear feller, with this crowd one can't be *sure* of anything. And I took one or two precautions on leaving the boat-train at Victoria, which ensured that I wasn't followed. But I must say that had I thought for an instant that they were favouring you with their attentions I should not have come here."

"No one would spot you in that rig."

"No," agreed Drummond, "I don't think they would. But although they're clumsy in their methods, there seems to be such an infernal number of them that one can't afford to take any chances. Moreover," he added savagely, "their manners if crude are drastic. When I think of poor old Talbot shot in cold blood, and in broad daylight in the Park, it fairly gets my goat."

"Same here," said Algy. "Well, old boy, what are orders?"

"First of all warn in the boys – Peter, Ted, the whole bunch. None of them are on the suspect list as yet. Get 'em to the club, Algy, and tell 'em the whole tale. They must cancel every engagement, and literally live at the end of a telephone wire."

"Interrupting you for a moment, Hugh, since the affair seems to be so damned serious, can't you get Scotland Yard straight on to this swine Burton?"

"Lawson has put them wise, of course. But at the moment there is nothing to go on. The mere fact that he took Menalin's girl friend to the Golden Boot, and that she jeered at us in Nice over the Chief's death, is not enough to hang a fly on. No, old boy, we've got to get something far more definite than that. And we're going to get it."

"Right ho! Go ahead."

"Warn 'em that this is no jest, but the grimmest thing we've ever been up against. I'll phone orders to Peter – not to you, since you are suspect. So under no circumstances must you be seen with Peter, or go to his flat. In fact, except for the meeting at the club, none of you must be seen together. When you get my orders you will come separately to the rendezvous I'll give Peter. Clear so far?"

"Perfectly."

"Where that rendezvous will be, I have no idea. When you will get the summons, I have no idea. But this matter is serious, Algy, and everything else must go by the board. Impress that on the boys."

"I will."

"If anything happens to me, leadership devolves on Peter. Tell him that."

"OK."

"As an additional precaution if it is easier to send orders by wire, I will sign the telegram HUD. Not Drummond; not Hugh. Just HUD. Over the telephone I will say 'HUD speaking.'"

"I get you. I'll warn everyone in. What are you going to do yourself?"

"Try and get on to Charles Burton's trail. What's the name of his house in Sussex?"

"Birchington Towers. It's a biggish place standing on a bit of a hill, and surrounded by trees."

"Sounds promising. Near Pulborough?"

"About two miles from Pulborough on the Arundel road."

"What's happened, Algy, about that girl you said he was keen on – Molly Castledon?"

"Nothing so far as I know. But she'll certainly give him the raspberry. And from what you tell me it'll be a darned good thing if she does."

Drummond looked at him thoughtfully.

"What sort of a wench is she, Algy?"

"Very nice. Charming girl. Why?"

"Reliable?"

"In what way?"

"Supposing she didn't give him the raspberry. At least, not yet. Supposing she played with him gently, and wangled an invitation to Birchington Towers."

"Hold 'ard, old man. Is it safe?"

"My dear boy, Burton is not going to be such a congenital half-wit as to hurt her. What possible object could he have in so doing?"

"Well, I can ask her. I can ring her up now and suggest a spot of alcohol. But I shall have to give her some reason."

"Why shouldn't you? You needn't tell her the whole thing. Just say that Charles is not all he seems on the surface, and that we are very anxious for any information we can collect about him. You can hint that it's a big thing, and that the country itself may be in danger."

"He's not likely to breathe a word of anything to her."

"Perhaps not. But a girl with her eyes open can frequently find out things. Especially if Burton has entered for the matrimonial stakes. Any scrap of news, Algy, might prove of value."

"Well, as I said, I can but ask her."

"Her people won't mind, will they?"

"Good Lord! My dear fellow, the old woman will swallow her false teeth in her excitement."

"Then get on with it," said Drummond rising. "Do you know where Burton is now?"

"No. But it's possible Alice might."

"Do you know her number?"

"I do."

"Then give her a ring on chance."

Drummond crossed the room, and peered cautiously out of the window, as Algy went into the hall. There on the opposite side of the road was a man rather obviously doing nothing. He was an inconspicuous individual, of much the same type as the man who had followed him in Piccadilly, but his occupation shouted itself aloud. And once again Drummond was struck with the extreme amateurishness of so many of the smaller fry on the other side. The man could never have shadowed anyone before in his life.

"She believes he's down in Sussex," said Algy coming back into the room. "In any case she knows he's going there for the weekend."

"Good. I've been watching your sleuth, old boy."

"Still there, is he? Let's have a look at the blighter. Ah! yes, I see him. A respectable looking fellow too, you know. Shall I go out and push his face?"

"No. But I'm going to let you leave the flat before me. I want to be quite sure that it is you and not me he's after. You barge on round to the club, old boy, and get busy."

"Suppose we want to get in touch with you, Hugh?"

"Agony column, *Morning Post*. Make it cryptic; address it to HUD and sign it P for Peter."

"It's a date. Well, so long, old man. I wish to God I could think who the knock-kneed girl is I'm supposed to be lunching with at the Ritz."

A faint smile twitched round Drummond's lips as he heard the front door slam, and a moment or two later Algy appeared on the pavement, and began to saunter slowly along the street. Sure enough the man followed him at a decent interval, and Drummond gave a sigh of relief. So far as he could see he had successfully lost himself. And how long that state of affairs continued would depend entirely on his own skill.

He poured himself out some more beer, and sat down in an easy chair. For the first time since the beginning of his hectic rush from Nice he really had leisure to review the situation; up till now his own getaway had occupied his whole mind.

The thing that worried him most was the failure of Standish and Gasdon to reach England. Particularly Gasdon; Standish, assuming he had returned to Cannes, would barely have had time. But that Gasdon, who should have been in England two days ago, was still in France was ominous. However, they were both men well able to look after themselves, and in any case there was nothing that he could do. His immediate job was to follow the advice he had given Algy and get busy.

The first thing to do was to have a talk with Ginger Lawson. But here a difficulty presented itself. They would almost certainly be shadowing him, and that meant running the risk of Drummond himself being picked up again. Especially as Ginger, though an excessively stout-hearted officer, was not very adept at work of that sort. As against that, to judge by the previous performers, nor were the other side.

"Marsh," he called out, "ring up the War Office and ask for Major Lawson."

A simple plan had suggested itself to his mind, and simplicity was advisable with Ginger.

"On the line, sir."

Marsh put his head in at the door, and Drummond went to the telephone.

"That you, Ginger? Drummond again. I've got to have a talk with you."

"Delighted, old boy. Come round now."

"Not on your life," said Drummond with a short laugh. "Things are much too serious for that. You've got to come and see me, but I don't want you followed. When you go to the club for lunch go in as usual by the entrance in St James's Square. Walk straight through and leave the club at once by the ladies' entrance in Pall Mall. Get into a taxi and drive to Heppel Street – Number 10."

"Where the hell is Heppel Street?"

"Behind the British Museum. I'll be waiting for you, and I'll have a lunch of sorts ready."

"All right," came Ginger's resigned voice.

"And should the necessity arise don't forget that my name is Johnson and I'm a plumber."

"May Allah help the drains. Right ho! old lad. I'll be there. About one."

Drummond replaced the receiver; so far so good. His next move must be to find out if his own house was being watched. It was almost a waste of time, but it was just possible that if they still believed him to be in France, they might not have bothered to do so. And if so, there were several things he would have liked to get hold of; in particular, a revolver, having left his other in Cannes.

"I'm off now, Marsh," he said picking up his bag of tools. "See that Mr Longworth behaves himself. No, don't open the door. I'm the plumber."

He let himself out, and standing on the doorstep, he proceeded to fill a singularly offensive pipe. His eyes darted this way and that; there was no sign of anyone suspicious. Then once more picking up his bag, he slouched off down the street.

One glance was sufficient as he neared his own house: they had not neglected the obvious precaution. But Drummond feeling perfectly secure in his disguise, determined on a bold move. He walked up the steps and rang the bell.

"Is this Mrs Rowbotham's 'ouse?" he demanded as Denny opened the door.

"No, it ain't." Came a pause. "Good Lord! sir, I'd never have known you."

"Dry up, you fool. I was told to come to Number 94... Mrs Rowbotham. Bring my revolver to 10, Heppel Street tonight... Where is 'er blinking 'ouse?"

"And watch that bloke opposite."

Drummond consulted a dirty note-book.

"There you are, see, Rowbotham. 94, Clarges Street. Bring some money too: twenty pounds."

"This ain't Clarges Street: it's Half Moon Street. Very good, sir. Next street along there."

"Thanks, mate."

At the bottom of the steps he paused to relight his pipe and take stock of the man on the other side of the road. It was a tougher-looking specimen this time, who might have been a professional bruiser. But he evinced not the smallest interest in the passing plumber, and he was still on sentry go when Drummond boarded a bus in Piccadilly.

As a residential quarter Heppel Street is not to be recommended. A row of dingy houses mournfully confronts another row of even dingier ones. At each end was traffic and life, but nothing ever came through that stagnant backwater. The arrival of a taxi was an event: the only wheeled traffic was the milkman's cart and an occasional tradesman's van.

Number 10 differed only from Nos. 11 and 12 in one respect: it was owned by Mrs Penny. And Mrs Penny had been in the service of the Drummond family for many years in days gone by. Why, when she was pensioned off, she had decided to live in such a repulsive locality, was one of these mysteries which he had long given up trying to solve. It remained that she had done so, and the fact had proved very useful to him in the past.

A better hiding-place it would have been impossible to find. Mrs Penny worshipped him with that touching and dog-like devotion so often displayed by old retainers on the children they have looked after. Torture would not have made her speak if she thought she was giving Master Hugh away. And though she sometimes expressed mild disapproval of his goings-on, as she called them, it was with a twinkle in her eye which quite belied her words.

One room in the house was permanently set aside for him. In it he kept half a dozen different disguises, and though he might not go near the place for a year he knew he would always find them in perfect condition whenever he wanted them.

So far as is known there had never been a Mr Penny. It was a courtesy title which lent, as Drummond always assured her, an air of respectability to their relations. But though he used to pull her leg about it in private, should a neighbour come in he was punctilious in his reference to the late lamented. On one evening it is true he had made a slight break by mentioning the grave at Wandsworth, and ten minutes later changing the venue to Hampstead, but in the wild hilarity of high tea the lapse had passed unnoticed.

"Darling," he called out as he entered the house, "put on your bonnet and shawl and trot off to the market. Get me two juicy, succulent steaks, and a nice bit of cheese. A gentleman is coming to lunch at one o'clock."

"That beard, Master Hugh!" The old lady emerged from the kitchen. "Can't you shave it off, lovey?"

"Not yet, Jane. Soon I hope it may be but a fantastic dream, but not yet. Let's have some onions and fried potatoes, and if you can get some celery I'll give you a kiss. And if any strange woman offers you a chocolate tell her she's a hussy. You can't be too careful these days."

"Will you be wanting some more beer, Master Hugh?"

"How many bottles are there left?"

"I ordered a dozen, dearie, last night. But I can only find four."

"Strange, Jane – very strange. How I can possibly have left as many as that is beyond me. Another dozen, darling."

"Who's the gentleman, Master Hugh? Do I know him?"

"No, Jane – you've never met him. He's a Major Lawson."

"Are you going on one of them wild pranks of yours again?"

"I am, my angel."

"Do be careful, dearie. You know what bad colds you used to have as a baby. And if you get your feet wet – "

Drummond burst into a roar of laughter.

"I shall borrow your elastic-sided boots, you old darling. Now pop along, and don't forget the celery."

He watched her waddle down the street: then picking up the morning paper he glanced through it. It was duller than usual, and he was on the point of throwing it down when a small paragraph caught his eye.

MYSTERY MILLIONAIRE
ARRIVAL IN LONDON

M. Serge Menalin, sometimes alluded to as the mystery millionaire, has arrived in London, accompanied by his beautiful wife. They have taken a suite at the Ritz-Carlton, and it is understood that they are staying there for two or three weeks. They have recently been in the South of France.

Drummond's eyes narrowed: so Menalin had appeared on the scene in person, complete with lady. Did that mean that things were coming to a head?

He lit a cigarette and began to pace up and down the little room. If only there was some ray of light in the darkness, some pointer to act as a guide. He heard Mrs Penny come in, and shortly after the wonderful smell of frying onions swept through room and house. But he was barely conscious of it; round and round in his brain turned the same unanswered question – what was at the bottom of it all?

A taxi drawing up outside brought him to the window; it was Ginger Lawson arriving, and he went out into the hall to let him in.

"Heavens above! old man," cried that outraged officer, pointing a finger at his chin, "why the grouse moor?"

"All in good time, Ginger. I want to make quite sure you haven't been followed."

Drummond was peering through the curtains, but there was no one in sight. And at length he came back into the room.

"I carried out your instructions," said Lawson. "Though what the devil anyone should want to follow me for is beyond me."

"They followed the Chief all right, didn't they?"

"The swine," cried Lawson savagely. "If I could catch those devils…"

"From what I read in the papers you're never likely to. When was the funeral?"

"The day before yesterday. What on earth is it all about, Hugh?"

Mrs Penny came bustling in with the steaks.

"Jane," cried Drummond, "this is Major Lawson. Short for antimacassar Jane, old boy. She has a passion for antimacassars which oversteps the bounds of decency. Put everything down, darling, and half a dozen bottles of beer and I'll shout when we're ready for the cheese."

"I got the celery, Master Hugh."

"Very good girl. Now, Ginger," he went on seriously as the old lady left the room. "Let's get down to things. Young Cranmer has, of course, told you about the show at the villa. Now have you made anything out of that mechanical device?"

"I sent it to an expert at the Yard," said Lawson. "And the utmost he could say was that as the thing stood it could fulfil no purpose at all. But that with the insertion of a spring it could be wound up just as a clock is wound up. Further, that it contained the additional mechanism which you only find in an alarum clock – that's to say it could be set to go off at a given time."

"Strange," said Drummond thoughtfully. "In conjunction with that fruit tin. And Jimmy's cryptic utterance."

"Are you playing with the idea that it is some sort of bomb that is intended?"

"Impossible to do otherwise."

"Then why go to all the bother of obtaining a proprietary brand of fruit tin? Any old tin would do."

"There's one very good reason, Ginger, so it seems to me. It's a stock size. There can be no mistake about its dimensions. And if these bombs are being manufactured in large quantities, possibly in different parts of the country, it might be most important to ensure that they were identical."

"But, good Lord! man – " began Lawson incredulously and Drummond held up his hand.

"I don't know if Ronald put it in his letter, but there was one remark that poor old Jimmy made to his girl friend out there that sticks in my memory. He said it was a plot which out-Vernes Jules Verne. And Jimmy was not an alarmist."

"That's true," agreed Lawson.

"You saw, didn't you, that Menalin has arrived in London complete with wife?"

"I did." Lawson pushed away his plate and stared thoughtfully at the fire. "By the way," he said suddenly, "who is this man Gasdon you were talking about on the phone?"

"An Englishman we met in Nice, again after Ronald wrote that letter. And full value, Ginger. He advanced a very remarkable theory. He suggested the possibility of a sudden devastating attack on England, financed, controlled and directed by the Reds."

"Rot, old boy: rot. We have accurate information of the whole of their movement here in England. It's blah, blah, and talk from the word 'go'."

"Here in England – perhaps. Gasdon's theory is that the thing might be engineered from outside, and be under the control of this man Menalin."

"He hates us, of course. We know that. But what could be his object?"

Drummond shrugged his shoulders.

"Ask me another. There I'm out of my depth. But it seems to me that there are quite a number of people in Europe who would not be sorry to see us down and out."

"That is perfectly true. At the same time, old boy, the whole idea seems most terribly far-fetched."

"That was my first reaction, but I've been thinking it over since. And now I'm not so sure. We're in a pretty helpless condition, Ginger."

"Absolutely helpless, I agree. True at long last we're re-arming, but most of our ships are antiquated, and as far as planes are concerned we're swamped for numbers."

"It's a funny thing," said Drummond thoughtfully, "but the very first night the Chief put me on to this job, when I was round at the Golden Boot, I had a most extraordinary experience. I suppose it only lasted a second or two, but it was the most vivid thing I have ever known. For a space I was actually back in France, with the flares lobbing up close to and the stink of death all round. The room had gone, the band had ceased. I heard the phit of a bullet; I heard the drone of a crump. And then as suddenly as it had come, it went."

"An omen?" Lawson looked at him curiously.

Drummond shrugged his shoulders again.

"I'm not a fanciful sort of bloke," he said, "but I wonder. Something pretty damnable is in the wind, Ginger. And the trouble, as I said to Algy, is that, officially, we haven't got a leg to stand on."

"Certainly not enough for the police to act."

"It would be fatal, Ginger, absolutely fatal. This has got to be done privately. The last thing we want to do is to arouse their suspicions. I'm hoping they think I'm still in France, but I'm not banking on it."

"Well, old boy, what do you want me to do?"

"Be the link, Ginger, between me and officialdom. And if anything happens to me – act immediately. I'll keep you posted in whatever I may find out. If Ronald or Gasdon ring you up tell 'em how matters stand, but be very sure that you're speaking to the right man. You know Ronald's voice, but you don't know Gasdon's, and they are quite capable of supplying a substitute. And don't forget that you're probably a marked man yourself."

Mrs Penny appeared at the door.

"Are you ready for the cheese, Master Hugh?"

"We are, my pet. And the steak was delicious."

The old lady beamed all over her face.

"Would you like a glass of redcurrant wine with your cheese?" she demanded.

"Jane darling," said Drummond. "I hate to hurt your feelings, but I cannot tell a lie. I can think of nothing I should abominate more."

"You used to be very fond of it when you were small," she cried indignantly.

"There you are, Ginger. There you see the woman who first set my toddling footsteps on the slippery path of drink. Away, temptress, and produce the celery."

Lawson glanced at his watch.

"I must be getting back, old boy. But I understand the position, and I'll do just what you've suggested. Anyway – here's luck."

He raised his tankard and drained it, then he rose to his feet.

"No, I won't have any cheese. I'm late already, and this is a day's march from the War House. Goodbye, Mrs Penny, and thank you so much for a delightful lunch. So long, Hugh, I'll let myself out."

"A good fellow, Jane," said Drummond as the front door banged. "And now, my love, I am going upstairs to sleep. I have a premonition that during the next week or so I'll have to go a bit short of that commodity."

"When are you going, dearie?"

"Tomorrow, Jane. Denny is bringing one or two trifles round for me tonight, and you can give him some of your redcurrant wine. I wonder," he added half to himself, "what luck Algy has had."

He was to find out next morning. For at that very moment Algy Longworth was handing in an advertisement for the Agony column of the *Morning Post*. And it ran as follows:

HUD. Filly agrees postpone raspberry. Will be there strong beginning. P.

Which was not difficult to interpret. Evidently Molly Castledon was going to play the game, and further would be at Birchington Towers for the weekend.

CHAPTER 9

Birchington Towers

"Stop snoring, George, and listen to me."

With a slight start Sir George Castledon sat up in his chair.

"Was I snoring, my love?"

"Should I have said so, if you were not? It was that second glass of port after lunch."

Resignedly Sir George watched the wife of his bosom lower her ample form into a chair facing him. The room was warm; he yearned for peace. But one glance at his wife's face had shattered that hope. A domestic storm was brewing.

"Are you aware that Molly is now playing golf with that young man?"

"What young man, my dear?" he said feebly.

Lady Castledon regarded him stonily through her lorgnettes and Sir George wilted. Small wonder; there was a story current in London that on one occasion her Ladyship had inadvertently entered a field tenanted by a bull. A few moments later it was tenanted by her: the bull had left, snorting with terror.

"Don't be more of a fool than God made you, George: you annoy me. What do you propose to do about it?"

"Do about it, my dear?"

The worthy baronet scratched his head.

"Don't keep on repeating what I say, George. Even if you are completely fuddled with alcohol you can surely grasp the fact that Molly is playing golf with that imbecile Algy what's-his-name, and that Mr Burton is all by himself."

"What's that? I'd better go and talk to him, my love."

He half rose from his chair.

"Sit down, George. Do you imagine he wishes to listen to your half-witted utterances? You must talk to him."

"But, damn it, Jane, that's what I suggested a moment ago, and you jumped down my throat."

"Not Burton. I mean that idiot with an eyeglass."

"What on earth am I to say to him? There's no harm in them playing golf if they want to."

"George. I shall shake you in a minute. Who said there was any harm in it? But this afternoon was a heaven-sent opportunity for Mr Burton to propose to Molly. If you'd had the gumption of an owl you would have taken that Longworth thing for a good brisk walk."

"My God!" Sir George shuddered violently.

"It would have been extremely good for your liver, and it would have got him out of the way. However, that can't be helped now: you must concentrate on after tea. The other guests do not arrive till about six, which should leave plenty of time. So as soon as tea is over you will suggest a game of billiards to Mr Longworth. He won't like to refuse a man of your age. And when you've got him in the billiard-room you will keep him there. Do you understand?"

"Yes, my love. Supposing Molly comes too."

"Leave that to me, George."

Lady Castledon rose to her feet.

"Leave that to me. Molly will not come to the billiard-room."

She swept out and Sir George sighed, a thing he had done frequently of late. Ever since that cursed dance Jane had had only one idea in her head. And the trouble was he did not like Charles Burton. The man seemed a gentleman and all that sort of thing, and he was certainly wealthy, but he did not like him. No definite reason: nothing particular on which he could put a finger: he just couldn't cotton to the blighter. As he had wittily said to old Lord Crumpleigh: "It's not the clothes that make the man, Bill: it's what's inside 'em."

A quick remark that: sized up the situation admirably. And he wasn't going to have Molly married to a shop in Savile Row, whatever Jane might say. True he had not actually put his foot down up to date, but on one point he was determined. There was to be no coercion. If Molly wanted to marry Burton she could, but he wouldn't have any pressure brought to bear on her.

He rose and walked over to the window. The floods were out, and below him there stretched a huge expanse of water from which trees rose like scattered islands. Away in the distance lay the South Downs, with Chanctonbury Ring showing clear in the setting sun. A glorious view, unequalled in that part of Sussex, and he was on the point of stepping out on to the lawn when two men came round a corner of the house in earnest conversation. So earnest was it that they did not see him until they were close to, and when they did so the conversation ceased abruptly.

"Good afternoon," remarked Sir George affably.

"Goot afternoon," answered one of them, speaking with a pronounced foreign accent.

"Lovely view," continued Sir George, wondering who they were. For neither of them wore a hat, and they both gave the impression of having just come out of the house for a stroll. Possibly some of the party who had arrived early. And if they were typical of the remainder of the guests it looked as if it was going to be a jolly weekend. For with a surly grunt from the man who had first spoken, the two of them resumed their walk and disappeared.

Sir George raised his eyebrows; then, lighting a cigarette, he stepped through the window. There was a faint and rather pleasant nip in the air, and he decided to have a stroll round the grounds. Doubtless, Jane would be entertaining their host, so that he was not wanted.

He left the drive that ran down to the main road on his right, and walked towards a summer-house about a hundred yards away. His path was bordered on each side with rhododendron bushes, which in the spring would be a blaze of colour. Just now, however, they seemed dank and gloomy, and the summer-house itself was even worse. Thick cobwebs covered the windows, and when he tried the door he found it was locked. Dimly inside he could see a pile of deck-chairs, but it surprised him that a man of Burton's money who must keep two or three gardeners, should allow such obvious neglect and untidiness on his property.

Turning round he studied the house. It was bigger than he had thought, with an unsuspected wing at the back which gave it a T-shaped effect. Thirty bedrooms at least, reflected Sir George, and wondered what the deuce Burton wanted a house of that size for. "Wouldn't have the damn place as a gift myself," he muttered, and even as he spoke he saw his host coming towards him.

"Inspecting the property, Burton," he said as the other approached. "Biggish place you've got here."

"Too big sometimes, Sir George, and at others not big enough. I often have parties here when my accommodation is taxed to the uttermost."

"Just met two of your guests a few minutes ago. Foreigners of sorts."

Charles Burton laughed.

"Not guests," he remarked. "They were two of my secretaries. I have so many connections in my business that I have to keep a foreign staff as well as an English one."

"Really! Which reminds me, you know, though it is an extraordinary thing to say, I'm dashed if I know what your business is."

The two men were strolling back towards the house, and for the fraction of a second a smile twitched round Burton's lips.

"Quite a number of people have asked me the same question, Sir George, but I can assure you there is no mystery about it. I am the English representative of a financial group – or house if you prefer the word – that has ramifications all over the world. There is practically nothing that we do not deal in; from real estate to raw materials; from armaments to agricultural machinery. And because our tentacles are so far-flung we have information at our disposal which no one firm in any country could hope to possess. And correct information is essential if you wish to make money."

"Very true," agreed Sir George. "I wish my damned broker would give it to me a bit more often."

Once again a smile flickered round Burton's mouth.

"You must let me give you a tip or two. And I hope that perhaps in the not too distant future I may be in a position where it will not only be a pleasure to do so, but even a right."

"Eh! What's that?"

The baronet stared at him.

"I have been talking to Lady Castledon," said Burton, "and I am glad to say that she has been good enough to approve of my suggestion. It concerns your charming daughter. Now I am fully aware that according to standards today, I am being old-fashioned: parents seem to be the last people who are consulted. I do not agree with that at all. And so I would like to know if I have your consent to approaching Molly and asking her to become my wife."

"God bless my soul," cried the baronet. "Most unexpected, my dear Burton: most unexpected." Must keep up the pretence of surprise anyway... And really it was decent of the man to have come to him and Jane first... "Little Molly... She's very young, you know: only just out... Not like these modern girls... Still, if her mother approves, and Molly herself is agreeable, I am quite prepared to give my consent."

"Thank you, Sir George. I am very sensible of the honour you have paid me."

"Not at all, not at all. Well, I must go and talk to Jane about it."

Charles Burton watched his retreating figure with an inscrutable look in his eyes. Now that the die was cast, now that he had put himself in such a position that he *must* ask Molly Castledon to marry him, he wondered if he had been a fool. What on earth did he want to tie himself up with a girl for? There were hundreds of other women to be had for the asking – or paying.

The trouble was that for the first time one particular woman was seriously interfering with his life. Ever since he had first met Molly Castledon she had intruded on his thoughts in a way he found most disquieting. It was strange, for he had met many prettier girls. Nevertheless, the fact remained that, try as he would, he could not get her out of his mind. He wanted her as he had never wanted anyone before. And being no fool he realised that in her case his intentions, on the surface, at any rate, would have to be strictly honourable. Afterwards... Well, it would all depend on how long it lasted.

That Molly herself would refuse never entered his head. Women did not refuse Charles Burton. Still it had been as well to pull out the dope with the old people; better to have everybody happy and satisfied. And there was no doubt that the horse-faced mother would prove a valuable ally, in case the girl did not jump to it at once.

The sight of a car coming up the drive brought a faint frown to his forehead; Algy Longworth and Molly were returning from golf. Now the reason he had asked that brainless idiot down for the weekend had certainly not been that he should take Molly off to the links. In fact when he had realised after luncheon that they had gone, he had felt definitely annoyed. Charles Burton disliked his arrangements being interfered with. However as he walked towards the car his face expressed only benign satisfaction at two of his guests having enjoyed themselves.

"Don't leave me, Algy," muttered the girl. "Stick closer than a clam. The blighter looks as if he was going to say his piece at any moment."

"Trust Algy. But you'll have to go through it some time, my pet."

"Had a good game?" said Charles Burton affably as he came up.

"Tophole, my dear old host," answered Algy. "And if I'd sunk my sixth putt on the last green I'd have beaten her. Pretty hot – what!"

"I wonder if you would care to see round the garden," remarked Burton turning to the girl. "Or are you too tired?"

For a moment she hesitated, then she handed her clubs to Algy. She *had* promised to go through with it, so it might as well be now.

"I should like to, Mr Burton," she said. "Take those in for me, Algy"

"Right, my angel. I feel honoured at the commission."

He turned towards the house, as the other two strolled off, and not for the first time he felt misgivings over the whole thing. True it was only pretence on her part, but if Burton was the swine that recent events made him appear to be, even pretence was over the odds. In fact, if it had been anyone except Drummond who had suggested it, he would have turned it down flat.

He entered the hall to perceive too late that it was largely occupied by Lady Castledon.

"And where is Molly, Mr Bugworth?" she boomed as soon as she saw him.

"Treading a measure midst the anemones with our host, Lady Castlegong," he burbled genially. "Good game this. What's your next fancy in nomenclature?"

He sauntered over to a side table and helped himself to a whisky and soda.

"What about a spot of Auntie's ruin for you? It clarifies the brain, and prevents the nose turning blue."

"I do not drink at this hour of the afternoon, young man."

"Don't you? You look as if you did. Or when I say that what I really intend to convey is that you don't look as if you didn't, if you take my meaning."

He came back to the fire with his glass in his hand.

"Nice wench – your daughter," he continued. "Definitely a nifty bit. I suggested the old wedding bells to her this afternoon, but as it made her miss her drive I didn't pursue the subject."

From the chair there arose sounds as of a cow elephant, suffering from asthma.

"Am I to understand" – words came at last – "that you have proposed to Molly?"

"Such is my recollection. It must have been her, because the only other woman I met had a purple face and muscles like walnuts. She was murdering her caddie in a bunker when I last saw her."

"Will you kindly cease talking for one moment and listen to me. Here and now I wish you clearly to understand that neither Sir George nor I would ever give our consent to Molly marrying a…a specimen like you. I believe you have a certain amount of money, but from what little I have heard about you, you represent a type of modern young man for whose continued existence I can see no possible object." She glared at him. "What are you waggling your finger for?"

"I was just trying to get the tempo and the first note of the seven-fold Amen," explained Algy. "No, it eludes me. But how right you are – how very right. There is just one academic point, however, on which I would like to join issue with you. Do we exist? Or is it just the figment of a disordered stomach? If you carefully study the works of Einstein and P G Wodehouse you will have to agree, that amongst the master brains there is considerable doubt on the subject. Are you really you, or are you a sweet ethereal wraith, wrapped round a central electron?"

Lady Castledon rose to her feet.

"If you were my son, Mr Longworth, and a little younger you would soon find out if I was an ethereal wraith wrapped round an electron or not. Don't forget what I said about Molly. Ah! Mr Burton, I hear you have been showing my little girl round the garden."

Charles Burton and Molly had just come in by the front door, and Algy stole a glance at his face. But he gathered nothing from it; as always, it was like a mask.

"Yes, we've been having a stroll round," he said.

"Begonias on the up grade?" asked Algy hopefully as Molly joined him by the fire.

"Move over in the bed, Algy," she remarked. "You take up too much room."

"Molly!" Lady Castledon gave a gasp of horror, "What was that you said?"

"Well he does, mother. Why men should always consider that they have a prescriptive right to the centre of the fireplace, is one of those things that defeats me. Algy darling, I need alcohol. What's on that tray?"

Charles Burton had gone upstairs and Algy looked at her with a grin.

"Have you something to confess to your mamma, my precious?"

"Shut up. And get me a drink. What's in that bottle?"

"Sloe gin."

"That'll do. And I want a lot."

"Molly dear," said her mother, "am I to understand that – "

"You are, darling; you are. Thanks, Algy."

"Oh! my dear, I'm so glad. And your father will be delighted."

"Good Heavens! I haven't accepted the man, if that's what you mean. But I haven't actually refused him. What are you pinching my leg for, Algy?"

"Only, my love, that I am sure it will merely be a question of time before you make him the happiest man alive."

His back was towards Lady Castledon, and he frowned horribly at Molly.

"We will resume our talk later, Molly," said her mother acidly, "when this impossible young man is not present."

She swept out of the hall, and Algy gave a sigh of relief.

"Sorry, my dear, if I nipped the old suspender," he said, "but you must remember one thing. On the face of it this has got to be a genuine affair. Your mother has got to believe that you really are thinking the matter over, if she's going to pull her weight properly. For, if that fellow Burton gets an inkling that this is a put-up job, we're absolutely in the *consommé*."

"All right, Algy; I'll remember. But I draw the line at him kissing me."

"I don't think that's necessary. If I was you, I'd just say with simple maidenly sincerity that you'll let him know when you've made up your mind."

"I can't make out why, if he's what you say he is, he wants to marry me," said the girl thoughtfully.

"Well, old dear, I've seen people with worse dials than yours, you know. What *I* can't make out is why the devil he's asked *me* down here this weekend."

"No; I don't see that either. Get me some more sloe gin, like a dear."

"I say, Molly," remarked Algy, returning with the glass, "as chap to chap, do you like your mother?"

"One gets used to her in time. Why?"

"Because I don't. I think she's dreadful."

"I know. So do a lot of people."

"I thought she was going to burst on me while you were doing the herbaceous border act with Charles. I told her I'd proposed to you on the links."

"Yes; that would cause an eruption. But why did you tell her that? I mean, you didn't, did you?"

"Nothing to speak of. Though every movement of my driver must have revealed my hopeless passion. You see we weren't getting on very well, and she'd just called me Bugworth. So I thought I'd give her a jolt in the corsets."

The girl began to laugh.

"You are a prize buffoon, Algy. But, tell me, while we've got the chance, what's the next move? I've done what Captain Drummond wanted, so far as Mr Burton is concerned, but what now?"

"His idea is, dear, that you *may* be able to find out something. If you don't, you don't; it can't be helped. But there's a chance. And I've never known Hugh Drummond so serious as he is over this affair. Hullo! here's another arrival."

From outside came the sound of wheels on the drive, and simultaneously Charles Burton came running down the stairs. And as the front door opened he reached it.

"Welcome, my dear fellow," he said. "I hope you had no trouble in finding the way."

He came in with another man, who was wearing an astrakhan coat.

"Let me introduce you to Miss Castledon," he continued, "and Mr Longworth... Mr Menalin."

The newcomer bowed without speaking, and allowed the butler, who had just appeared, to divest him of his coat. Then he turned to Burton.

"Would it be convenient," he asked, "for us to have a little chat as soon as possible? A matter of business." He bowed again to Molly Castledon.

"At once, if you like," said Burton. "Let us go to my study."

They crossed the hall and disappeared, and the girl looked at Algy.

"Who's that?" she said.

"According to Hugh," answered Algy gravely, "the big noise who is at the bottom of the whole thing. I'd give a lot to be in the study at the moment."

The girl glanced at him curiously.

"You're a funny mixture, Algy," she said. "You're looking quite the strong, silent man."

"Good Lord!" he laughed. "Not as bad as that surely."

"Tell me more about Hugh Drummond," she said after a pause. "He sounds rather a pet."

"He's a topper," answered Algy simply. "You'd love him."

"What's he look like?"

"Great big chap. Ugly as be damned, and frightfully powerful. He and I and one or two others have always hunted together, but it's Hugh who gives the orders."

"But what makes him suspect this Burton man?"

"I can't tell you more than I have told you already, my angel, because I'm not allowed to. But you can take it from me that Charles is a nasty bit of work."

"I hate the man: he's so dreadfully in love with himself. But I should never have thought he was a criminal."

"Nor did anybody else until quite recently. Which is why he's so dangerous."

"And you've got no idea what he's trying to do?"

"Not the slightest, dear. Nor has Hugh. That's what we're trying to find out."

"Does he know that Captain Drummond is in England?"

"Good Lord, no! And he mustn't, either. What is it, Molly?"

She had suddenly gripped his arm.

"That window beside the front door, Algy. A man had his face pressed against it."

He rose and crossed the hall; then, opening the door, he peered out into the darkness. There was no one to be seen, and after a while he came back to the fire.

"Probably a gardener," he said reassuringly. "Or one of those funny-looking birds I've seen creeping about the place."

"I've seen some too," she answered. "I wonder who they are."

"Ask me another, my pet. Since they didn't come in to lunch, I suppose they're servants of sorts."

Molly Castledon got up.

"I don't like this house," she said. "It's very comfortable, but there's something about it that gives me the shivers."

"You aren't leaving little Algy, are you?"

"I am, my sweet. I'm going to have a bath."

He watched her as she went up the stairs; then, with a slight frown, he helped himself to another whisky and soda. For the first time in his life he found himself at variance with Hugh Drummond. He did not like the part the girl was playing. True, Hugh would never have suggested it without good reason, and so far as he could see, Molly was incurring no risk. At the same time it went against the grain.

After a while he lit a cigarette, and his thoughts turned to the other subject that worried him. Why had Charles Burton asked him down? The invitation had come quite unexpectedly the morning after he had seen Drummond; and had it not been for the fact that he had persuaded Molly, much against her will, to accept the preceding day, he would have refused. And now that he had arrived, he was even more surprised.

He had expected a large party, similar to the one he had been to before. But, so far as he could make out, save for this man Menalin, the Castledons and he were the only guests. And since Burton was not a man who did anything without a reason, he asked himself what that reason could be. That his host had conceived a sudden and violent friendship for him he dismissed as improbable, to put it mildly.

The sound of voices interrupted his train of thought: Burton and Menalin were returning to the hall. And immediately Algy's face became vacant.

"All alone, Longworth," cried his host as he entered.

"Deserted, dear old host, by men, women and children," he said mournfully. "Come and chat to me on this and that."

"I tried to get that pal of yours down for the weekend," continued Burton, splashing some soda into a glass. "Captain Drummond. I looked him up in the book, and dropped him a line, but I've had no reply."

"You wouldn't. The old scout is in France. At least, he was the last time I heard from him."

"Really! When did he go?"

"About a week ago."

"I want to get in touch with him rather badly," said Burton. "You haven't by any chance got his address?"

"I'm afraid I haven't. I tore up his letter. But in any event it wouldn't have been much use even if I'd kept it. He was just passing through, if you take my meaning, from hither to thither."

"Did he happen to mention when he was returning to England?"

"No. But he's an uncommunicative old bean, you know. Just said he couldn't shoot last Wednesday."

"I see. Well, I'd be very much obliged, Longworth, if you'd ask him to ring me up when he does come back."

"Certainly. I'll let him know the instant he returns. How goes the Golden Boot? I haven't seen you there lately."

"I was in a couple of nights ago. You use it a good deal, don't you?"

"Yes. I've masticated quite a number of kippers there. God bless!" He finished his drink. "I'm for a spot of hot water."

He lounged up the stairs and Burton looked at Menalin with a faint smile.

"That, I think, settles the matter," he remarked as Algy disappeared. "The two are great friends, which is really why I asked that idiot down here. He, if anybody, would know Drummond's whereabouts. So I think we can assume that the gentleman is still in France. The point is – how much does he know or guess?"

"Exactly," said Menalin, lighting a cigarette. "How much does he know or guess? One of my principal reasons for coming here was to discuss that very matter."

"So I gathered from your letter. And as I said a moment or two ago my sole reason for asking Longworth here was to try and get in touch with Drummond."

"The manoeuvre does not seem to have been very successful. However, for the moment we will let that pass. How much does he know? It is a matter to which I have given a good deal of thought, and *at present* I do not think we need worry. All that he can *know* is what Madame Pélain told him."

"Which may have been a lot," said Burton uneasily.

"I don't think so," answered Menalin. "Had she told him anything of real value it would have been contained in the letter which Standish wrote to Talbot from Cannes. Since, however, you have observed nothing suspicious since the receipt of that letter, we can assume, I think, that it did not contain any such information."

"It would have been well if you could have got that letter."

"Had it been possible we would have. But Standish registered it himself at the main post office."

"And where is he now?"

"He was caught as I informed you at Evian, and taken back to Cannes. And when the police had finished with him I intervened. You need not trouble about Standish: he is safely under lock and key."

"I'd far sooner he was dead."

"Possibly. But we do not all of us possess your method, my dear Burton, of causing – er – natural death. And murder always excites the police."

"You got Gasdon in Paris?"

"He was picked up as he came in by the Porte d'Italie driving Drummond's car. He is still in hospital with a bad knife-wound."

"So only Drummond remains."

"As you say – only Drummond remains. And that, Burton, is a state of affairs that has got to be rectified as soon as possible. That man is dangerous."

"But if he knows nothing…"

"I said that I don't think he knows anything of importance *at present*. But if I'm any judge of human nature, that will merely spur him on to greater activity. Drummond, my friend, must go."

"Once I can lay my hands on him he will trouble us no more."

"Ah! – once you can. He has, I take it, no reason to suspect you?"

"None whatever. No one has. It was a nuisance that I had to give my name going up in the boat-train, but it couldn't be avoided."

"And how goes this new venture of yours – the night club?"

"Hardly a venture, Menalin. The Golden Boot is a blind. The fact that it's a paying blind is all to the good, but I should keep it going even if it wasn't. Like the parties I throw: and this house. Also, in a different way, like my marriage to that girl you met. They all help to keep my real activities out of the limelight."

"I see the idea. Dorina told me that for an English night club yours was much better than the usual abomination."

"I think she enjoyed herself. Funnily enough that was the last time I saw Drummond."

Menalin stared at him.

"What's that you say? Was Drummond at the Golden Boot the night you took Dorina there?"

"Yes. What of it?"

"And he saw her?"

"Of course he did. Why shouldn't he?"

"Because she was with me in the bar of the Negresco on the occasion that I saw him."

"But why the devil," said Burton, "did Dorina go into the bar if Drummond was there?"

"Because she didn't know him from Adam. How could she? He was never introduced to her at the Golden Boot. He was merely one man in a crowded night club. What was there to make her notice him? You never drew her attention to him."

"That's true. I didn't know anything about him then."

Burton began to pace up and down the hall.

"Perhaps he didn't recognise her," he said at length.

"Not recognise Dorina! Don't be a damned fool. No one could fail to recognise her. It didn't matter if Madame Pélain realised that Dorina was the woman who had been at Chez Paquay that day, so long as she was only seen with me. But that Drummond should have seen her with *you*, is awkward."

"Was the Pélain woman with Drummond at the time?"

"No."

"Then it is possible that Drummond does not know that Dorina was at Chez Paquay. You see what I'm getting at. Dorina as a link between you and me I don't mind; Dorina as a link between Latimer and me would be infernally dangerous."

Menalin shrugged his shoulders.

"I fear it is a possibility that you've got to consider," he remarked shortly.

The two men stared at one another.

"Moreover," continued Menalin, "should it prove to be so, your pleasant conceit that you resemble Caesar's wife rather goes by the board. You'd better get Drummond, Burton, dead or alive. And now I think I shall follow that young man's example and go and have a bath."

"I will show you your room," said his host, leading the way up the stairs.

And once again, pressed against the window beside the front door, there appeared for a second the face of a man.

CHAPTER 10

Limerick by Algy

It cannot be said that the evening was a success. Some ten people from the neighbourhood came in for dinner, but though Charles Burton's chef was as famous as his cellar, conversation flagged. And the fault lay in the host himself.

This sudden disclosure on the part of Menalin had upset him more than he cared to admit. It had transported him from a mood of absolute confidence and security into one of doubt and uneasiness. He had returned to the subject in Menalin's room, and though the Russian had told him that he was almost sure Madame Pélain had *not* seen Dorina in the Negresco there was an element of uncertainty about the matter which worried him.

At the time he had been doubtful as to the wisdom of taking such a singularly striking woman to the Golden Boot. But she was a lady who possessed a very decided will of her own, and when she expressed a wish to go there he had agreed. And the fact that Drummond should have selected that particular night to go there himself, was one of those chances which no one could legislate for.

Then a further disquieting thought occurred to his mind – one, which oddly enough had not struck him before. Was it chance that had taken Drummond that night? The interview with Talbot must have taken place *before* he arrived at the Golden Boot. Was it possible that some deeper motive had caused his presence at the night club? If so, it meant that Talbot had suspected him then.

He ran over the chain of events from Latimer's arrival in Paris to his death on board. From the moment he had left the Gare de Lyon he had never been out of observation. He had put through a call to London, but it had been so short that it was out of the question that anything really incriminating could have been mentioned. And that was confirmed by the fact that nothing had subsequently happened. For although there was no mention of him by name on the papers in Latimer's possession there was a very vital clue to his present activities. And had that come out Charles Burton would have known about it at once; the police would have been buzzing like a hive of bees.

The same thing applied to the letter which, so Menalin told him, Standish had written to Talbot from Cannes. Though it was most improbable that a man like Latimer could have passed on valuable information to a woman he had only known a fortnight, it was possible. In which case Madame Pélain would have passed it on to Standish, and it would have been in the letter – a letter which, though Talbot himself never received it, must have been opened by somebody else. In short, he was convinced that the contents of the papers had not been passed on; Latimer's death had ensured that.

Once more his thoughts reverted to Drummond's presence at the Golden Boot. And with growing irritation he realised all that it might entail if Drummond with the help of Madame Pélain, had realised that the woman of Chez Paquay was the woman who had been with him that night. True, there could be no question of proof; Latimer had died of natural causes. They could exhume him till they were black in the face; they would find no trace of anything. But they might suspect, and he did not want suspicion. No one desired to blush unseen for the next few weeks more fervently than did Charles Burton.

An abstemious man as a rule, tonight he was drinking more than usual. And after a while the champagne began to take effect. He was worrying unnecessarily; what could Drummond do anyway? The instant he showed up in England he was a doomed man; if he was still in France the police were bound to get him sooner or later and then Menalin would do the rest.

A sudden sentence caught his ear; they were discussing the murder of Colonel Talbot.

"A dastardly outrage," cried a retired general. "I've known Harry Talbot since we were subalterns together. Member of my club. And that he should have been murdered in cold blood in broad daylight in the middle of the Park reveals a scandalous state of affairs. You might expect it with gangsters in America, but that it should happen in London is simply unbelievable."

For the fraction of a second he caught Menalin's eye; that, too, had been a well-planned bit of work. And even if he had not been fortified by his own excellent champagne, he knew that no shadow of suspicion could attach to him over that. The orders had passed through too many channels for him ever to be traced.

And it had been necessary – or, at any rate, expedient. Talbot had been far too clever and able a man to leave alive. But for Latimer he might have risked it; as things stood, it had been impossible. And so...

"I beg your pardon."

He suddenly became aware that his prospective father-in-law was in vocal labour.

"What do you think of the state of affairs, Burton? You're one of these international financial fellahs. Any chance of another war?"

"Perhaps my friend, Mr Menalin, is better informed than I am, Sir George," he murmured.

With an effort the worthy baronet shifted his focus. "Of course, of course," he grunted. "Well, sir – what do *you* think?"

"It is an interesting field of thought," answered Menalin. "So much depends on the *chef*."

"The *chef!*" spluttered Sir George. " 'Fraid I don't quite get you."

"Liver, my dear sir; liver. Have you never realised the appalling danger of a dictator with too much bile?"

"Deuced good. 'Pon my soul – that's deuced clever. Must get that off at the club."

"Where the members will be greatly edified, no doubt," said Menalin with a smile. "Seriously though, has it never occurred to you, that the ordinary factors which used to govern international relations are quite dead today? War used to creak into being; next time it will flash. Hence the danger of a bad egg at a crucial moment. And now most moments are crucial."

"Horrible," shuddered Algy. "You make me go all goosey. Me for the bottom of a disused well."

"It would be hard to think of a more suitable place for you, Mr Longworth," remarked Lady Castledon acidly.

"Anyway, mother," cried Molly Castledon, "he got a bar to his Military Cross. Don't look sheeplike, Algy; I know you did. What did you get it for?"

"Saving the rum at divisional headquarters, darling. But joking apart, Mr Menalin, do you really think we're going to get all hot and bothered again?"

"I am not a prophet, Mr Longworth. All I say is that when supreme power over a nation is vested in one man the situation is dangerous. And you must admit that your country has not gone out of its way to ease it. Actuated doubtless by the highest motives you have, as your first contribution, successfully turned an old friend into a bitter enemy without achieving the slightest result…"

"A moral one surely," remarked the vicar.

"Assuredly," agreed Menalin with a smile. "But hardly in the way you think. Had you closed the Suez Canal you would, at any rate, have done something, even if it was only to start a European war. But doing what you did do in the sacred name of justice produced, if I may say so, one of the most Gilbertian situations of recent centuries. That is why I said that the moral result was hardly what you intended. The benefit was entirely to Italy."

"Don't hold with sanctions," grunted the General. "Damn foolishness. For all that I don't quite follow you, Mr – er – Mr Menalin."

"And yet, General, it is very simple. At the beginning the Abyssinian war was intensely unpopular in Italy, except among a minority of hot-headed boys. And then the League applied sanctions. Immediately the war became a crusade – not against the Abyssinians, but against what the Italians considered injustice. The entire country closed up: every dissentient voice was stilled. A united nation with a common ideal came into being as a result of your action. And the fact that it was the unfortunate Ethiopians who were left to carry the baby was, of course, nobody's business."

"Rather a novel way of looking at it," remarked Sir George.

"My dear sir, I should have thought it was obvious. True, I know Italy better, perhaps, than most of you here, but even without that knowledge it is difficult to see how anyone could have expected a different result. You may take it from me that the powers that be in that country mention you with gratitude in their prayers every night. To keep up appearances they have to pretend you are the villain in the piece, and the *hoi polloi* believe it. But in reality you have saved them at what one must admit was a trifling cost. You only ruined two or three of your own fishing centres, and caused a coal mine or two in Wales to close down. In fact, I don't suppose helping Italy to win the war has cost you more than six or seven millions."

"Do you suggest that we should have stood aside and done nothing?" demanded the vicar.

"I fear, sir," said Menalin, "that I am a practical man. Until this world becomes Utopia, judgment goes by results. And when I see a policy pursued, from no matter what exalted motives, that produces the result your policy did I can only sit back and thank Heaven that the balance sheets of my companies are compiled by business men. Would you excuse me, Burton?"

A footman was standing beside him with a telegram on a salver.

"The worst of being one of those unfortunate individuals – business men," he murmured to the woman on his right as he opened the envelope. And as he read the contents two pairs of eyes were unobtrusively fastened on him. One pair belonged to his host: the other to a guest who wore an eyeglass. And it seemed to Algy that for the fraction of a second, Menalin's face registered uneasiness. However, as he thrust the wire in his pocket and turned to his neighbour his expression was as impassive as ever.

To Algy the entire party was becoming like a dream. Numbed by the two women he was sitting between, and who mercifully were discussing county affairs with their other partners, he felt a curious sense of detachment. Here, seated round Burton's table, was gathered a group of people who, save for a difference in clothes, might have been sitting there fifty years ago. To them England was England – a thing as constant as the sun itself. That anything serious could really happen to their country literally never entered their heads. Other nations might bicker and fight, have revolutions, don different-coloured shirts – but not England. The whole thing was rather vulgar and ridiculous.

And since Algy was born and bred in the same caste himself he understood their point of view. Understood, too, the veiled hostility engendered in all of them by Menalin's remarks. For whatever criticisms they might feel disposed to make on their country's actions themselves, it was a totally different matter for a foreigner. Any disparagement from an outsider was sufficient to unite the most rabid enemies against the common foe.

He stole a glance at Menalin, who was apparently engrossed in conversation with the general's wife. Was it possible that behind that inscrutable mask some amazing plot was being hatched that threatened the very foundations of their life, so far as the rest of the party was concerned? It seemed fantastic, and yet Hugh Drummond was not in the habit of making fantastic statements.

"Sweet, sir?"

He looked up: a footman was offering him a dish – a footman who stared him straight in the face and then gave the barest perceptible wink.

"Your napkin is on the floor, sir," murmured the man and passed on.

It was a prophecy, if not a fact. A moment later it was on the floor, covering a twisted scrap of paper: two moments later the napkin was restored to its proper position and the floor was bare.

Not in vain had been Drummond's teaching: Algy's face, as he unrolled the message under cover of the table, was more asinine than usual. But no one had noticed anything: conversation was still general.

He straightened out the note, and glancing down he recognised the writing with a sudden thrill.

Mention island of Varda. Get reactions B and M – HUD.

So ran the note: concise and to the point. But, Algy reflected, as he put it in his pocket, not the easiest order ever. A: he had never heard of the darned place. B: suddenly to interject a remark about Varda in the middle of a description of last Tuesday's hunt might cause aspersions to be cast on his sanity. However, it had to be done, and that was that. So Algy came out of his stupor, and gave his celebrated imitation of a horse neighing.

In his usual haunts it was a certain winner; on this occasion the effect was electrical. A dead silence settled on the room and everyone stared at him.

"Molly, my angel," he burbled, "I've got it."

"Got what, you fathead?"

"The last line of that limerick, darling. The one we were trying before dinner. Not your sort, Lady Castledon. This one is quite proper. And one gets a guinea for the best effort. Hence my recent silence; my brain had been in action."

He beamed genially on the company.

> "There was a young lady called Mahda
> Who had hidden her stays in the lahda
> When asked to explain
> She said it might rain –

"Now here's my effort:

> "I'm going back to the island of Vahda.

"Pretty hot that – what? I suppose," he added anxiously, "there *is* an island called Varda."

"Have you been drinking too much, Mr Longworth?" remarked Lady Castledon ominously.

"Of course. I always do. But I haven't reached the Plimsoll line yet. You know – half-way up the tonsils. Well, people, what do you think of it?"

He gazed round hopefully.

"No bon! No guinea! Tum-tum-ti-ti-tum-ti-ti-tum-tum. I think it's dashed good myself. Witty; cryptic; neat. What say you, old host?"

"I had no idea you were so accomplished, Mr Longworth," said Burton suavely. "I should think it will certainly win the prize."

"There you are, Molly, my dear," remarked Algy complacently. "You can put your shirt on little Algy every time."

"And in what paper is that interesting competition?" asked Burton.

"Not one that you're ever likely to see, Charles," said Molly calmly. "A fashion paper, my poor dear, which gives you patterns for garments no nice girl ever mentions. Personally, Algy, I think it's a rotten line."

"Take it or leave it, my child," said Algy airily. "Possibly it wants a bit of polishing, but the basic idea is good. Don't you agree?"

He turned to his dinner partner who was regarding him dispassionately through lorgnettes.

"Are you by any chance mental?" she asked with interest.

"Only at high tide; then I bark like a dog. My grandmother was the same, only she carried it further and bit people in the leg, until she had finally to go about on a lead, poor old soul."

"It seems a great pity that you don't follow your grandmother's example," she remarked acidly.

With relief he contemplated a bony shoulder blade; evidently the only reaction felt by the guests was that he was half-witted. But what about Menalin and his host? Had he been *too* damned stupid?

That he had succeeded beyond his wildest expectations was beside the point. The reaction of the two men had stuck out a yard, though it had passed in a flash. Menalin had stiffened like a pointer marking a bird, only to relax instantly; Burton had given an unmistakable start. So he had carried out Drummond's order all right. But did they suspect him?

Another thing; where was Drummond? Presumably somewhere in the neighbourhood since he had got a note through to the footman. And who was the footman?

Algy glanced at him; he had never seen the man before in his life. But that he was in the show on their side was obvious. And

161

presumably it would have to be through him that he'd get the answer back to Drummond. Which might be difficult unless he was the footman who was valeting him.

His clothes had been laid out that evening when he went up to dress, so he didn't know who was looking after him. And he would not know, in all probability until the following morning when he was called.

Came a sudden pushing back of chairs and the ladies rose to leave the room. For a second he caught Molly's eye; what a girl! How marvellously she had played up, with her yarn about a fashion paper! And then the door closed and the men were left alone.

It came as no surprise to him when Menalin rose and, coming round the table, took the next chair.

"Do you often indulge in these poetical flights, Mr Longworth?" he asked with a smile.

"Rather," cried Algy. "Must do something, don't you know, to keep the old grey matter up to scratch."

He was conscious that the other man was watching him like a lynx, but in his own particular line Algy was unbeatable. No man living could look such a completely congenital idiot at will.

"Quite," murmured Menalin. "A very praiseworthy idea. But tell me, Mr Longworth – I ask out of idle curiosity – why did you select the letter V? You might have had Garda, or Sarda, or Tarda, which would all have rhymed equally brilliantly. Why Varda?"

" 'Pon my soul," cried Algy. "I never thought of that."

He gazed at Menalin with rising excitement.

"I believe Garda is better. Much better. You see, you get a play on the words. By Jove! you're a genius – a blinking marvel. In the second line there's that snappy bit about her stays in the lahda. You remember that!"

"Yes, thank you," said Menalin.

"Well now, that's where your notion hits the roof. Garda sounds very like garta. So you've got stays and garter. Gad! I must remember that. If that doesn't knock 'em for the count, nothing will. I say," he asked anxiously, "you haven't any objection to my using your idea, have you?"

"Not the smallest," Menalin assured him.

"Well, I call it deuced sporting of you," said Algy with feeling. "I don't mind telling you that there are mighty few fellahs who wouldn't insist on fifty-fifty. But I tell you what I will do though. I mean fair play's a jewel and all that sort of bilge. Now have you heard the story of the charwoman who had tripe for dinner... I say, don't go, old friend. That story is an absolute wow."

"I'll take your word for it, Mr Longworth," said Menalin grimly. "At the moment I fear it might prove too much for me."

"Well, well," murmured Algy resignedly, as he watched Menalin take a vacant chair by his host, "this doesn't seem to be Algy's night out."

"What did you say?" grunted the man on his other side.

"An airy nothing," answered Algy, "tossed into the port-laden atmosphere. I say, what do you think would happen if we started to flick bread pellets at the General?"

"Bread pellets at the General! Good Gad! sir – are you mad? Are you aware that his coverts march with mine?"

With an effort Algy controlled his face: he was beginning to enjoy himself.

"Where to?" he asked.

"How d'you mean – where to?"

"Where do they march to? And do they have a band?"

His neighbour swallowed twice.

"Coverts, sir, are woods. And the phrase 'march' means that his land adjoins mine."

"Oh! I see," said Algy. "My father has a wood on his land... Near Wigan..."

"Indeed! Does he preserve? Birds, I mean – not jam."

"Rather... I shot some starlings there the other day... And a fox... We've got its tail hanging up in the downstairs lavatory."

For a space there was silence, broken only by the sound of heavy breathing. Then: "You shot a fox! Tail! By God! sir, where were you dragged up?"

"It was a lady fox, too," said Algy hopefully.

"Lady fox! Lady fox!! By Heavens, sir, you ought to be in prison."

"What's the matter, John?" called out the General. "You seem excited."

"Excited, Henry – excited! So would you be. Are you aware that this – this gentleman has just told me that he shot a vixen – I beg his pardon, a lady fox – the other day and that her tail – her tail, mark you – is hanging in the downstairs lavatory."

The General took it in slowly.

"Deuced bad form, my dear John," he remarked at length, "deuced bad. But these boys know no better. Gad, young man, it's a good thing for you that you weren't in Poona in 'eighty-three. Or was it 'eighty-four? Old Shirty Ramsbotham would have put the wind up you. Damn' good fellow – Shirty," he added reminiscently. "Used to eat wineglasses after mess."

"Why?" asked Algy brightly.

"Why!" The General glared at him. "Confound you, sir: what d'you mean – why? Just to show you that he could, of course... Why!"

He subsided into a heavy rumble of disgust, and Algy viewed him with alarm.

"Have I said the wrong thing?" he murmured to his neighbour.

"Have you ever said the right?" answered that worthy witheringly, and at that moment Burton rose.

"Shall we join the ladies?" he remarked to the room at large. "Hope you found the port to your liking, General."

"Very good, Burton. Excellent. Wish I could say the same of your guests," he added darkly.

The disgruntled warrior hoisted himself to his feet, and moved towards the door.

"We'll have our coffee and brandy in the hall," continued Burton.

It was at that moment that Algy caught the footman's eye. He had suddenly appeared, and was standing in such a position that Algy would have to pass close to him. And as he got abreast of him, having lagged a little behind the others, he heard a whisper: "Your room; ten-thirty."

Algy glanced at the clock; just a quarter-past ten. Presumably the zoo would break up about eleven; until then would it be safe to talk to Molly? Must keep up the fiction about the limerick, of course, but they'd better not seem too matey... Just in case...

She was sitting by herself near the fireplace and he strolled over to her.

"Grand idea, my pet, about the limerick," he announced. "Straight from the horse's mouth. Not Varda, but Garda."

He was conscious that Burton was watching them.

"Mr Menalin's own," he continued. "You see the great notion. Garda – garter. Pretty hot – what?"

"You complete idiot," she laughed. And then without altering her voice: "What on earth is the game? Careful, Algy."

"Send it up tomorrow," he said. "Right-ho, my dear. Don't worry."

"What would be a good thing to do?" remarked Burton as he joined them. "Invent more limericks? It seems to be Longworth's strong point."

A burst of laughter came from the other side of the hall, and the words "lady fox" and "tail" floated across.

"You're entertaining a real sportsman unawares, Burton," said Algy's dinner neighbour coming over. "He tells us he's just shot a lady fox in his father's wood and hung the tail in the – er – hung it downstairs."

For a moment there was silence, while Burton stared at Algy through narrowed eyes.

"Really," he remarked softly. "Now I wonder why you said that, Longworth."

Inwardly Algy was cursing; he had been a fool to go so far. Actually he had completely forgotten that Burton hunted in the shires himself. But his face remained its usual vacant self.

"Bit of a leg-pull, old host," he burbled genially. "Wanted to see if anyone would have apoplexy. And this sportsman damn near did."

"What do you mean?" The harbinger of *bon mots* had got even redder in the face.

"Merely, my dear Livermore," said Burton quietly, "that it seems a peculiar pastime for a man who hunts with the Pytchley."

He turned away, leaving Mr Livermore gasping like a fish.

"Deuced good!" he said at length. "You had me that time, Mr – er – Mr –"

"Longworth," remarked Algy politely. "Algernon to my friends."

He took out his cigarette case from which he had taken the precaution to remove the cigarettes.

"Dash!" he murmured. "Must go up to my room. No, thank you, Mr Livermore; I only smoke my own poison."

He crossed the hall, and began to mount the stairs. Burton and Menalin were both engaged in conversation with different people, and there was no one in sight as he opened the door of his room. The footman was laying out his pyjamas.

"Who are you?" said Algy quickly.

"Talbot. It was my father they murdered. I got special leave and shaved my moustache."

Algy whistled.

"How the devil did you get in here?"

"Drummond fixed it. By God! that man would fix anything. Burton was advertising for another footman, and Drummond arranged it somehow."

"Where is the old scout?"

"Don't know. But he's somewhere about. Saw him this evening. Listen for you mustn't be too long. First, I was to tell you that Standish has escaped."

Once again Algy whistled.

"I wonder if that's the wire Menalin got at dinner. It shook him – that message."

"It may have been. Second, this Varda business. Incidentally I darned near dropped the whole outfit with laughing over that limerick. What's your report?"

"They both definitely reacted," said Algy.

"I agree. Quite definitely."

"Where is the blasted place? I've never even heard of it."

"No more have I. For that matter no more had Drummond when he gave me that note to give you. But you're to insert an advertisement in the *Morning Post* as to the reaction."

"Can't get it in till Tuesday's issue," said Algy. "However, that's OK."

"Third. You're to go to the Golden Boot on Monday night, and see one Alice Blackton."

"Right. Anything more – for I must go downstairs again?"

"No – that's the lot."

"And you don't know where Hugh is? Drummond, I mean." Talbot shook his head.

"My hat! What a man!" he cried.

"You're telling me," said Algy. "By the way what's your name here?"

"Simpson. Henry Simpson."

"Are you looking after me?"

"Yes."

167

"A new job for you, Henry," grinned Algy. "And I don't mind warning you, old lad, that you won't get fat on your tip."

He crammed some cigarettes into his case and sauntered out of the room. The passage was still deserted: no one appeared to have moved in the hall. In fact his absence seemed to have passed unnoticed. And a few minutes later, to his intense relief, signs of a general departure began to manifest themselves.

"Don't overdo the village idiot stuff," came a low voice in his ear. "I don't think dear Charles is amused."

Molly Castledon drifted on past him, but he had got her warning. And she was right; he knew that. Neither Burton nor Menalin were gentlemen with whom to run unnecessary risks. And he had no desire to share Latimer's and Talbot's fate.

Not that anything was likely to happen to him in that house: Burton would hardly dare to do anything actually on his own property. But the weekend would not last for ever, and after that it would be a very different matter.

The last guests had gone as he crossed to the drinks table and helped himself to a whisky and soda. Molly had disappeared, and so had Burton. Menalin had been buttonholed by Sir George, and was regarding him with intense disfavour. So that an imperative summons from an armchair near the fire came as no surprise.

"Mr Longworth," boomed Lady Castledon, "come here. I wish to speak to you. I have noticed," continued the voice as he approached the presence, "with great disapproval, your habit of addressing my daughter by such titles as 'darling' and 'angel'. In public too. Tonight, for instance, at dinner, when you produced that idiotic and vulgar limerick – was a case in point. Kindly understand that it must cease at once."

"It will break her virginal heart," said Algy sorrowfully. "So is it fair? Is it just? Has she done anything to deserve such cruel punishment? I beg – nay, I implore you – as her mother, not to let the poor child think that she has incurred my displeasure. If she puts her head in a gas oven it will be your fault."

Lady Castledon rose majestically.

"George," she remarked, "I am going to bed. I will leave you to deal with this case of arrested mental development."

"Certainly, my love, certainly."

"And remember what I said, Mr Longworth. Good night, Mr Menalin."

The Russian bowed, and at that moment Molly came in from the billiard-room. Her face was slightly flushed and there was an ominous glint in her eyes.

"Going to bed, mother? I think I'll come too. Night-night, Algy."

"Too-te-loo, scab face. Mind you wash under the ears."

"What did you call me?" demanded the girl, pausing at the foot of the stairs.

"Mother's orders, my pet. She doesn't like me calling you 'darling'."

He was looking at her closely: something had evidently upset her.

"Now pop up and lower your Glaxo like a good girl," he continued. "And then Algy will come and kiss you good night."

And even as he spoke there came from some way off, though perfectly clear and distinct, a sudden cry of "Help."

CHAPTER 11

The Sleepwalker

For a moment there was silence. Lady Castledon had disappeared, and Molly, one hand on the banisters, stood staring at Algy.

"What was that?" cried Sir George. "Sounded like someone shouting."

"It did," agreed Menalin. "I wonder where our host is."

Not a muscle in his face had moved; hearing calls for help might have been part of his daily routine.

"We must renew our discussion tomorrow, Sir George," he continued, lighting a cigarette.

"Yes; but oughtn't we to do something about that shout?" said the baronet uneasily.

"I feel sure that Burton... Ah! here he is. What's the trouble, Charles? We heard a cry a few moments ago."

"Please don't be alarmed," said Burton. "No damage done. One of the men who looks after the electric-light plant got his hand jammed. But no bones broken, I'm glad to say."

"That's good," cried Sir George. "Well, I think I'm going to bed. Good night, my dear fellow: good night. Are you coming, Molly?"

He went up the stairs with his daughter, whilst Algy crossed to the drinks and helped himself to another whisky. That Burton was lying he felt convinced: you don't get your hand jammed in an engine and have no damage done. So who was it who had shouted, and why?

"Do you hit the old golf ball, Mr Menalin?" he asked casually, as he resumed his position by the fire.

"I fear I do not," said the Russian.

"A pity. Darned good links those, Burton. Absolutely first-class. We might have a round tomorrow if you feel like it."

"I'm afraid I shall be too busy, Longworth. But doubtless you'll be able to fix up a game."

"I'll have a dip at it," he answered. "Perhaps Molly would care for a return."

The two men were standing, one on each side of him, and in spite of himself he found that his pulse was going a little quicker. Not that they could do anything to him – such an idea was absurd. But with his knowledge of what Drummond had told him, he rather wished they were not quite so adjacent.

"Longworth," said Burton abruptly, "both Mr Menalin and I are a little worried over what I am sure is a small thing. That limerick of yours. Now what was it that made you think of the island of Varda?"

Algy stared at him blankly.

"It rhymed, old host: that's all. And now we're not using it; it's Garda, thanks to Mr Menalin. But anyway, why should you be worried? I mean, is there anything particularly fruity over the island of Varda, wherever it is?"

"Only this. Very few people know of its existence, and we discovered it quite by accident when cruising in Mr Menalin's yacht. We were immediately struck by its immense possibilities as a health resort – it's a second Madeira. And amongst some other activities we are floating a company for its development. Which brings me to the point. As you will naturally understand, the fewer people who know about it, with matters in their present stage, the better. And what we feared was that you might have heard the scheme being discussed owing to some leakage, and that that had put the name into your head."

"Good Lord, no!" cried Algy. "Never heard of the bally place in my life. Rest easy in your beds, my jolly old financial magnates. Your secret is locked in my bosom. All I ask is that the bridal suite should be reserved for me when you open."

He yawned cavernously, and put down his glass.

"Well – I'm for bed. And tomorrow, refreshed and invigorated by a night of dreamless sleep, we will all dance a merry roundelay in the garden before breakfast."

He strolled up the stairs and paused at the top.

"I must warn you of one thing, chaps: I sing in my bath."

He disappeared, and the two men stared at one another.

"I suppose," said Menalin thoughtfully, "that he really is not quite all there. Though why," he continued irritably, "you should have asked any of these unbelievable individuals at all passes my comprehension. The girl's the only possible one and it struck me that you weren't getting on quite as well as might be expected in that quarter."

Burton flushed at the sneer, but said nothing.

"What actually was that shout?" continued Menalin.

"He'd slipped his gag somehow and got in one cry before they stopped him."

"I see. Well, my friend, this is disquieting news about Standish."

"It doesn't reflect too well on your staff work out there," said Burton, getting some of his own back. "Have you heard how it happened?"

"Only the bare detail that he has escaped. Do not worry; he will not get far. And even if he does he knows nothing. I am much more concerned about Drummond. I have heard something new, Burton, which I have had no chance to pass on to you as yet. Tosco was in my room before dinner and told me."

"I didn't even know he'd arrived," said Burton. "What is this news?"

"It concerns the murder of Maier in Territet," went on Menalin. "Apparently Tosco managed to get into communication with our agents who, as you know, were arrested. And from them he got a description of the two men who were in the house when they returned. It appears that they were both English, and that one of them was a big, strong man who was remarkably ugly. It was he who knocked out Number ten as if he'd been pole-axed."

"You mean it might have been Drummond."

"Exactly. We know that Standish was making for the Lake of Geneva; isn't it more than likely that Drummond did the same? And that Drummond got into Switzerland whilst Standish didn't?"

Burton nodded thoughtfully.

"In which case any chance of catching Drummond in France may be eliminated. He would naturally return to England via Germany and Holland."

"That is so," agreed Burton.

"Moreover, he will have brought with him Maier's model, which as you know was missing."

"Why should he?" demanded Burton. "For that matter why should he go to Maier's house at all?"

"On the face of it – quite true. And I don't say for a moment that it *was* Drummond. But *if* it was the affair is disquieting. Not so much that Maier is dead, and the model missing, but because it reveals a knowledge of certain parts of our organisation which I had not suspected the other side possessed. Who put them on to Maier in the first place?"

"Do you think that little rat of a barber overheard anything and passed it on to Talbot?"

"Possibly. I cannot say. But the bald fact remains, Burton, that *if* it was Drummond, it shows there is a leakage somewhere.

Fortunately that leakage can only be on the fringe of our scheme, but one never knows when one thing may not lead to another. And whatever you may say about the English, you cannot deny that their Special Service men are second to none, and that once they've got on to a thing they never let go."

He lit a cigarette.

"I suppose it is necessary to remove our friend below?" he asked.

"Absolutely. He has suddenly developed scruples, and he knows too much. God! I wish I'd got Drummond down there as well."

Menalin laughed shortly.

"Well – you haven't. And from what little I've seen of the gentleman, I don't think you're likely to. Shall we adjourn? There is a lot to be discussed, and I am anxious to see this method of yours in action."

They crossed the hall towards Burton's study, and Algy who had been lying with his ear glued to the banisters on the first floor landing, rose and dusted his trousers. Except for an acute attack of cramp he had gained nothing. One or two odd words here and there were all that he had heard, and they had been of no help.

The house was very silent as he walked to his room. From the further end of the corridor a faint roaring noise proclaimed that Sir George had given up the labours of the day; a suddenly extinguished light under the door of the adjacent room indicated that his wife was about to imitate him.

A fire was burning brightly in the grate, and throwing himself into an easy chair he lit a cigarette. He had half hoped to find some message from Talbot concerning the shout, but there was no sign of one. And the possibility that it was Talbot himself who had called out, struck him for the first time.

He rose and began to pace up and down the floor. That something was going on he knew; how to find out what it was –

that was the point. And it was no question of fear or danger that deterred him, but just ordinary horse-sense.

In the first place, save for the hall and the sitting-rooms, he did not know the geography of the house. It would, therefore, if he had a look round, be a blind search. And was the bare chance of discovering something worth the risk of being discovered himself? For if that happened, no amount of pretended buffoonery could possibly save him. He would stand self-convicted as a spy, and, apart from anything they might do to him, his value to the side would become nil on the spot.

He drew back the curtain and looked out. It was an overcast, rather unpleasant night, and very dark. From a room at one end of the annexe, light was filtering through a blind, and it seemed to him that he could catch the faint murmur of voices. The room was on the same floor as his own: if only he could see inside. But it was impossible, and once more he started pacing restlessly up and down.

After a while he got undressed, but he knew that sleep would be out of the question. So, putting on a dressing-gown, he again flung himself into a chair, and picked up a book. But he could not concentrate. Round and round in his mind went the ceaseless questions. Where was the island of Varda? What was really happening there, for he no more believed Burton's explanation about that, than he believed his story about the electric-light plant? Where was Drummond? Was he outside there in the darkness prowling round the house?

Suddenly he put down his book and leaned forward, listening intently. And this time there was no mistake: a board had creaked in the passage outside. Like a flash Algy was across the room and had switched off the light. Then, crouching behind the bed, he waited tensely.

Came another creak – this time just outside the door, and the handle was gently tried. The flames were throwing dancing shadows, as with every muscle taut he watched the door slowly open. Watched and waited, only to relax suddenly with a gasp.

With her eyes open and staring and her hands groping in front of her, Molly Castledon closed the door and came on into the room. She moved with a strange impression of sureness – slowly, but unfalteringly, and Algy watched her with some dismay. By now he realised what had happened; she was walking in her sleep. And his only coherent prayer was that her gorgon of a mother would not follow her. He felt that explanation would be difficult...

But what on earth was he to do? Dimly he remembered that the one thing you must *not* do is to wake a sleepwalker. He had an idea that one took them by the hand and led them gently back to their own room. And one slight difficulty was that he had no idea which was her room. The prospect of a hand-in-hand search for it, and encountering mother minus hair and teeth in the process, made him break out in a cold sweat. Especially as, somewhat naturally, Molly had omitted to put on a wrap and was clad only in pyjamas.

Algy drew a deep breath: something had to be done quickly as, to make matters worse, she was now preparing to get into bed. Wild thoughts of singing "You can't do that there 'ere" he dismissed as impracticable, and then the tension broke.

"Are you never going to speak, fathead?" demanded the girl.

"What the... Why the –" spluttered Algy. "I thought you were walking in your sleep."

"Bright boy," she said sitting on the edge of the bed. "That's what I meant you to think. I used to when I was a kid, and I was afraid I might have forgotten how. Did I do it well?"

"My angel woman – magnificently," he remarked. "But what on earth is the notion?"

"Give me a cigarette," she said.

"But, Molly," he cried, "you can't stop here. What on earth are people going to say if you're found out?"

"Who's going to find out? Father had too much port, and mother's taken her usual sleep dope."

"Thank God for that," breathed Algy fervently.

"And if it eases your mind I'm not going to stop here. You're coming to my room when I've finished this cigarette. Algy, that little performance was a dress rehearsal."

"Go on, dear heart," he said resignedly. "I suppose I'll get this right sometime."

"Did you notice I was a little annoyed when I came in from the billiard-room?"

"It did not escape Algy's attention."

"I don't know if the gentleman had been liquoring up, but the result left much to be desired."

"I guessed it was that."

"Much," she repeated. "His ideas of fun and laughter and mine do not coincide. And when I told you I'd play I did not bargain for that."

"I'm sorry, dear," said Algy quietly. "Very sorry indeed. And I know that Hugh will be too."

"Don't you worry about that; this child can look after herself. But, Algy I want to get a bit of my own back. Hence the sleepwalking."

"I'm afraid I'm a bit dense, my love, but..."

Algy looked frankly bewildered.

"Come over here."

She took him by the arm and drew him to the window.

"You see that room with the light on. I can see it much better from mine than you can from here. There's something going on in it. And I'm going to find out what that something is."

"But how the devil do you propose to do it?"

"If I can sleepwalk into this room, I can sleepwalk into that."

For a moment or two he stared at her speechlessly.

"My dear girl," he gasped at length, "don't be such an ass. It's out of the question. I absolutely forbid you to do anything of the sort. You're to go straight back to bed."

She blew out a cloud of smoke.

"Algy, my pet, you're rather angelic when you do the caveman stuff. Now listen to me, big boy. First of all what was all that Varda business about?"

"Hugh got a note to me through one of the footmen. Incidentally he's not a footman at all, but the son of Colonel Talbot who was murdered the other day. And in the note I was told to get Burton's and Menalin's reaction to the island of Varda."

She began to laugh.

"And was that the best you could do, my poor lamb? However, we'll let that pass, and go on. Do you believe what our charming host said about that man who screamed?"

"No," admitted Algy. "I don't."

"Good. Two points. A third you've just told me yourself; this show is sufficiently big not only for a man to come masquerading as a footman, but for me to have been given the job I've got. OK up to date?"

"You little devil," grinned Algy. "You're not going to get me that way."

"Shut up," said the girl. "So much for that side of the situation; now for the other. I never liked Charles, but you can take it from me that, compared to my feelings for him now, those of yester year were like a crooning mother's. So you see that everything adds up: no subtraction anywhere."

"But Molly, my dear," he said, "it's not safe. There are probably a lot of men there."

"What if there are? They won't eat me."

"And the chances are very small that you'll find out anything if you do."

"The chances are non-existent that I'll find out anything if I don't."

"Besides – your rig."

"What's the matter with it? I'm decent, ain't I?"

"Of course you are, my dear," he said feebly.

"Perfectly adorable, but…"

She rose and pitched her cigarette into the fire.

"Algy dear," she said quietly. "My mind is absolutely made up. There's no good pretending that if you thought you had half a chance of getting into that room successfully yourself you wouldn't take it."

"I suppose you're right," he admitted grudgingly.

"Of course I'm right. Well you haven't half a chance – not the hundredth part of a chance. They're more than a bit suspicious of you already. So the only hope is me. I may find out nothing; the door may be locked; they may be holding a Bible meeting. But I'm going to have a look see."

"You are a fizzer, Molly," he cried. "But it's all wrong, you know. And if anything happens to you, I'll never forgive myself."

"Don't be an ass. What can happen to me? Now come along to my room, and we'll have a preliminary investigation. Then once I'm away you must come back here, and wait for me."

"I'll wait in your room."

"Don't be silly. When Charles leads me back by the hand it'll look grand, won't it, if the first person he sees is you. Come on."

Side by side they crept along the passage till they came to her door. And it was as they got to it that Algy suddenly stiffened: from close by he had heard a faint sound of movement. His grip on her arm tightened, and she paused pressing close to him in the darkness.

"What is it?" she whispered.

"There's someone here," he breathed. "Go into your room; shut and lock the door. I'll come in later – if it's safe."

He crouched back against the wall as she opened the door. And in the faint light that filtered out from the fire he saw for a second the outline of a man not a yard away. And seeing – sprang.

Came a grunt and a stifled curse as he closed, and the next moment he was fighting in earnest. And then more light: Molly had reopened her door.

"Good God!" muttered Algy, letting go. His opponent was Talbot.

"What's the game?" he demanded suspiciously. "What are you doing here?"

Talbot raised his eyebrows, and Algy frowned. It had just struck him that, on the face of it, the same question applied to him even more forcibly. Then he realised Molly was still standing in the open doorway.

"Molly," he said, "this is the footman I told you about. Captain Talbot: Miss Castledon."

She gave an amused little laugh.

"How d'you do," she remarked, holding out her hand. "Don't look so embarrassed, you poor man. I can assure you that Algy's intentions are strictly honourable. Come in: we can't all stand about in the passage."

"You see," explained Talbot, when the door was shut, "Drummond didn't know that Longworth was going to be here when he first sent me. And so, amongst other things one of the jobs he gave me was to look after you, Miss Castledon. He told me what you were doing – leading Burton up the garden path and so forth – and – er – I – er – happened to be passing the billiard-room tonight when you were in there. So I thought – er – er – "

"Exactly," said Molly quietly. "You thought he might endeavour to follow up the good work."

"Something of the sort," he admitted.

"Thank you very much, Captain Talbot. It was sweet of you. So far I am glad to say I have been spared that. This is something quite different. Explain to him, Algy."

Talbot listened with a look of admiration growing on his face.

"But it's super," he cried, enthusiastically. "Simply super. I congratulate you, Miss Castledon."

"Rot," said Algy. "She oughtn't to do it."

"But she's going to, my pet," answered Molly.

"And I shall be on hand," said Talbot.

Algy stared at him.

"That makes it better," he said thoughtfully. "Much better."

"But how can you be?" cried Molly. "You can't be sleep-walking too."

"Not exactly," laughed Talbot. "But I am a footman. I can be in parts of the house, quite safely, where Longworth couldn't possibly be without raising suspicion."

"Have you got any idea how many there are in this party?" asked Algy.

"There's a permanent staff here of six men," said Talbot. "They've got a dining-room of their own, and four of 'em are foreigners."

"What do they do?"

"Secretarial work apparently. But it's really only guess-work on my part, because they've got a special staff who look after them."

"And was it one of them who screamed?" asked the girl.

"I don't know," answered Talbot. "I heard it, of course, but there's one thing you soon discover in this house. Curiosity is not encouraged."

"Burton said it was someone getting tied up in the electric-light plant," remarked Algy.

"That I can assure you it wasn't," said Talbot. "The engine is a hundred yards away in the wood. No: that scream came from the house."

"Come on, Captain Talbot," cried Molly. "If we stop here talking all night, their meeting will be over."

"Dash it, Molly," said Algy. "I *don't* like it."

"Dry up," she laughed. "Now what are you going to do?" She turned to the soldier.

"Go with you and show you the room. Then lurk round a corner out of sight, but within hearing. And if anything happens, just give a call and I'll be with you."

"And you, Algy?"

"I'll watch from here for a bit, but I'll be away before there's any chance of your coming back. It's all wrong this, but good luck, bless you."

The door closed behind her and Talbot, and Algy crossed to the window. The girl had been right: he could see straight into the room opposite. But the blind was pulled down, so that the fact did not avail much. And then to his amaze and delight a thing happened which he would not have dared to hope for. With a click the blind flew up, and there was Menalin leaning out of the window.

Algy crouched down still lower, though he knew he could not be seen. What an unprecedented stroke of luck! Every detail of the room was plainly visible. Facing him, and sitting at one end of a table was Burton, and the six men mentioned by Talbot were flanking him, three on either side. Nearest to him was a pushed-back chair, evidently the one which Menalin had just vacated.

At the moment Burton was doing the talking, though it was impossible to hear anything he said. Occasionally one of the others would make a note, or consult a paper, whilst Menalin, his back to the room, stood quietly smoking. It might, reflected Algy, have been the most ordinary common or garden business meeting, with the chairman addressing his board of directors.

Suddenly Algy grew tense; the moment had come. Menalin had swung round: the other men had all risen and were staring open-mouthed at some obviously amazing spectacle. And then

Molly herself came into view. Heavens! but she was superb. Even at that distance he could see the outstretched hands, sense those wide-open staring eyes as she moved across the room.

She came to a chair, and began slowly to feel her way round the table. And it was then that Burton seemed to come out of his stupor. He lifted one hand in an imperative signal for silence, and moved swiftly towards the girl. For a moment Algy's heart stood still. What was he going to do? And with unspeakable relief he saw that all was well: Burton had been taken in even as he had.

Very gently he took the girl's hand, and began to lead her towards the door. Which, reflected Algy, was his cue not to linger on the order of his going. Five seconds later he was back in his own room, marvelling at the pluck which had carried a girl of her age through such an ordeal. Whether she had found out anything or not was beside the point: nothing could detract from the merit of the performance. In fact he was still taking off his hat to it when Talbot shook him into consciousness next morning at eight o'clock.

"Wouldn't have believed it possible that I could have slept," Algy announced. "God! man – she was immense. Did you see it?"

Talbot shook his head.

"But I followed back to her room at a discreet distance to make sure Burton didn't try any funny stuff."

"He didn't, did he?"

"No. I'll give the swine credit for that. I wonder whether she's got on to anything."

"We'll find out this morning. Jove! That girl can act."

Algy lit a cigarette.

"All the six worthies you told us about, and the great Menalin himself, gaping at her like a group of dead codfish."

"I wish I'd seen it," said Talbot.

"The incredible bit of luck was that just before the performance started Menalin went and loosed up the blind. So that I saw the whole outfit from A to Z. Look here, old lad, we'll have to keep up the fiction. D'you mind turning me on a bath?"

Talbot grinned.

"As your lordship wishes. Shall I carry in the ducal loofah?"

"Go to hell," said Algy amiably. "You're a foul valet, and if the water isn't the right temperature I shall report you to that pompous-stomached butler."

The male members of the party were already down when he arrived for breakfast an hour later.

"Good morrow, my dear old proprietor and fellow guests," he burbled, wandering over to the hotplate on a tour of inspection. "What is the popular line in nourishment?"

"Eggs in silence," said Burton. "You'll find papers on the sideboard."

"Eggs in silence!" Algy guffawed. "By Jove! That's good; I must remember that one."

He glanced sideways as the door opened and Molly came in.

"Good morning, Miss Castledon." He bowed deeply and realised that not for nothing did she pass her hand wearily over her forehead, and give him the barest suspicion of a wink. "We are in great heart, are we?"

"Please don't get up." She turned to the others who had risen. "Not very great, Algy."

"My angel – you shake me to the core. What ails thee?"

"I had the most extraordinary vivid dream last night," she said.

"Really." Burton looked at her solicitously. "Nothing to do with the dinner, I hope."

"It was about you," she went on. "And Mr Menalin. You were in a room which had a big table in it, and there were six other men with you. There were chairs round the table, and a lot of papers scattered on it. And you were all standing up and looking at me. I know it all sounds very stupid and ordinary, but it was so vivid that it might have been real."

"Not at all stupid, Miss Castledon," said Menalin. "In fact very interesting. And I'll tell you why in a minute. Was that all you saw in the room?"

"No. There was a man asleep on the sofa."

"Very interesting," repeated Menalin. "Isn't it, Charles?"

Burton nodded and the girl looked in bewilderment from one to the other.

"What do you mean?" she said at length.

"Because it wasn't a dream, Miss Castledon," answered Menalin. "Tell me, do you often walk in your sleep?"

"No. I don't, do I, Daddy?"

"What's this? What's this?" Sir George came out from behind his paper with a start. "Walk in your sleep! You haven't since you were a child."

"She did last night, Sir George," said Burton. "We were having a business conference which lasted rather late, and suddenly the door opened and your daughter came in. I'd never seen a case of sleepwalking before: in fact none of us had. But she went quite peacefully back to her room and never woke at all."

"God bless my soul!" cried the startled baronet. "You don't say so. She used to do it when she was small, but she hasn't for years."

"And why I said it was interesting," remarked Menalin, "was that Burton and I had a little argument as to how much anyone in that condition really sees. From what Miss Castledon tells us, everything is imprinted on the brain, just like a camera exposure."

"You mean to say that it really *was* you I saw last night?" cried Molly.

"Undoubtedly," said Menalin. "And our host. And the six other men. And the man asleep on the sofa."

"Then that probably accounts for my feeling so tired this morning," she said. "You poor people! I'm sorry I was such a nuisance."

"A very charming one, at any rate," laughed Menalin. "I wish we could always have such delightful interruptions to prosaic business meetings."

"Do you feel up to golf, old thing?" asked Algy.

"Rather. Of course I do. Ring up for caddies. You see, Algy," she said half an hour later as they swung out of the drive in his car, "I thought it was safer to take the bull by the horns. Telling the whole thing like that, and looking a bit washed-out ought to dispel any possible suspicion. And in view of everything, it's advisable."

"My dear!" he cried enthusiastically, "you were superb. I watched the whole thing through the window." He glanced at her as he spoke. "What's the matter, kid? In view of everything... Is there..."

She was staring straight in front of her.

"There was one moment, Algy, when I nearly gave the whole show away."

"Was there? When?"

"The man who was asleep on the sofa..."

"What about him?"

"He wasn't asleep. He was dead."

CHAPTER 12

Caddie Most Foul

Algy pulled into the side of the road and stopped the car.

"What is that you said?" he asked very quietly.

"I said that the man lying on the sofa was not asleep. He was dead."

"Look here, dear," he continued. "I don't want you to think I'm being stupid or unbelieving. But this is serious. Are you sure?"

"Absolutely."

"Have you ever seen a dead man?"

"No. Not till last night."

"And you're quite certain he wasn't asleep?"

"A man breathes when he's asleep, doesn't he, Algy? He doesn't lie motionless with his mouth open, and his eyes wide and staring... Oh! God, I nearly screamed."

"May He be praised that you didn't," said Algy gravely. "You wouldn't have been here now if you had, Molly: nor would Talbot, nor would I."

He lit a cigarette and leaned forward over the steering-wheel.

"What did they kill for, Algy?" she cried.

"Ask me another," he said. "Same as you can over everything connected with this show. He was probably the poor blighter we heard shout for help earlier on."

All around them stretched the floods, the water lapping idly against the sides of the road.

"You do believe me, don't you?" she cried.

"Yes, my dear, I do – in view of what we know of these gentlemen. The point is – what to do?"

There came the faint swish of a bicycle approaching from behind, and a man rode slowly past them.

"Get on, Algy, you fool," said a well-known voice. "You're in sight of the house. Go to the golf club. Play a round. Look out for me there."

As silently as he had come the cyclist departed, without even having turned his head. And as they overtook him again half a minute later, a typical caddie was still bicycling stoically along the road towards the links.

"Who was that?" gasped the girl.

"Hugh Drummond," said Algy shortly. "I *would* make an idiot mistake like that."

"But I don't see what was wrong," she cried.

"Darling," he said, "you don't see what was wrong, because you don't know what we're up against. Why should we stop and talk in the middle of a ruddy lake, unless we had something very important to discuss, especially as ostensibly we're on our way to play golf? We're fighting a gang of utterly unscrupulous men, and once let them think that we're in collusion, it's all U P."

"So that was the mysterious Captain Drummond," she said after a pause. "I want to meet him."

"You evidently will – this morning. But don't forget that so far as you are concerned he's just an unknown man of the caddie type. This is a game of no mistakes, Molly, in spite of the fact that I've just made a crasher."

There were some twenty cars parked when they arrived, and Algy, taking out the two bags, walked over to the pro's shop.

"Bit short this morning, sir, I'm afraid," remarked that worthy. "There's a match on. I can manage one caddie for the lady, but..."

"Excellent," said Algy casually. "If anyone else turns up send him out to me."

A bit of luck, he reflected as he strolled over to the club house... Left Hugh to do as he liked...

His eyes narrowed; coming up the road was a car he knew well – Charles Burton's. And the owner was inside.

"Changed your mind?" he called out as the car stopped. "Come and play a three ball."

"No, thank you," answered Burton. "I've only come up to see the secretary, and get my clubs."

Algy wandered into the bar looking thoughtful. On the face of it Burton might have telephoned the secretary and asked Algy to bring back his clubs. So was that the real reason that had brought his host here, or was it to make sure the golf was genuine? And at that moment he noticed the group by the bar: Peter Darrell, Ted Jerningham, Toby Sinclair – the whole of Drummond's gang. Moreover, everyone of them glanced at him as if he was a stranger... The game was beginning in earnest. He ordered a pint of beer, and stood leaning up against the bar and almost touching Peter Darrell.

"Quid corners, boys?" Peter was saying.

"Goes with me," answered Jerningham.

"By the way, steward," went on Peter, "is there any good hotel nearby where we could put up for the night?"

"Yes, sir. Two or three. I can give you the names if you like."

Algy strolled over to the window; certainly the game was beginning. And as he looked out, he saw Drummond standing by the caddie master's hut shouldering his bag of clubs.

"Steward," he called out, "would you telephone through to the professional and ask him to give my caddie a couple of Bromfolds. Hud something or other is his name."

"Very good, sir."

The steward turned away, and for an instant the eyes of all of them met. Then Algy put down his tankard and went out into the hall to find Charles Burton talking to Molly.

"Come on, you boozing hound," she cried. "I don't believe you've even got a ball down."

"I hope you have a good game," said Burton politely.

"Sorry you won't make a three ball, old host." The door had flung open behind him and the others were coming out of the bar. "Come on, Molly. I've got a caddie after all."

"Algy," she said as they walked to the tee, "wasn't that Ted Jerningham I saw in the hall?"

"It was," he answered.

"Why did he look straight at me and cut me dead?"

"Because I got in 'old host' just in time," grinned Algy. "You wouldn't have thought, would you, that I'd known the whole crowd for fifteen years?"

"What d'you mean?"

"Drummond, dear. They're all his gang – same as I am. And you're our latest and most priceless addition. So for today you don't know Ted, and he doesn't know you. See?"

"You know," she said happily, "I'm beginning to like this. What are they doing down here?"

"Stopping for the night for one thing. But I'll know more by the end of the round. Goodbye, darling. I think you've hooked into Kent."

"A grand girl, Algy," said Drummond, as Molly and her caddie disappeared. "That show of hers last night was magnificent – simply magnificent."

"You saw it, did you?"

"I was up in a tree. Did she find out anything?" He fumbled suddenly with the bag. "Bit to the right of the 'ole, sir. Gaw blimey – wot a putt!"

"Not up to your usual form, that one, Longworth?" From nowhere, apparently, Charles Burton had unexpectedly materialised.

"D'you mind if I stroll round with you for a bit?"

"An honour, dear old boy, an honour. I admit that putt was not struck with my usual fluent form, but the round is yet young."

"I had an idea," remarked Burton a little later, "that you knew Peter Darrell."

"Peter Darrell!" Algy frowned thoughtfully. "What do I want here, caddie?"

"Yer driver," answered that worthy contemptuously. "It's more'n a 'undred yards. 'Ere – try a number five. The young laidy's dead. Caw!" He viewed the shot dispassionately. "Wot you wants is a 'ockey stick. Now, Mr Darrell, sir – wot this gentleman was talking abaht – he *can* play. Caddied for 'im, I did, sir, last Hamateur up at Prestwick. 'E ain't down 'ere today, is he, sir?"

"Are you speaking to me, my man?" said Burton.

But Algy's caddie was not listening; he was staring at a four ball coming up the last fairway.

"That's 'im," he announced triumphantly. "That tall gent in the levver jacket. Know 'im anywhere I would, though I've only met 'im once or twice."

"When you've quite finished your interesting reminiscences," said Burton coldly, "would it be too much to hope that you could keep your mouth shut for a minute or two?"

"Sure I begs yer pardon, sir."

"As I was saying, Longworth, I thought you knew Darrell."

"Like our loquacious friend here, I have met him once or twice," said Algy as if searching in his memory. "That's the crowd who were in the bar, isn't it? I thought I recognised one of them... Of course it was Darrell, now I come to think of it...

Silly of me... We sort of stared at one another... Can I go yet, caddie?"

"Yus. But you'd better not. Yer *might* 'it it this time."

The four ball had reached their tee and sat down on a bench.

"Remember me, Mr Darrell, sir?" Algy's caddie touched his cap. "Caddied for you, I did, sir, last summer at Prestwick. 'Udson's my name."

"Of course, Hudson. I remember you perfectly. How's the world treating you?"

"So-so, sir. Been 'aving a spot of trouble with me kidneys, but not too bad."

"Sorry about that." Darrell got up as Algy approached him.

"Stupid of me not to recognise you in the bar, Darrell," said Algy. "I forgot where we met, but..."

"So do I. And d'you know I'm ashamed to confess it, but I've completely forgotten your name."

"Longworth. We must have a spot afterwards. Can't I go now, Hudson?"

"Well, yer ain't Bobby Jones, are yer? Nor Cyril Tolley. If yer keeps yer 'ead dahn for once yer might clear the rough. Cripes! That one's killed a rabbit orl right."

Muttering darkly he plunged into the heather brandishing a niblick.

" 'Ere we are," he announced morosely. "Can't even see the perishing ball, though it don't make no odds seeing as 'ow yer never looks at it."

"For God's sake shut up, you awful mess," muttered Algy in a shaking voice. "If I begin to laugh we're ungummed."

"I didn't realise Burton would be coming up to the club," said Drummond. "Look out – here he is. Well aht, sir; good one, that was."

"Well, Longworth," said Burton with a laugh, "if you aren't stunned by your caddie's verbosity, I'll expect you both at lunch."

"Going back?" cried Algy. "Right ho! old host. We'll masticate the rissoles later."

"By God! that bloke wants watching," said Drummond as Burton disappeared over the rise in the direction of the club house. Then he looked across at Molly Castledon, who was searching for her ball in the rough on the left. "Tell me, Algy, did she find out anything last night?"

"You know she was pretending to sleepwalk?"

"Yes. Talbot told me that this morning. But what did she hear – or see?"

"A man lying dead on the sofa," said Algy quietly.

"What!"

Drummond for one second halted dead in his tracks. Then, true to his role, he ambled forward again.

"Is she certain?"

"Absolutely. We were discussing it when you rode past us this morning."

"So they've got him, have they?" muttered Drummond.

"Do you know who he was?" asked Algy.

They were converging on the green, and the girl came towards them.

"How many have you played, Algy?" she called out.

"Three, my love," he answered.

"Pretty foul player, aren't you? D'you see the man," she continued as she joined them, "standing by the tree at the next tee?"

"I do," said Algy, missing his putt by a yard.

"He was in the room last night. One of the six. Have I got this for it?"

"You have, darling. Well holed: in all the way. You heard that, Hugh?"

"I did. Gad! that girl's a fizzer."

He said no more until they had topped the hill in front of the seventh tee. Behind them the watcher at the sixth green seemed to be growing a little bored, and was showing signs of following them. And then the crest of the bunker hid him from sight.

"Listen, Algy," said Drummond quietly, "obviously this isn't safe. How much they suspect, I don't know – but they suspect something. Luckily – here comes the rain. Quit your game at the next green, and go back to the club house.

"This afternoon you have got to go to London. I will arrange for a telephone call to come through to you."

"Don't forget," put in Algy, "that there are extensions all over the place, and it's more than likely to be tapped."

"Right," said Drummond. "Molly Castledon will remain here: she'll be perfectly safe, especially with Talbot in the house. Arrived in London you will ring up Alice Blackton and arrange to meet somewhere. That's instead of Monday night. You'll have to watch it; she will almost certainly be followed. And that you've got to dodge. You will then bring her down here."

"Here?" cried Algy.

"Yes: here. Go back to the Black Horse at Storrington and await further orders. Here's a brassie, and, for Heaven's sake, hit it. I've got a lot to say yet, and this is our last chance.

"Now," he continued, when Algy had despatched the ball towards the green, "the situation is this. As Talbot told you, Ronald Standish has escaped. Incidentally you needn't worry about the *Morning Post*: Talbot told me their reaction to the word Varda. It was Ronald who cabled me about it: he too is in ignorance of where it is. And that is what we have got to find out: so far as I can see, it is not mentioned in any atlas. Which is where Alice Blackton comes in."

"Does she know where it is?" asked Algy.

"No. But she knows a man who probably does. The trouble is that, unless I'm much mistaken, that's the man Miss Castledon saw lying dead last night."

Algy whistled.

"The devil it is," he muttered.

"I don't know him by sight," continued Drummond, "so it's useless for me to work on my own. Alice is the only person who does, so she's got to do the identification."

"But where?"

"Unless I'm much mistaken," said Drummond quietly, "he was killed even as Latimer was killed. Earlier in the evening, from my point of vantage, I caught a glimpse of Burton with a hypodermic syringe in his hand. Now the body was not moved last night, and they won't dare to do so today. So he'll be deposited somewhere tonight. Almost certainly not in the grounds – that would be too close home; but they'll dump him on the Downs. That's where the boys come in: lucky I got 'em down. Tell Peter he'll get his orders in due course, and that it's an all-night job tonight for everybody."

"What's the great point over the identification?" asked Algy.

"If it's Alice Blackton's man they've killed, we're no further on than we were before over locating this island. But if it isn't, we needn't worry."

"I get you. Hugh, are you any nearer what's going on?"

"A few months ago France wasn't far off a revolution," said Drummond grimly. "Nor was Belgium. Let's leave it at that. Stopping, sir?" he continued in a louder voice. "It is coming dahn a bit."

Molly Castledon took her cue instantly.

"Not much fun, is it, Algy?" she remarked. "Let's go back to the club house."

"Right, old dear."

Out of the corner of his eye he saw the watcher approaching.

"Dry the clubs, caddie," he continued, "and put 'em in my car, please."

"Very good, sir. Thank you, sir."

His hand closed round his fee, and for the fraction of a second his lips twitched.

"A bit of my own back," said Algy happily to Molly as they started to walk back. "I gave him a farthing and a trouser button."

"What's it all about, Algy?" she asked eagerly.

Briefly he told her, and she began to frown mutinously.

"But I wanted to be in it," she said. "It's not fair of Captain Drummond."

"Darling," he assured her, "you shall be later. Tonight you *can't* do any good, and if you were found to be missing from the house, the whole outfit goes west. Don't forget that Hugh has had very little time; all these orders have had to be worked out since I told him that man was dead. He's simply raving over what you did."

"All right," she said. "I'll forgive him this time. Let's have a drink."

"It will be interesting to see what our friend the watcher does," he murmured, as they sat down in the lounge. "Here he comes."

With his coat collar turned up, for the rain was now coming down in earnest, the man came in through the swing doors and went into the cloakroom.

"I wonder what the deuce he thinks he's going to find out," said Algy. "Burton I can understand; obviously he suspected Peter and me. But this bloke defeats me."

"Just watching, I should think," said the girl, "to see if there's any reaction between you and the others when you might think it was safe."

"There's no doubt," remarked Algy thoughtfully, "that Hugh is right. We're suspect. But I must say it amused me today – the old boy caddying right under that swab Burton's nose. Now what do you suggest we should do, my pet? Here comes Peter and Co., and I've got to get a message through to him. But after that?"

"Let's go back as late as possible," she said. "I dread the thought of that house without you there to support me."

"Pretty foul, I agree," said Algy. "Still, you can always plead a head and get to bed early tonight... And lock your door, my dear; don't forget."

The lounge was filling as more people came in out of the rain. The watcher, engrossed in a paper, was sitting inconspicuously in a corner; Peter Darrell, passing on his way to the bar, had been formally introduced to Molly Castledon. And in the process thereof had been given Drummond's message... But since it had been contained in a story of apparently sultry hue, which had given rise to much ribald merriment, the watcher was blissfully ignorant of it. In fact he was blissfully ignorant of anything, save that he had spent a wasted morning, when at a quarter to one Molly and Algy rose to go back to Birchington Towers.

The rain had ceased, and Algy proceeded to offend God and man by singing as they drove along.

"Feed me with ortolans; nurture me with the wines of Cathay," he declaimed. "You know, darling," he continued, relapsing into speech, "the more I think of it, the more unutterably foul do I regard that limerick last night."

"That's something, anyway," she agreed kindly.

"Nevertheless it succeeded in its object. The name Varda stabbed 'em both in the stomach."

"And you think this girl, Alice Blackton, will know where it is?"

"Such seems to be Hugh's idea."

"And if she does, or can find out?"

"Presumably we go there, and the fun really begins."

She lit a cigarette thoughtfully.

"Do you always follow Hugh Drummond blind?" she asked.

"Always. The only time that I've ever faintly jibbed was over his suggestion that you should dally with Burton. However, up to date, there's no harm done."

"I'm not going on with it much more, my lad."

Algy turned in at the drive.

"My angel child," he said quietly, "don't worry. If I'm any judge of matters you won't need to. It won't be long now before things come to a head. We're on the warpath properly."

"Who is telephoning you from Town?"

"Haven't an earthly. Hugh is fixing it."

It proved to be Algy's Uncle William who was leaving for Egypt next day. A faint click as he picked up the receiver when the message came through after lunch, assured him that another person had done likewise, elsewhere in the house, but Uncle William was foolproof. His seat was reserved; his cabin was booked; and it was essential he should see Algy before he went. There was some business connected with the estate which he wanted cleared up at once. So he would await Algy at his club, and if he wished would give him dinner that night.

"That's torn it," said Algy, re-entering the hall. "Little Algy must leave you for the metropolis. Uncle William has escaped from the home we keep him in and would fain see his nephew before leaving for Egypt. So if you will excuse me, old host, I will see about getting my things packed."

Talbot answered his bell, and there was a faint grin on his face.

"The secretary was listening in to your London call," he remarked. "Was it OK?"

"Quite," said Algy. "Dear Uncle William was word perfect. Have you seen Drummond?"

"Yes. For a minute before lunch on the road."

"You know about the dead man?"

Talbot nodded.

"Do I take off my hat to that girl? I'm asking you."

"Look after her, old boy," said Algy.

"Leave me to it," answered Talbot. "I only wish I could talk to her openly."

Then his face set grimly.

"By God! Longworth – I'm just waiting for the moment when I can get my own back on these swine. My dear old guv'nor – who'd never harmed a child..."

"Trust Hugh Drummond, old boy," said Algy. "It'll come sooner than you think. Put the bags in my car, will you! And I may be seeing you tonight..."

It certainly seemed as if Uncle William had pulled it off. Burton was politely disappointed at his having to go: Menalin did not even appear on the scene. Even Lady Castledon, overjoyed at the prospect of Algy's departure, so far forgot herself as to ask him to call in London.

But for all that Algy was taking no risks. It was a Sunday and traffic was heavy on the main Bognor road, even though it was late in the year. An easy day, in fact, to follow a car, however fast it was, since high speed was out of the question.

So he swung into a network of lanes, when he had gone a few miles, and slowed up his pace. And a few minutes convinced him that he was safe; no one was on his heels. He pulled up and lit a cigarette; a plan of campaign was necessary.

To begin with, his own flat and club would almost certainly be under supervision. To go to London at all, therefore, seemed foolish. The point was whether Alice Blackton could smuggle herself out of town without being spotted. And the only way of finding that out was to get through to her on the telephone.

He drove on, keeping well clear of the London road, until he came at length to a village which a notice-board proclaimed was Rodsworth. It appeared to be wrapped in slumber, though one dilapidated Ford stood outside the Chequers Inn. It would serve, he decided, as well as any other, and backing his car into the so-called garage, he entered the hotel and booked a room, to the evident amazement of the landlord. Then he put through a telephone call to Alice.

199

By an amazing stroke of luck he caught her just as she was going out: in fact, he gathered the boy friend was even then blaspheming in the hall at the delay.

"He must blaspheme, dear," said Algy firmly. "Has he a motorcar? He has. Outside the door at the moment? Good. Now listen, Alice. Is your place being watched? Not that you know of. Not good enough, my dear. We can't run any risks. Tell your pal that he's got to cancel any plans he may have made for this afternoon. He is to start off in any direction he may think fit – preferably as if he was going to John o' Groat's – and then after devious detours he is to arrive with you at the Chequers Inn, situated in the fascinating old-world village of Rodsworth in Sussex. Got that? Good. You must make absolutely certain you're not followed... No. I don't want to be more explicit over the phone... What time? Any time before it's dark. Goodbye, my angel."

He replaced the receiver, and crossed to the window. The village street was still deserted, which confirmed his own safety. Would Alice and her escort be equally fortunate?

Slowly the hours dragged by. A watery sun had come out, throwing fitful shadows on the stuffed horsehair furniture of the parlour. Over the mantelpiece his host, encased in his wedding glory of frock coat and bowler complete gazed at him sheepishly from the wall: whilst flanked on each side of him, two masterpieces depicted shoals of fat and very naked babies floating hopefully in space.

It was six o'clock when he awoke, cramped in every limb, from a painful doze. A car was thrumming softly outside the window, and in the gathering darkness he could just see Alice and a man getting out.

"Great," he cried, meeting them at the door. "Sure you've not been followed?"

"Certain," said Alice. "This is Jimmy Parker...Algy Longworth..."

The two men shook hands.

"Run her into the garage, Parker," said Algy. "Then we'll have a drink."

"What's the great idea, Algy?" demanded the girl, as Parker rejoined them. "Jimmy's been breathing blood all the way here."

"Sorry about that," said Algy with a grin, "but it was unavoidable. You're for a job of work tonight, Alice."

"What d'you mean?" she asked.

"And incidentally so are you, Parker," he added. "What is it, chaps? Two pints and a gin and french, please. Now," he continued as the landlord left the room, "is this bloke reliable, Alice?"

"Quite," she said. "He's an NO."

"Grand. Couldn't be better. Have you told him anything, my dear?"

"Vaguely. I guessed it was to do with the Drummond show."

"Right. Well, please keep that to yourself, Parker. It's a case of murder, Alice, and you've got to identify the victim."

"What's that?" cried Parker sharply. "Why should she?"

"Dry up, Jimmy," said the girl. "Tell me, Algy."

They listened in silence while Algy told them briefly what had occurred, and when he'd finished Alice Blackton sat twisting her pocket handkerchief in her fingers.

"I wonder if it's Mrs Cartwright's husband," she said in a low voice, and Algy looked at her quickly.

"Who's he?" he cried.

"I'll tell you later," she said. "What does Captain Drummond want me to do?"

"Come with me to the Black Horse at Storrington to start with," answered Algy. "We'll get further orders there."

"And what about Jimmy?"

"I want him, if he will, to do a much more uninteresting job," said Algy, "but a very important one. It's my own idea, I admit, because no one knew he was coming into the picture till this afternoon. Now it will be of the greatest advantage if the other side think I'm safely in my flat tonight. So if you will, Parker, what I'd like you to do is this.

"Drive my car back to London, leaving yours here for me. At about ten or so go round to my flat – I'll give you the address – and leave the car outside the door, where in due course its number will be noted by the gentleman on guard. Then go straight indoors – here is the latchkey – keeping your coat collar turned up and your face away from the light. Once inside you will encounter a large and forbidding-looking man called Marsh. To him you will hand a letter I will give you, which will say that you are stopping the night in the flat, and that *he* is to put the car away in the garage. After that my cellar is yours, but don't go near enough to the window to be recognised."

"Well, I'm damned," remarked the Navy. "It sounds a perfectly riotous evening. Is this what I came up from Pompey for?"

"Anyway, old man," laughed Algy, "it's better than hiding in a gorse bush on the Downs, which looks like being our portion."

"Can't I come too?" pleaded the sailor.

"No, Jimmy," said the girl firmly. "Algy is right. You've got to do as he says."

"It's big stuff, Parker," put in Algy quietly. "You can take that from me."

"Orl right," said Parker resignedly. "I'll play. What's your bus?"

"A Lagonda. She can move."

"And what will you do with mine tomorrow?"

"Leave her in St James's Square at eleven o'clock."

"OK," said the sailor. "Gawd 'elp all poor blokes at sea. What ho! without, mine host. Send in thy tire-maidens bearing foaming goblets. The poor, bloody Navy is in the chair."

CHAPTER 13

Burglars in Battersea

"And now, bless you, I'm just waiting to hear how you've come into it again."

Algy drew up his chair to the fire and lit a cigarette. Dinner at the Black Horse was over, and the sitting-room was empty. Outside, the West Sussex darts championship was in full swing; a low hum of conversation, punctuated by an occasional jovial laugh, provided the unbeatable setting of the old English coaching inn.

He had arrived there with Alice Blackton an hour before, having first seen Jimmy Parker safely on the road to London from Rodsworth. As yet no orders had arrived from Drummond, but the night was still young. And until these came there was nothing more to be done.

"There's not much to tell, Algy," said the girl. "But for what there is, here goes. Last Wednesday night just before I was starting off for the Golden Boot, I happened to go into my landlady's room. She's an awfully nice woman is Mrs Turnbull, and I often go and have a talk with her. On this occasion there was another woman with her, and a glance at her face showed that she'd been crying.

"Of course I felt a bit embarrassed, and was on the point of going out again when Mrs Turnbull suddenly turned to me.

"'What's the name of the man who owns the Golden Boot, dearie?' she asked.

"'Burton,' I said. 'Charles Burton. Why?'

"She looked at the other woman triumphantly.

"'What did I tell you?' she cried. 'I was sure I knew the name. This is Mrs Cartwright, dear. Sit down and have a cup of tea.'

"Well, Mrs Cartwright was an elderly body who looked rather like a prosperous cook, and, under ordinary circumstances, I should have made some excuse. But the instant I heard dear Charles' name, I determined to hear more. So I sat down.

"'A devil he is – that Burton,' sniffed Mrs Cartwright. 'You be careful of him, my dear.'

"'What's he done to you, Mrs Cartwright?' I asked.

"'It's her 'usband,' explained Mrs Turnbull – two h's in succession generally defeat her, poor dear. 'Tell Miss Blackton, Amelia.'

"So Amelia, bless her heart, gave tongue. I won't attempt to give it verbatim, but what it boiled down to was this. Her husband, Samuel Cartwright, was a working watch-and clock-maker, living down Battersea way. And some months ago he'd begun to dabble in politics in a mild way. At first she'd been rather pleased; it kept him quiet, and got him out of the house. But after a while she began to notice a change in him. He became morose and secretive, and what upset her most of all was that he began to ask some funny sort of men to their house – men she didn't like at all. And when she reasoned with him about it he used to fly into a passion.

"Another thing, too, that worried her was this. In their little backyard he had a shed where he did a lot of his work. In the past the door had always been open, and she had never thought twice about walking in if she wanted to ask him anything. And then, suddenly, for no apparent reason, he had begun to keep the door locked.

"That there was something on his mind, was obvious, but try as she would she couldn't find out what it was. His appetite fell away. He began to sleep badly and, in short, the man was clearly ill. But any suggestion of a doctor was met with a flat refusal.

"'Not that a doctor would have done any good,' as she admitted. 'Sam's trouble was in his mind.'

"And then, a few days before I met her, matters had come to a head. Sam had announced his intention of going down to the country for the night – alone. Well, I gathered from Mrs Sam that such a proceeding was almost as amazing as the descent of Nelson into Trafalgar Square. He loathed and detested the country; even on Bank Holidays Epping Forest was the farthest he would ever go. And here he was proposing to venture forth alone into places full of uncharted terrors. Moreover – and this is what upset her most – she was convinced he didn't want to go. He was going because he had to.

"So the old girl decided to get at the bottom of matters once for all. She couldn't follow him herself, since he'd have recognised her – but she got hold of a young nephew whom Sam didn't know. And, having pointed Sam out to the boy, she gave him some money and told him off to do the job.

"The boy was a cockney and quick on the uptake, and had no difficulty over following his uncle. And, my dear Watson, you will have no difficulty in guessing where Sam went to – Charles Burton's house near Pulborough.

"By this time I was beginning to look at my watch, for the old girl had taken about half an hour to get that lot off her chest. But it was important to hear everything, so I stayed on. And it appeared that far from his visit to the country having done Sam any good, it had made him much worse. The very night he came back he started shouting, 'I won't; I won't,' in his sleep, and woke up bathed in perspiration.

"So the next day she really got down to it with him. And this time, apparently, he proved a bit more amenable, and she did get something out of him. It appeared that, without intending to, he had got mixed up in some secret society, and they were compelling him to do something he didn't want to do. That he hadn't known when he joined them what they really were, and that now it was too late to draw back. But what the something was he wouldn't tell her."

Alice Blackton lit another cigarette.

"Now that was last Friday week – five days before I met Mrs Cartwright. And it struck me, of course, that it was vital to let Captain Drummond know at once. I'd had a line from him, saying where I could get hold of him – Mr Hudson, c/o GPO, Petworth – and I was just wondering whether to write him before going to the Golden Boot, when the door opened and in walked Sam himself. He'd come to fetch his wife, and I took stock of him.

"Algy, if ever a man was frightened unto death, he was that man. He must have lost stones in weight, if his clothes were any criterion; they hung on him like sacks. His hands were shaking, and he reeked of whisky. So, after a moment or two, I got up and left, and that was that up till last Wednesday night."

"You got it all through to Hugh?" asked Algy.

"Next day."

"And has anything else happened?"

"One thing. On Friday – that's the day before yesterday – Mrs Turnbull came into my sitting-room about lunch time.

"'You remember Mrs Cartwright, miss,' she said.

"'Of course,' I cried. 'What about her?'

"'Samuel's going down to the country again tomorrow,' she said. 'And Amelia is fair worried to death.'"

"Tomorrow," remarked Algy thoughtfully. "That is – yesterday. And last night a man was killed. Things become clearer, my dear."

"Can it be him, Algy?" she cried.

"Anything can be anything with this crowd," he answered. "But it's now obvious why Hugh wanted you. You're the only player on our side who can identify the poor devil."

He rose and strolled over to the window.

"Thank the Lord, it isn't raining," he said. "The stars are out, and with luck it will keep fine. Hullo! what do you want?"

A young farm-hand was standing by the door, fingering his cap.

"Mr Longworth?" he said.

Algy nodded.

"Bloke called 'Udson told me to give you this. Said as 'ow you'd give me 'alf-a-dollar if I did."

Algy held out his hand for the note, with the coin in view.

"Here you are, my lad," he said. "Thank you. And shut the door when you go out."

He came back to the fire, slitting open the envelope.

"Orders, my dear – at last."

He grinned faintly as he looked at them.

"Got a warm coat, my love? You'll need one."

"What does he say?"

"Be at the cross-roads quarter of a mile north of main entrance to Birchington Towers by eleven p.m. Remain in car, which hide in entrance to quarry. No lights. If nothing happened by three, return London. HUD.

"There you are, my dear. Terse and to the point. And it looks like four hours of fun and laughter for the chaps."

"You know where it is?" she asked.

"I know the quarry," said Algy, once again crossing over to the window. "It's not going to be too bad; you can do a bit of shut-eye under the rug."

And as it turned out the night proved almost muggy. Punctually at eleven Algy backed the car into the narrow track that led to the sand quarry, taking it far enough in not to be visible in the lights of any passing car. Away to the right, on the high ground, lay Birchington Towers, almost invisible in the trees. Only a faint general light gave its position, and after a time that was extinguished.

Occasionally a car roared past on the main road homeward bound, but they grew fewer and fewer, and when midnight chimed out across the low ground from a neighbouring church, the whole countryside seemed asleep.

Interminably the time dragged by. Alice Blackton, tucked up in the back of the car, was dozing, but Algy, afraid of doing likewise, kept on sentry go between the car and the road. And he was just wondering if he dared risk a cigarette under cover of some bushes, when he heard, in the distance, the sound of a car coming from the direction of the Downs. It came nearer: then abruptly the engine stopped.

He waited: peering along the road. Once he thought he heard footsteps, but it might have been imagination. And it came as a shock, when, from close beside him, he suddenly heard a low voice.

"That you, Algy?"

It was Hugh Drummond: small wonder he'd heard no sound.

"Here I am," he answered.

"Got the girl?"

"She's in the back of the car. I'll wake her."

But she was already with them, and Drummond shook hands.

"Good for you, Alice," he said. "Leave your car here, and we'll get into Peter's, which is down the road."

"What's happened, Hugh?" asked Algy.

"As I thought, they moved the body tonight. I had Peter and Toby watching one drive, and Ted the other. They brought him out in a large car, and they've dumped him in some wooded ground on top of Bury Hill. Then the car went on towards London. Peter knows the exact spot where they left the road.

And that is our destination now. Sorry I've got to ask you to do it, Alice, but you're the only one of us who can. Ahoy, Peter…"

A car, standing in the road, loomed out of the darkness.

"You don't know Miss Blackton, do you… Mr Darrell… Let's get to it…"

"Where's Toby?" asked Algy.

"On guard by the wood," said Drummond.

They settled into the car, and Peter drove off. It was just a quarter to one and they did not meet a soul in the four-mile run; the only sound they heard was a dog barking furiously in a farm they passed. And at the top of Bury Hill they stopped.

To their right stretched the open Downs, and it was from here that after a moment or two Toby Sinclair materialised.

"OK, Toby?" cried Drummond.

"OK. Shall I lead the way?"

He plunged into the trees, and Drummond took Alice Blackton by the arm.

"Careful, my dear," he said. "We don't want you spraining your ankle."

It was not far to go: the body had been dumped about thirty yards from the road, in an open grass clearing. Actually it was hidden from the road itself, though anyone going a few feet into the trees would see it.

"Clever," said Drummond quietly. "They don't mind it being found: that's why they haven't concealed it. He died naturally just like Jimmy Latimer, and a man who dies naturally don't hide himself… He was hiking… You see his boots are dirty, and his clothes sodden with rain – though there hasn't been any since this morning… Probably put the poor devil in a bath before they started… Well, Alice?"

He switched his torch on the dead man's face, and the girl shuddered.

"Yes," she said. "It's Samuel Cartwright, all right…"

"I'd have betted on it," remarked Drummond. "Well, there's no more to be done here, so we may as well go home."

"But aren't you going to do anything about it?" she cried.

"What can we do, my dear?" said Drummond. "Nothing can bring him back to life. And the instant the matter is mentioned to the police, we've got to come into it. Which is the thing of all others I want to avoid."

"Have you been through his pockets, Hugh?" asked Algy.

"With a vacuum cleaner. And found nothing. Come on, chaps. You can drop me, Peter, at the quarry…"

"And what are we to do tomorrow?" asked Darrell. "Play a round in the morning, and come up to London in the afternoon. There's nothing more to be done down here."

"What are you going to do yourself?"

"Go up tonight with Algy… Hell!" he muttered. "To think that poor blighter knew what I'd give my eyes to know…"

He relapsed into silence till the car drew up at the entrance to the quarry.

"Night-night, boys," he said. "I'll get in touch with you tomorrow."

He watched Darrell's tail lamp disappear: then he walked towards Algy's car.

"Hullo!" he cried. "What's this bus? Good for you," he continued, after Algy's explanation. "We'll go to Heppel Street and our Mrs Penny for what's left of the night."

And they were running into London before he spoke again.

"Do you know Mrs Cartwright's address, Alice?"

"No. But I can easily get it from Mrs Turnbull."

"I'm thinking of that shed," said Drummond. "That shed in the backyard. I'd like to see inside that shed very much."

"Well, as I say, I can get the address quite easily."

"I wish you would. But you mustn't say that Cartwright's dead. That's a thing you know nothing about. It's our best chance, Algy," he continued thoughtfully. "That poor devil knew enough for them to kill him. Has he left any record behind?"

"The only way to find out is to go see," said Algy.

"Exactly. But how to do it is the point. Once Mrs Cartwright realises her husband is dead she's going up in steam. In addition the police will be buzzing round like a swarm of bees. Burglary, old boy, is the only hope. I'll think it over and let you know later. But the first and main thing is the address."

And that, as Alice had prophesied, presented no difficulty. It transpired next day over the telephone to Mrs Turnbull, that Mrs Cartwright lived in a street off the Albert Bridge Road, and, moreover, that she would be at home that night. Further, that she was worried to death over Sam's continued absence.

"It's going to be a little awkward for Burton," said Algy, "if she goes to the police. She'll tell 'em he was going to Birchington Towers, and, when his body is ultimately discovered on Bury Hill, what does Charles say?"

"That he never arrived," answered Drummond promptly. "That he knows nothing about the man at all. That from enquiries he has made a man with some fancied grievance asked for an interview last week, but was turned away, and on identification of the body by one of his servants it transpires that it is the same individual. No, Algy – they won't catch Charles that way. You see there will be no trace of murder on Samuel... And if the widow mentions his nervous state, the answer is that obviously it was some strange case of hallucination. What could Charles Burton have to do with a clockmaker in the Albert Bridge Road?"

"Perhaps you're right," said Algy. "So what do we do about it?"

"Will you still help us, Alice?" asked Drummond.

"Of course," she answered.

"Your job this evening is to keep Mrs Cartwright occupied whilst I explore that shed. If necessary take that female of yours

– Mrs Turnbull – with you; in fact it will seem more natural if you do. Algy will come with me, and will be on hand in case you should want him."

"What time shall I go there?"

"I suggest nine o'clock. And keep the lady occupied for an hour."

"That won't be difficult," said the girl.

"Your excuse for going, naturally, is her husband. You can invent some stuff about Burton to keep her interested, but don't, under any circumstances, let her come into the shed…"

"Right," she nodded. "I'll do just what you say."

"Grand girl! Jane!" he shouted, and Mrs Penny waddled in. "I'll want some lunch today, my pet," he announced. "And Mr Longworth and I will be sleeping here tonight."

"That'll be all right, Mr Hugh… And the young lady?"

"I think you'd better lunch here too, Alice, and not go back to your rooms till later."

"Just as you like," she said. "I could do with some more sleep."

"Algy, you take the car to St James's Square – and then come back here. We've got to alter your appearance before tonight."

"What are you going to do, old boy?" asked Algy.

"A little spot of exploration," said Drummond with a grin. "My knowledge of the Albert Bridge Road is not all it might be. But I shan't go till after lunch."

It was six o'clock when he returned in excellent spirits.

"Luck is in," he announced. "I do not think our burglarious adventure is going to be very difficult."

At seven o'clock Alice Blackton left; at eight, two typical dockyard natives slouched out of Number 10, Heppel Street, and were soon lost in the busy traffic of Tottenham Court Road.

"There is a pub of reasonable excellence, Algy," said the larger of the two, "not far from our destination, where we might while away a few fleeting seconds. And then – what luck? I wonder…"

It was just after nine that they swung out of the saloon bar and slouched along the street towards the Cartwrights' house. A few scattered groups were congregated under the lamp posts, but the night was raw and most of the inhabitants were indoors. The houses were small, but the street was in no sense a slum. Shops alternated with private dwellings, and suddenly Algy saw on the other side of the road the notice – "S CARTWRIGHT, WORKING CLOCKMAKER."

Drummond led him on about fifty yards; then he abruptly crossed over, and retraced his footsteps slowly. A wireless was blaring forth from an open window as they passed, but no pedestrians seemed near at hand. And with a quick movement Drummond turned into a narrow path along a fence that terminated in a wooden door.

"The back entrance," he whispered.

Cautiously he pushed the door open and in a second they were both through with it closed behind them.

"The yard," he muttered. "And there's the shed in front of us."

From above their heads light was filtering out from a curtained window, and they could hear the sound of women's voices. Evidently Alice and Mrs Turnbull had arrived and were holding the fort.

Like a shadow Drummond moved over to the shed, and for the fraction of a second a pin-point of light shone on the lock. Then it was extinguished, and he jumbled in his pocket. Came one short sharp crack, which sounded like a pistol shot to Algy, and the door flew open.

They paused motionless; had it been heard? But no sign came from the neighbouring houses, and the faint drone of voices from Mrs Cartwright's room was still audible. From his pocket Drummond took two pieces of felt and pinned them over the cobwebby windows. Then he closed the door and made Algy stand with his back against the crack.

"We must chance the rest," he said, switching on his torch, and letting the beam play around.

It was a small shed, not much larger than a bathing-hut. The whole of one side was occupied by a bench, on which was fitted the ordinary implements of the owner's trade. A large open box containing drills and other tools stood in one corner, and two upturned packing-cases apparently constituted the seating accommodation. Of papers there was no sign.

The walls were bare of shelves or cupboards; there was no drawer in the bench. And with a muttered curse Drummond was on the point of giving it up, when he gave a sudden exclamation. A board under his foot had moved. He turned his torch on to it; it was loose. And even as he did so there came the sound of a door closing gently, somewhere close by...

He switched off his torch and straightened up. He could hear Algy's breathing; otherwise everything was silent. And suddenly it struck him that the voices from the house had ceased.

He moved over to Algy, and pulled him back against the bench.

"Did you hear that?" he breathed.

"Yes," came the answer. "Back door, I think."

"Take the torch. Switch on if I tell you."

They waited tensely; outside a twig snapped. And then came the sound of fingers fumbling at the door, followed by a stifled exclamation of surprise. The newcomer had evidently discovered the broken lock.

For a moment or two he hesitated; then very cautiously the door was pushed open inch by inch, and framed in the faint light they could see the outline of a crouching man. At length he was in, with the door closed behind him.

As it happened he missed them both as he moved forward. Then he knelt down and they could hear him fumbling on the floor. He was breathing heavily, and muttering imprecations to himself. And at last he struck a match.

His back was towards them, and beyond him they could see a dark cavity in the floor. The board Drummond had trodden on had been removed, and from the hole underneath the man was pulling out some documents. He did not trouble to examine them, but just laid them beside the opening. Then, having satisfied himself that he had the lot, he replaced the board and stood up.

Which so far as he was concerned constituted the end of a perfect day. He felt two vice-like hands grip his neck; was aware dimly through the roaring in his ears that a torch was flashing on his face – and then blackness. And he was quite unconscious when he was deposited in a corner.

"Saves bother," said Drummond, cramming the papers in his pocket. "He won't come to for half an hour."

He was crossing the yard as he spoke and suddenly he paused.

"They've stopped talking, Algy," he whispered, "which is unlike women. We'd better go and see."

The back door was open, and they crept into the passage. In front of them light was shining out from a half-shut door, and they stopped outside it; stopped to see reflected in a mirror a woman sitting in a chair, whose terrified eyes met theirs from above the gag in her mouth.

"Just in time," muttered Drummond as he entered. A man, who had been leaning out of the window, swung round and stared at them, his jaw dropping as he did so. And then, he too was spared any further worry for a space. Drummond was not wasting time though this one struggled more than his friend outside.

"Undo the women, Algy," he said, as he dropped his limp opponent on the floor.

They were all three there, tightly bound and gagged.

"They came in suddenly on us," said Alice Blackton as she stood up. "Have you got the other?"

"Yes," answered Drummond. "I don't know who you ladies are," he continued, staring straight at her, "but if I was *you* I'd go home before the police come."

The emphasis was clear and she nodded.

"And if your name comes out you must disappear for a time."

Again she nodded, and then smiled faintly at the outburst in the corner. For it was going to be even money whether Mrs Cartwright or Mrs Turnbull had hysterics first.

"Come back with us, lovey," sobbed Mrs Turnbull, "and we'll telephone the police from my house."

"I couldn't stop here," sniffed Mrs Cartwright. "In my own parlour too."

"Excellent," whispered Drummond to the girl. "Get 'em back. And postpone telephoning as long as you can. If possible I *don't* want these men caught. And, of course, you don't know us…"

He beckoned to Algy and they faded silently away.

"Much better if they are not caught," he repeated as they walked along the street. "For if they are, Burton will know they've failed: but if they're not, they'll pretend they've succeeded and destroyed the papers."

"Where to now?" asked Algy.

"Back to Heppel Street to examine our catch," said Drummond, hailing a taxi. "Jove! Algy, what we'd have done without those two girls in this show don't bear thinking about."

They were met at the door by Mrs Penny.

"That gentleman that lunched with you the other day, dearie," she said, "rang up half an hour ago."

"Ginger Lawson," said Drummond to Algy. "What did he want, Jane?"

"To see you, Master Hugh. I said you were out and he's coming round at eleven."

"Ten-thirty now. All right, Jane. Show him in when he comes. Now, Algy, let's get to it."

216

He drew up a chair to the table, and from his pocket he pulled out the bundle of papers. There were five in all, and picking up the first he opened it.

It was a blueprint such as is common in engineering plans. But this one seemed to consist entirely of wheels and springs. There was one central diagram, and a series of smaller ones which seemed to represent parts of the main design enlarged. Drummond stared at it: then he suddenly rose and pressed the bell.

"Jane," he said, "do we patronise Petworth's Fruit Salad?"

"I've got a tin in the house now, dearie."

"Then bring it here, like an angel," he cried. "Don't open it."

Somewhat mystified, the old dame retired and brought the tin.

"All right, Jane, leave it here. As I thought, Algy," he said when she had gone, "it's the exact size of the central diagram. This is the print of the mechanism we got from Maier's house in Switzerland – or at any rate, something of the same type."

"On which, presumably, Cartwright was working," remarked Algy.

"Precisely. But since we've got the actual machine itself, the print doesn't seem of much importance, except that it brings the actual doings to England. Let's go on."

The second and third were in the nature of lists of stores. They were compiled in pencil with numerous erasions and alterations. 250 No. 1 wheels had been altered to 320; 150 D. springs had been half rubbed out and the number 200 substituted; 1,000 nuts various were a few of many similar items.

"It fits in so far, Algy," said Drummond, lighting a cigarette. "Even to my limited brain it is obvious that there are not 150 D. springs, whatever a D. spring may be, in that one machine. Therefore Cartwright was employed in making a number of them. And I think we can take as a working theory that Mr Maier of Veytaux was the original pebble on the beach. He it was who designed the first mechanism – the one that he kept, and which for some reason or other was stolen from him the night he was murdered, and which we've now got. Why they murdered him, we don't know – since he must have been in their confidence to start with. Perhaps he started opening his mouth too wide: perhaps he threatened them. Anyway, that doesn't matter. Maier produced the original, a blueprint of which was sent to Cartwright to copy. How's that?"

"Sounds perfectly feasible to me," answered Algy.

"So let us to Number 4," said Drummond. "By Jove! Algy," he cried excitedly. "Look. One of the very papers Jimmy Latimer got hold of."

He spread it out and they both pored over it. It was an outline map of England and Scotland, with dots sprinkled all over it. No names were printed at all, but it was easy to see that the dots represented towns. And as Madame Pélain had said, they were far more numerous in the Midlands and north than in the south.

Against some of them numbers in red were written. And the area so filled in on the map before them comprised Bristol and the South of Wales, and a few isolated ones in Somerset, Devon and Cornwall. Further, in the margin, was a total which read 320.

"And we have 320 No. 1 wheels," said Drummond thoughtfully. "Listen, Algy. In the map Madame Pélain saw, these numbers were entered everywhere – not only in one district. What do you make of that?"

"That the district marked here was Cartwright's?" remarked Algy promptly.

"Exactly," agreed Drummond. "In which case, he was only one of several employed on the same game – all working on identical blueprints. Very possibly each of them was given a district far removed from where he lives, to prevent any personal feeling coming into the matter, and the finished map is never seen by the underlings."

Algy nodded.

"It all sounds perfectly feasible to me," he said.

"At any rate, there's nothing wildly fantastic so far," remarked Drummond, picking up the last paper.

"What's this?" he said, staring at it. "Helverton: where or what the deuce is Helverton?"

There came the sound of voices in the hall.

"Come in, Ginger," he called out. "You arrive in the nick of time. Where, or what, or why is Helverton?"

Ginger Lawson stood in the doorway eyeing him queerly.

"Strange you should ask that," he said at length. "Helverton is a village in Cornwall, near which there have been strange doings of late. So strange that it's filtered through to the Yard."

It was Drummond's turn to stare.

"What sort of doings?"

"They say that a headland not far from the village is haunted, and undoubtedly a man who went out to investigate was found dead."

"How did he die?"

Ginger Lawson closed the door.

"He was washed ashore four days later. The body was beginning to decompose, and the natural assumption was that he had been drowned. But when they came to examine him more closely, they came to the amazing conclusion that he had been burned, if not to death, at any rate very near it."

CHAPTER 14

The Trail Narrows

He came on into the room.

"And how, might I ask, did *you* come to hear of Helverton?"

In silence Drummond pushed the documents over to him, and Lawson studied them.

"Where did these come from?" he said at length.

"A gentleman who was murdered the night before last by Burton," answered Drummond. "His body, which may or may not have been discovered by now, is in a wood on the top of Bury Hill in Sussex. Unfortunately his death, as in Jimmy's case, will, apparently, have been due to natural causes."

"Who was the man?" asked Ginger.

"Samuel Cartwright – if that conveys anything to you. A working clock-maker, old boy" – and Drummond put a significant finger on the blueprint. "We're getting warm, Ginger," he continued. "Unless I'm much mistaken, that print represents Maier's model. And that district" – he pointed to the map – "is Cartwright's district. Now we happen to know that Cartwright joined some so-called political society a few months ago. We also know that recently he has been an extremely worried and nervy man. And now he's dead. What do you make of it?"

"That he showed signs of splitting and had to be put out of the way," said Lawson.

"Exactly. Now take that figure 320. My idea is that he had to make 320 similar machines to the one we took from Maier's house. Other people in other districts had to make their quotas also, so that the total would be sufficient to account for the whole map. And then these various contributions have been or will be collected at one central depot."

"And after that?"

"I wonder if it would be possible," said Drummond thoughtfully, "to find out if any large order from a new customer has been given recently for Petworth's Fancy Quality Fruit Salad?"

"It could probably be done," answered Lawson.

"And where it's been despatched to... Ginger," he continued gravely. "I'm no ruddy engineer. But what would be the result if you took a dynamo or a fly-wheel, rotating at speed, and exploded a bomb on one of its bearings?"

"Hell let loose backwards, I should say. The whole thing would fly to pieces and smash up the entire shooting-box."

"Just what I thought," said Drummond. "We've got to find where that central depot is."

"What price this place – Helverton?" remarked Algy.

"Why such a remote spot?" objected Lawson.

"Ask me another," said Drummond. "But it's a strange coincidence – this paper, and what you've just told us about the man being burned."

"Didn't you find out anything about the island of Varda?"

"Algy, with great brilliance, took that on. Both Burton and Menalin reacted to it."

"So Ronald is on the track," said Lawson.

"What news of him? I've heard nothing except that he's escaped."

"That's the main reason that I came round to see you," answered Lawson. "Somehow or other he got away from the place where Menalin was holding him as a prisoner, and swam out to a private yacht. He must have heard Varda mentioned in the house before he escaped, I suppose. Anyway he got a wire through to me from the yacht, whose owner he must have bluffed into keeping him. And he's on his way home now…"

"What about Gasdon?"

"He was knifed in Paris as he drove in. He was taken to hospital, but I gather it's not serious."

Drummond shook both his fists in the air.

"By God! Ginger – what a day of reckoning there's going to be. And it's not going to be put off long, either. In fact, I seem to feel that the overture is playing for the last act…"

With eyes half closed he stared across the smoke-filled room.

"Do you remember what I told you once, that strange vision of a fleeting second that I had in the Golden Boot? It's coming; I know it. And it will be battle, murder and sudden death before we get through to the end…"

"What about bringing in the police now?"

"We can't, Ginger – yet… We don't *know*. It's all guesswork. We've *got* to find out first. Otherwise we'll merely put them on their guard."

"And how do you propose to do so?"

"Go to Helverton. I'll take Algy and Peter with me. This *can't* be coincidence."

"I wish to Heaven I could come with you," said Lawson.

"I know you do, old man – but you can't. If Ronald arrives, or Gasdon, tell them where I am. I'll keep in touch with you. I'll send you a wire every day, signed HUD with just the day of the week on it. If you don't get it you'll know something has happened, and you can get gay."

Ginger Lawson nodded, and rose.

"Trust me, Hugh. How shall I get at you if I want to?"

"Where is this place, Helverton?"

"On the coast – not far from Bodmin."

"Then send anything you want to Hudson at the post office, Bodmin, Night-night, old boy… We shall start tomorrow."

He came back into the room after he had locked the front door.

"It's big stuff this time, Algy," he said quietly. "Very big. I think we're going to get our money's worth. Ring Peter up at his pub tomorrow morning, and tell him to motor straight to Exeter. Chuck over that AA book… Here's a one-star pub. He is to go to the Lowestoft and wait for us there. I'll bring a gun for him and a disguise."

And when Algy went to bed five minutes later, Drummond was still sitting hunched in his chair staring at the embers of the dying fire. Strange – this premonition of his, for he was one of the least fanciful men in the world. But try as he would he could not shake it off. And the thought that worried him was whether he was justified in what he had said to Ginger Lawson about the police… Was he justified in trying to tackle the show on his own?

That he was itching to get at it was neither here nor there. But supposing they got him and Peter and Algy – what then? There might be delay – fatal delay. On the other hand, if the police started making enquiries Menalin and Burton might close the whole thing down for a time, and come back with it again later under more favourable conditions.

He lit a cigarette and poured out some more beer. Balancing the two alternatives he felt he was right. The delay would not be great if he had bad luck; just one day when Ginger got no wire. And, in any event, he felt certain that there was one big point he would be able to clear up. Was this village of Helverton a spot of importance, or not?

At the bottom of his mind he felt it must be. That Cartwright – a confirmed Cockney – should have troubled to write down the name of an obscure Cornish village without some good reason, seemed very improbable. And, even if he had, why put the paper with documents connected with the other affair? This mystery, too, of the burned man…

"Helverton has it," he muttered to himself. "All Lombard Street to a china orange on it… Go to bed, my boy, go to bed."

It was Algy who woke him the next morning at nine o'clock.

"I've just got through to Peter," he said. "He lost three quid to Ted yesterday, and is blaspheming with rage at not getting it back this morning. He's going straight to Exeter."

"Well done, Algy. So we shan't want another car there. Go and look up the trains, while I dress."

"There's a ten-thirty-five from Paddington," sang out Algy from the hall.

"Couldn't be better," answered Drummond. "We will honour it with our presence."

Gone completely were the doubts of last night; life was just a hundred per cent.

"Money, fool," he roared. "Have we any? If not, go out and cash your maintenance order."

"Is forty quid enough to keep you in beer?"

"No. Tell Jane I'll be down in ten minutes. And, Algy, look in the papers and see if they've found the body on Bury Hill."

Came a pause and then Algy's voice: "Don't see any sign of it. But there's a paragraph here about last night."

He came upstairs with the paper in his hand.

"A strange outrage occurred last night at the house of Mrs Samuel Cartwright, who lives near the Royal Albert road. She was entertaining two friends after supper when the house was entered by two men, who bound and gagged all three of them. One of the men remained on guard, whilst the other went into the yard at the back.

"Shortly afterwards two other men appeared…"

"Damn!" said Drummond. "I'd hoped we might have been left out of it. Go on."

"...appeared, who overpowered the man on guard and stunned him. Then having set free the three ladies these men disappeared. Mrs Cartwright, who was overcome with the shock, accompanied her friends to their house, from where she rang up the police, who at once went to the scene of the outrage. Unfortunately they were too late; the house was empty, the miscreants had fled.

"The motive of the crime is obscure. The door of a shed in the yard, which is used by Mr Cartwright, a clock-maker, and at present away from home, had been forced. But since nothing had apparently been taken from it, or from the house, the whole matter is difficult to understand.

"Unfortunately, the descriptions of the men, as given by Mrs Cartwright, are so vague as to be almost valueless. The most she can say is that the second pair, who liberated her and her friends, looked like dockyard hands."

"Good up to a point," said Drummond, brushing his hair. "There's no mention of Alice. But I wonder if the old girl said anything about Burton. And the police have suppressed it. For if so, Master Charles won't feel so good, when Cartwright's body is found and identified."

"He can still bluff it," remarked Algy.

"Oh, yes! he can still bluff it," agreed Drummond. "But I've got a sort of idea that our Charles is not quite as happy as he was. After you went up for your bath on Saturday night, he and Menalin were having a little heart to heart chat in the hall..."

"Was it you," interrupted Algy, "that Molly saw looking through the window by the front door?"

"Who the hell did you think it was? An anthropoidal ape? As I say, they were having a little chat. I couldn't, of course, hear what they said, but it struck me that Burton was a bit worried."

"He was damned silent during the early part of dinner," said Algy.

"So Talbot told me. By the same token," he added with a grin, "it strikes me that Captain Talbot would not be averse to a spot of walking out with little Molly Castledon. I definitely caught the love-light in his eyes when discussing her. And before breakfast, too, which takes a lot of getting round."

"How on earth did you manage to get him there?"

"A sheer lucky break. A pal of Denny's was engaged, so I wangled the change. You see, Algy, I didn't know you were going there for the weekend… Let us to our eggs."

"I'm still in the dark as to why he asked me."

"To pump you about me, of course. And, my dear old lad, you did magnificently. Talbot swears that he distinctly heard Burton tell Menalin that you were a cross between a Mongolian idiot and that monkey at the zoo with the purple bottom. Jane darling – don't listen. Algy would like a tumbler of your redcurrant wine – hot."

"You're very rude about my redcurrant wine, Master Hugh," said Jane indignantly.

"Jealousy, my sweet; jealousy." He peered suspiciously at his plate. "A little on this egg might be a good thing; I think the hen gave up halfway through."

She snatched up the dish.

"That there Johnson at the corner," she cried as she sniffed it, "swore they were new laid. Leave it to me, dear."

"I will, Jane, if you will substitute one of this year's vintage. Your baby boy needs building up."

He picked up one of the papers and opened it.

"Hullo! Algy," he said quietly. "Here's a little item of possible interest. All in the Court Circular column too.

"Mr and Mrs Serge Menalin have left the Ritz-Carlton for a few days' tour in the West Country. No letters will be forwarded.

"Now, isn't that strange, boy?" He stared at Algy thoughtfully. "That means they went yesterday. And it means another thing as well. Up till then they had no reason to be secret over their movements. Until yesterday everything in their garden was lovely. Which is all to the good... Long may it continue."

"They'll smell a rat over the account of the Cartwright affair," said Algy.

"Perhaps: perhaps not. I think that if we were in the position of the two blokes we laid out, we should pretend that we were the dockyard hands who had done the laying. There would be no one to call us liars, and we could pretend we'd succeeded."

He glanced at his watch.

"Come along, Algy: time we pushed off. I've got everything in the suitcase."

"What are we going to be?" demanded Algy.

"Hikers, old boy. Scoutmasters in shorts, covered with badges. You'll probably have to make a fire by rubbing sticks together. And then we shall eat poisoned berries and die, and the robins will cover us with leaves. Bye-bye, Jane: don't take in any male lodgers while I'm away."

They arrived at Exeter to the minute, and sought out the Lowestoft. It was a small hotel in a back street, but clean and comfortable, and they found Peter in a front room building up nature with something in a glass. And having ordered likewise, and closed the door, Drummond produced a half-inch ordnance map of Cornwall and spread it on a table.

"Just as well to get the lie of the country before we start. As the crow flies this place Helverton is about fifteen miles from Bodmin, so that, judging by the way the road twists, it's about twenty miles by car. To the east and west of it the ground rises steeply, so that it really lies in a gap in the cliffs."

"And a bit back from the sea," said Darrell. "Presumably it's a little fishing village."

"In which case the arrival of three strangers will go the rounds," remarked Drummond.

"We might pretend to be journalists," suggested Algy.

"Probably lousy with them already over the burned man episode," said Drummond. "However, we'll see. Anyway, there's the rough lay-out. Obviously the coast is rocky and deserted, except for Helverton itself. Let's get changed here, and leave the suitcases with mine host. Then we'll motor to Bodmin, leave the car, and get off the mark."

Dusk was falling when they arrived at Cornwall's county town, and parked the car in a garage.

"Walking tour?" said the proprietor, scratching his head. "Well, for them as likes it, it may be all right. But it ain't my idea of fun. Which way be you going?"

"Thought of starting off from Helverton," answered Drummond.

"You be on it too, are you?" laughed the other. "The drowned man that was burned! Rot – sez I. Haunted, indeed. Them villagers would imagine anything..."

"I'm afraid we haven't heard anything about it," said Drummond.

"Well – you will, if you goes there. Won't they, George?"

A shock-headed individual emerged from the back of a carrier's van.

"What do'ee say?" he asked.

"These gents are going to Helverton. I was telling 'em about the ghost."

The van driver spat thoughtfully.

" 'Tis more in it, sur, than that," he said. "Be you gentlemen new to these 'ere parts?"

"We are," said Drummond. "We're on a walking tour."

"Well, sur – if you takes my advice you'll walk elsewhere…"

He retired inside his van again and the owner of the garage smiled at Drummond.

"Just like the rest of 'em," he said confidentially. "As a matter of fact he's going to Helverton tonight. He's the local carrier."

"The devil he is," remarked Drummond. "I wonder if he'd give us a lift."

"Sure," cried the other. "George – you'll give these gents a lift, won't you?"

Once more the head emerged.

"Aye – if they're wanting to come. I'm starting now…"

"Then we'll leave the car here," said Drummond, "and call for it in a few days."

"Very good, sir. It'll be quite safe with me."

The ancient Ford van wheezed into life, and the three men clambered inside. A number of motley parcels comprised the load: two big packing-cases on the floor afforded some sort of seat. But springs were non-existent, and by the time they had crashed and rattled through the night for about a quarter of an hour they were all partially winded.

It was a slow journey. Every mile or so they stopped, and the driver appeared and searched for a parcel. This was duly handed to someone in the darkness: a book was signed, and the health of everybody's relations was discussed at length. But after they had been going for an hour only the two packing-cases remained.

Suddenly the van halted, and Drummond peered through a tear in the cover. They seemed to be in the middle of a large open moor: no house or cottage was in sight.

" 'Ave to wait 'ere, gennelmen, for them cases to be picked up. Sends a van 'e does for 'em."

"How far are we from Helverton?" asked Drummond.

"Two miles, sur…"

"And who is this who is sending a van?" continued Drummond thoughtfully.

"Mr Stangerton, sur... The artist... 'Im who 'as the 'ouse called Hooting Carn... Where the terror is..."

"What terror?"

"The ghost, sur..."

"I see," said Drummond. "You say you have to wait here for the cases to be picked up. Have you delivered many before?"

"A tidy few, sur."

"Get out of the van," muttered Drummond to Peter and Algy. "Listen, George: do you want to earn a pound?"

"Sure I do, sur."

"Then don't mention the fact that you've given us three a lift to whoever comes for the packing-cases."

"They be a-coming now, sur. I see the lights."

In front, a dim grey streak, stretched the road to Helverton: away up to the left, coming down from the high ground, were the headlights of a car. And as they got out they realised they had stopped at a fork in the road.

They slipped into a ditch as the car reached the spot and proceeded to turn. Then two men who had come in it, assisted by George, lifted each case in turn out of the van and put them in a trailer that was attached. A book was signed, cartage was paid, and in a minute the car was on its way back up the hill.

"Pretty heavy – those cases, George?" said Drummond casually.

"Aye, sur. A tidy weight."

"And you say you've delivered a good many of 'em?"

"Them two makes eight, sur."

"Do you know where they come from?"

"Different parts, sur. I picks 'em up at the station. Them two came from Leeds."

"I see. Stangerton, you say, is the name of the gentleman?"

"Ess, sur: that's right."

"And what's this terror you talk about, George?"

" 'Tis an old fable, sur. My father heard it, and his father afore him. 'Tis the ghost, they do say, of a Spaniard. Hundreds o' years ago a big Spanish ship was in danger of driving ashore here in a gale. And the captain 'e sold 'isself to old Nick if so be his ship was saved. A wicked man he was, and when the officers and crew, who were praying to the Holy Virgin, heard what he had done, they threw him overboard. And just as soon as he was in the sea the wind shifted and blew them off the lee shore into safety. But the captain he was drowned, and his body was washed ashore on the little island... And because he had sold 'isself to the devil he can't rest in his grave, and his ghost is sometimes seen flitting round Hooting Carn, and sometimes on the island itself... And them as sees it had best mind out – for it means death..."

"That's very interesting, George," said Drummond. "And has it been seen much lately?"

"That be the funny thing, sur," answered the driver. "Just a legend it was till a few months ago: I can't rightly recollect anybody who had actually seed it. All the chaps used to talk about it at times, but it was allus somebody else who had told 'em they'd seed it. And then lots of 'em started to see it."

"Very strange," agreed Drummond quietly. "And what was it they saw?"

"A yellow figure, sur, that seemed to glide over the ground – and then suddenly disappeared. Afeard they were – until young Jan Penderby said he weren't. Ghost or no ghost he was going to lay it. And 'tis him who is dead. Aye, sur – dead... Drowned they say, but it's burned he was – just as you'd expect. For isn't it the devil himself that Captain Varda sold his soul to?"

"Captain – who?" Try as he would to speak calmly, Drummond's voice shook.

"Varda, sur... Don Miguel Varda – his name is on the grave at Hooting Carn. The grave from which he walks and into which he disappears."

"This island you mentioned," said Drummond.

"What is it called?"

"Varda, sur... After the Spaniard... Not that it's really an island; 'tis just a big rugged rock that sticks out of the sea eighty yards from the cliffs. And sometimes, as I was telling 'ee, the ghost can be seen flitting over the top of it for 'twas there he was beaten to death by the waves."

The van pulled up outside the Jolly Fisherman.

"Here we be, sur... You'll be hearing all about Jan Penderby from the lads inside..." He pocketed his pound note. "Thank 'ee kindly, sur... I'm out here every day, if so be there be anything you're wanting."

The street was long and straggling. Lights filtered out from the cottage windows, and in the distance they could hear the lazy roar of breakers on the rock. Most of the male population of Helverton seemed to be assembled in the bar as they entered, and a sudden silence fell at the appearance of three strangers.

"What about a pint, George?" cried Drummond cheerfully; and the arrival of the carrier broke the awkward pause. As their link with the outside world, who daily brought them spicy tit-bits of gossip from Bodmin, he occupied an unassailable position in the community. And the sight of him drinking with the new arrivals was a sufficient introduction.

A little man with a straggling grey beard appeared to have the ear of the meeting. Even the landlord, after drawing the beer, returned to his position at the other end of the bar, and resumed his air of interested attention.

" 'Ess, sur," cried the speaker, banging his tankard on the table. "I seed 'un orl rit. I went out night arter young Jan were washed ashore. It were dark, an' I told meself I were a fool to go poking me 'ead in at all. Still I kept on. And I'd just got to that li'l' rise afore you comes to Hooting Carn, when I looks to me left. An' there I seed 'un. There 'ee were as 'igh as a 'ouse, an' gleamin' all over 'ee were – from 'ead to foot. For a bit I couldn't move – struck frozen I were, and then 'ee started to walk towards me. I gave one yell an' turned on me 'eels an' I never stopped running till I got back – an' that's all of two mile."

"Tall as a 'ouse, Mr Dogerty?" said someone doubtfully.

"Tall as a 'ouse," repeated greybeard firmly, "an' gleaming all over. I tell 'ee it's the devil 'isself that got young Jan."

"You be new to these parts, sur?" said the landlord, coming back to Drummond.

"We are," answered Drummond. "George has been telling us about your excitement here."

"Bad affair it was, sur... Very bad... Young Jan Penderby was as nice a boy as you could meet."

"They say he was burned," remarked Drummond.

"Well, sur – I did see the corpse. An' there sure was something mighty odd about it... I've seen drowned men before, but never a one like Jan. All yaller 'e was, as if 'e'd been scorched with fire."

"Have you seen the ghost yourself, landlord?"

"I have not, sur. An' I don't want to neither. Be you gentlemen on a walking tour?"

"That's the idea," said Drummond. "Hope it keeps fine."

"The weather will be all right. But if you takes my advice you'll not walk past Hooting Carn save by daylight..."

"Belongs to a Mr Stangerton, doesn't it?"

"That's so, sur. Rented it, he did, about a year ago... Been empty some time afore that."

"And what does he say about the ghost?"

"Bless you, sur – we don't never see him. Keeps 'isself in 'is 'ouse, he does; never goes out at all, so far as I knows."

"This little island Varda," continued Drummond, "that George was telling us about. Does anyone live on it?"

"Bless you, no, sur. Only the seagulls. Rises well nigh sheer out of the sea. They do say as 'ow in the old days it was used by smugglers. But them be old tales."

"It's not marked on any map, is it?"

The landlord laughed.

"Marked on a map? No, sur. 'Tis only a small rock. And the name is just a local one – given after the Spaniard who was drowned there."

He turned away to supply another customer, and Drummond looked at the other two.

"Can you beat it for luck?" he muttered. "I just want to ask him one or two more questions, and then we might have a pow-wow. Do you happen to know, landlord," he continued, "if this Mr Stangerton is married?"

"Never heard as how he was, sur. But that's not saying he ain't."

"An artist, so George was saying. Is it a big house?"

"Middlin', sur. About a hundred yards from the top of the cliff."

"Does he keep a large staff?"

"Can't say as I rightly knows, sur. As I was telling you, he keeps 'isself to 'isself."

"One would have thought that tradesmen delivering goods would have known," said Drummond casually.

"That's where you're wrong, sur. He gets all his stuff from Bodmin. Sends in for it, he does."

"Quite a mystery man," laughed Drummond. "And when did the ghost first begin to show itself?"

"Nigh on two months ago, sur. Regular walk it used to be for couples courting. But now not one of 'em would go near it…"

"Don't blame 'em," agreed Drummond. "Could you let me have some bread and cheese, and another pint all round. Over in that alcove would do nicely."

"Certainly, sur… Will you be wanting rooms for tonight?"

"Yes, please," said Drummond. "Well, boys," he went on as they sat down in their corner, "as I said before, can you beat it for luck?"

"What do you make of this ghost business?" remarked Darrell.

"Ghost my foot," cried Drummond. "You heard what the landlord said. All the necking pairs in Cornwall were using it as a lovers' lane. Which did not suit this man Stangerton. So, having heard about the legend, he produced the ghost."

"And this fellow who was killed?"

"Happened to find out too much," said Drummond quietly. "That's how I read it. What was in those packing-cases, chaps? They seemed damned heavy."

"Some of Mr Sam Cartwright's little machines," hazarded Algy.

"That's what I think, old boy. And there have been six before those two. But it isn't that," he continued after a pause, "that is making me scratch my head. You heard what mine host said about this little island. He said it rises well nigh sheer out of the sea. But, according to our friend George, the ghost has been seen flitting over the top of it. How did it get there?"

"Boat and rope ladder."

"Which presupposes someone on the top of the island beforehand, to let down the ladder. Further, even to a superstitious crowd like these people, the spectacle of a ghost laboriously climbing up the side of a cliff would shatter 'em a bit. No – I'm wondering…"

"We'll buy it."

"You heard what the landlord said about smugglers in the old days. Is it possible that there is a connection between that island and the mainland – under the sea? And that that is what Jan Penderby found?"

"I like it," said Algy. "Definitely – I like it. Starting from the house, or something of that sort?"

Drummond nodded.

"You've got it," he said. "Though probably not from the house itself, as I don't see how a local man could have got inside. But he found it, and being a courageous lad he followed it up. And that was his death-warrant."

"What puzzles me," remarked Darrell, "is this burning business. Why go out of your way to draw attention to the thing? Why not knock him on the head and throw him in the sea? Then it's plain drowning."

"I agree," said Drummond. "That's been worrying me. And from what we know up to date, there's no answer…"

"If you're right about the passage," reverted Algy, "how are we going to find the entrance?"

"How did Jan Penderby?"

"Stumbled on it by chance."

"At night! Again – I wonder. I think he happened to see the ghost go to ground. Is there any reason why we shouldn't do likewise?"

Peter Darrell began to rub his hands together ecstatically.

"Good boy," he cried. "Very good boy… Go right up to the top of the class. Teacher is pleased with you. So your suggestion is…?"

"Same as yours."

"Tonight?"

"As ever is," said Drummond. "Let's have some more ale."

CHAPTER 15

The Ghost Walks

The weather was warm and almost muggy when they started. The last visitor had left the bar: the landlord of the Jolly Fisherman was preparing to shut up for the night. It was useless to try to conceal their intentions from him, even had they wanted to, and he regarded them with a pleasingly benign toleration.

"Well, gents," he said, "everyone to their own way of thinking. Give me my bed. I'll leave the door open, and the candles on the table."

At first the rise was almost imperceptible; then it grew steeper. And a quarter of an hour after they had left the inn they reached the top of the cliff. Behind them lay the village, though no light could be seen: from far below came the monotonous beat of the sea on the rocks.

The going was smooth and springy, and they swung forward in silence. From the map they knew that Hooting Carn lay just on two miles from Helverton, but they were still some way short of that distance when they saw in front of them a solitary light. It was shining through trees and lay in a hollow.

"The house, presumably," remarked Drummond. "I think a little closer – " He paused suddenly. "What's that noise?"

They listened intently, but the other two could hear nothing.

"I can," said Drummond, lying down on the ground and pressing his ear to the grass. "Why, it's unmistakable."

They followed his example, and then it was obvious, too, to them. Very faint, but perfectly distinct, there came to their ears a gentle, rhythmic thump – thump – thump. Almost could they feel a faint tremor in the ground.

"An engine of sorts," said Algy.

"Exactly," remarked Drummond. "But what sort? And where? No electric-light machine ever made that noise. It might be a pump for water, but it seems a rum time to have one going. However, let's investigate further."

They walked on, their footsteps making no sound on the soft turf. Dimly they could see the outline of the house, against the ground that rose again on the other side of it. And at last they got near enough to see into the room from which the light was shining.

A man was seated at a table smoking. In front of him were a batch of papers and a ledger which he consulted from time to time, and in which he made periodical entries. He was not a prepossessing-looking individual, and evidently the thought of water with his whisky was not one that appealed to him. His features were red and coarse, but the breadth of his shoulders denoted strength.

"Is that our artist?" whispered Drummond.

"I should think his sole claim to painting ability," answered Darrell, "would be covered by disinfecting the chicken run."

After a few moments the door opened, and another man entered. He was obviously an underling as he did not venture to sit down, but stood waiting for orders. And, having received them, he left as abruptly as he had come, Twice more the performance was repeated; then the leader lit a cigarette and rose to his feet.

He was a bigger man than he had seemed when sitting down, and for a while lie stood looking out into the night. Then, pitching away his cigarette he closed the window and switched off the light. And a moment or two later a gleam from an upstair room proclaimed that he had gone to bed.

"Evidently he doesn't mind being seen," said Drummond quietly. "Though when all is said and done the whole proceeding was perfectly harmless. Let's explore a bit more."

Cautiously they circled round the house, keeping some fifty yards away from it, but there was nothing to be seen. There were lights in a few of the top rooms, but one by one these went out. And at length the place was in darkness.

"What do we do now?" asked Algy.

"Sit down and wait," said Drummond. "It's only just eleven. The trouble is we mustn't smoke. Incidentally that engine is still going strong."

"I wonder where the deuce it is," remarked Darrell. "It's not loud enough to be coming from the house."

"It sounds to me," said Drummond with his ear again pressed to the ground, "as if it was underneath us somewhere. My God! look there."

Motionless they sat staring at the house. Out to sea a siren blared mournfully: nearby a fitful eddy of wind stirred the trees. But the three silent watchers had only eyes and ears for one thing.

Behind a clump of bushes near the house a light was gradually beginning to materialise. It rolled and swirled, shapeless to start with, until it seemed to take the form of a gigantic man. And then, abruptly, with a curious gliding movement, it passed from behind the screen of undergrowth out into the open.

Fascinated, they watched it as it passed over the ground. Its height was fantastic – twice that of an ordinary man, and as it moved it seemed to be dripping fire. It went away from them, up the rise they had come down, then, making a detour, it circled round towards them.

"No wonder the locals were frightened," muttered Drummond. "It's a fearsome-looking object."

It passed about twenty yards away from them, and at that range, they could see how the effect had been produced. The luminosity was obviously caused by a preparation of phosphorus; the great height by some form of superstructure carried on the shoulders. But it was in the apparent movement of gliding that the cleverness lay. For the ghost's legs were covered with a voluminous skirt reaching almost to the ground, which effectually prevented the actual feet being seen.

It drifted on aimlessly first in one direction, then in another until, at length, it halted. But only for a second; even as they watched it, it sank into the ground and disappeared.

"Quick," said Drummond. "Now's our chance."

They walked towards the spot from which a faint glow still emanated. Then, as if a light had been turned out, all was dark again.

They groped forward cautiously, and suddenly Drummond paused. Just in front of them, from what seemed to be a crack in the ground, there still filtered a chink of light. And then that, too, went out; everything was dark.

"Run to earth," said Drummond quietly. "What the deuce have we here? It feels like a stone. Form a scrum, boys, between me and the house; I'm going to chance the torch for a second."

It flashed out; at their feet was a mildewed, moss-covered stone slab. But three words cut in it were sufficient to show what it was:

DON MIGUEL VARDA.

"The Spaniard's tomb," breathed Drummond. "Well, I'm damned! It bears out what George said. The grave from which he walks and into which he disappears. And Jan Penderby found it."

He was staring out to sea as he spoke.

"Give it a minute or two, yet chaps, and we'll see if I was right. I was; by God! I was."

Floating, apparently in space, over the sea was the gliding yellow figure. Twice, three times it went backwards and forwards some three or four hundred yards away; then, even as it had done on the mainland, it sank down and disappeared.

"Yes; I was right," repeated Drummond. "That was the ghost doing its piece on the island of Varda. Which means that if the ghost can get there, we can."

"Is it likely to come back this way?" said Darrell thoughtfully. "Because, if so, we'd better allow a few minutes. We don't particularly want to meet it in a narrow passage."

"Agreed," said Drummond, who was fumbling with the tombstone. "Got it," he muttered suddenly. "The whole thing slides back."

They retreated a little distance and sat down to wait. And it was not for long. Barely five minutes had elapsed before there came a faint rumble from in front of them, and a dark figure emerged from the ground. The ghost minus its make-up had returned. Came another rumble; a faint clank as of a metal bar being shot into position – and silence. The ghost had departed to bed.

They gave it another quarter of an hour before they again approached the grave. And then one gleam from the torch was sufficient to show the cause of the clank. A steel bar had been shot home which bolted the stone slab in position. It was not locked in any way; evidently Mr Stangerton relied on superstition to prevent any undue curiosity about the tomb. And it was a simple matter to slide the bar from its sockets and lay it on the grass. Then very cautiously they pulled back the slab.

Below them yawned a black hole, and one after another they lowered themselves down into it. And then, having pulled back the stone into its normal position, Drummond switched on his torch.

They were standing in a small vault-like cave. In places the walls had been shored up with baulks of timber, and the work was obviously recent. A ladder, which they had not seen led to the stone above them; in front was a black opening that looked like the entrance to a mine shaft. From it, descending sharply, ran a tunnel. And in this, too, the walls were supported in various places with new timbering.

The going, though steep, was good. The roof was high enough to allow them to walk without stooping, but caution was necessary. And every few yards Drummond stopped, torch switched off, to listen. But no sound could be heard; the engine they had noticed earlier, had ceased.

It was at the third halt that they struck another gallery coming in from the right – a gallery completely shored with mine cases, which was obviously all new work. And here they paused for a space; there were points of considerable interest to be noted.

First – from its direction it could lead to only one place, the house. Second – the wires. Looped to the roof ran half a dozen – some thick insulated cables, others which might have been telephone connections. And they all stretched away into the darkness in front of them. Moreover at ten-yard intervals there now hung electric light bulbs from the top of the tunnel.

"They evidently feel pretty safe here," whispered Drummond. "Which is not to be wondered at seeing we must be fifty feet underground by now. But there's no doubt about one thing, boys, this has taken a bit of doing. Even granted the original foundation which they had to work on, a hell of a lot of labour has been put into this show. And what I'm wondering is where all that labour is. Have they got a young army billeted about the place? Or did they chance letting the men who did this job go?"

The angle of descent became steeper after the junction. In places rough steps had been constructed, with lengths of rope attached to the wall as an additional help. And as they descended lower the air grew dank and cold.

At last the shaft flattened out; they were under the bed of the sea. And here the timbering was far more elaborate and powerful, though the roof dripped water in places, and puddles lay on the floor. For about a hundred yards the tunnel continued horizontal; then it began to rise steeply again. And with a feeling of relief the three men ascended into drier air.

Suddenly Drummond switched off his torch; a faint light was beginning to filter down the shaft from an opening in front, which grew stronger as they got higher. They were moving with the utmost caution, their rubber-soled shoes making no sound as they climbed. And at length, inch by inch, Drummond hoisted himself up so that he could see what the shaft led into.

"Great Scott!" he breathed. "Look at that."

The other two joined him, and side by side they lay staring at the scene in front of them. And assuredly it was an amazing one.

They were looking into a large cave, from the roof of which hung two electric bulbs, throwing an eerie white light into the gloom below. Fantastic shadows lay across the floor, and as their eyes grew accustomed to it they began to see the details of the place more clearly.

Around the walls various types of machines had been erected – lathes and the like, each one of which must have been carried along the passage that lay behind them. In the centre there stood what looked like a crushing machine, with a heavy vertical rod moving in guides – the machine that had probably been making the thumping noise they had heard on the mainland.

Close by it stood a huge pile of tins neatly stacked, and on which they could see the label of Petworth's Fruit. Packing-cases – some open and some shut littered the floor, and in the far corner was a wooden partition marked "Danger".

Of human beings there was no sign; evidently work had ceased for the time. And after a moment Drummond rose and crept forward followed by the other two. They skirted round, keeping as much as possible in the shadows, and as they investigated further the whole gigantic scheme became clear. One packing case labelled Leeds – one of the two that had come with George – was open, and contained as they had guessed a number of clockwork machines similar to the one Drummond had found in Switzerland. Another was full of unopened fruit tins all of the same Petworth brand.

The tins stacked in the centre were empty, and a thing like a pig tub close by was full of lemon cling peaches, slices of banana, apricots, and pink cherries; Mr Petworth's Fancy Quality Fruit Salad had come to an undignified end. And picking up a few of the tins Drummond noticed that some of them had three little cubes inside, while others were plain.

He walked over to the wooden partition labelled "Danger": there was a door in it which he tried cautiously. But it was locked, and he made no attempt to force it.

"Presumably the explosive for this jolly little scheme," he muttered, and even as he spoke the unmistakable sound of a human snore fell on their ears. It came from the other side of the cave, and looking across they saw a blanket hanging in the wall.

Creeping over they listened; from behind the blanket came sounds as of a barrack room at night – heavy breathing and an occasional creak as a sleeper turned over in bed.

"Fitted with dormitory complete," whispered Drummond. "I wonder how many of the swine there are."

The other two laid hands on him.

"Come away," muttered Darrell firmly. "None of your charge of the Light Brigade here. We've found out all we want to find out, old lad; let's hop it."

"Perhaps you're right," agreed Drummond with a grin. "We'll go."

With one last look at that converted smuggler's cave they began the return journey down the shaft. Details might be – were

– lacking, but the main outline of the plot was clear. And as Drummond went along, once again did those words of Jimmy Latimer come back to him – "Out-Vernes Jules Verne."

"Not this time, my friends," he muttered to himself; "not this time."

And at that moment all the lights in the tunnel went on.

They halted dead in their tracks; the thing was so utterly unexpected as to stagger them momentarily. They were in the horizontal section under the sea, and no one was in sight. Only the bulbs gleaming dully through the moisture that covered them showed that somewhere someone was awake. But was it in front, or was it behind? Had the lights been switched on from the mainland or from the island?

Drummond produced his wire cutters.

"Better anything than light," he muttered, as he cut the flex. "They may think a fuse has blown, or that there's a short."

They stood motionless – listening. Around them pressed the darkness – so black that it could be felt. And then, step by step, they began to feel their way towards the mainland end of the shaft.

From behind them came suddenly the faint sound of voices, and Drummond swore under his breath. Cutting the wire had put not only the lights in the tunnel out of commission, but also the two that had been on in the cave. And, presumably, somebody who had been awake behind the blanket had given the alarm. Which meant, if the original switch-on had come from the house end, they were caught between two fires.

Undeniably the situation was awkward. To use a torch was out of the question; they could only grope blindly on by feel. And the trouble was that if the men from the island did come to investigate there was no reason why *they* should not use a torch, which meant instant discovery. The shaft ran straight; there was no recess in either wall which would hide one man, much less three.

They were climbing now – scrambling up the steep slope as silently as they could. There was no sign, as yet, of any light ahead, and hope began to rise in their breasts. Once over the steepest section progress would be quicker; if only they could make the grave they were safe. And at last with a sigh of relief Drummond, who was leading, topped the rise and felt the ground become flatter under his feet. Just in time; a torch was flashing down below them as the island contingent came into view.

His pace quickened; speed was essential. Half running, half stumbling, their hands outstretched to feel the walls, they pushed forward. And at last they reached their goal.

"Heave," he muttered, "heave like hell. Those blighters will be in the straight soon."

And they might as well have heaved at solid rock; the tombstone would not budge an inch. Someone had replaced the bar; they were caught like rats in a trap.

"'Pish!' said Eric, now thoroughly aroused," remarked Drummond with a short laugh. "That, chaps, would seem to have torn it. Especially as hounds are in sight."

It was true. The island party led by two men with torches had come into view. As yet they were too far off for the light to pick them up, but it would only be a question of moments before they were spotted. And then there occurred an unexpected development. The whole pack swung away up the gallery leading to the house.

"Now what the devil is that for?" said Drummond thoughtfully. "Is it a trap, or…"

They were not long in getting the answer. Came a vicious phut, and a bullet buried itself in the ground behind them – followed by another, and yet a third – a third which ended with a different note. Too often in the old days had they heard it in France.

"Sorry, old man," said Algy with a groan. "They've got me through the shoulder."

"Lie down," came Drummond's quiet order. Then he cupped his mouth in his hands. "We surrender," he called out.

The object of the move up the branch gallery was clear; they could be shot at without being able to answer. A man firing round the fork of the two shafts would be bound to get them in time, and they had nothing to fire back at.

"Hurt, old Algy?" he asked gently.

"Only a Blighty," answered Algy. "Blast their eyesight."

There was a silence from the other end; then with a sudden spluttering noise a tiny search-light flared into life. The beam shifted, then focussed and grew steady on the three prone men.

"Stand up," came a harsh voice. "I am watching you through a periscope."

They rose to their feet.

"Hold up any revolvers or other weapons you possess. Now put them on the floor beside you."

The voice waited until the order had been carried out.

"Now come along the shaft until you are within two yards of the search-light. I warn you that you are covered, and that on the slightest sign of your doing anything foolish, you will be killed."

In silence they did as they were told.

"Bind their wrists behind them," continued the voice.

Three men stepped forward, each with a length of cord, and though Algy turned white no sound escaped his lips as one of them wrenched his wounded arm back.

"So we scored one bull, did we?" went on the voice. "A foretaste of more to come. We will now show you to your temporary quarters."

The man behind Drummond gave him a jolt in the back.

"Move," he grunted.

He jerked Drummond's arm and pushed him into the gallery leading to the house. At the far end was a square of light, and as he got up to it he saw that the shaft opened into a big cellar. A flight of stone stairs opposite him led up into the house, but the room itself was empty, save for a table and some chairs. The walls were of stone and were also bare, except for a small switchboard flanked with coloured bulbs.

"How are you feeling, Algy?" asked Drummond as the other two were pushed in beside him.

"Fine, to what he will do," remarked the voice materialising. It was the man who they had seen working in the downstair room earlier in the evening.

The rest of the men came in behind him, and Drummond took stock of them. And with one or two exceptions he was struck by their appearance of respectability. This was no collection of gangsters or toughs; they looked like a bunch of hard-working mechanics. Save for the exceptions, who were the men who had bound them. And they looked what they were – rough stuff who would bump off anyone for a dollar.

"And now," continued the leader, "may I ask what you were doing down below?"

"By all manner of means," said Drummond frankly. "We are, as you see, on a hiking tour, and this evening we reached the Jolly Fisherman at Helverton. There we heard stories of a mysterious ghost that had been seen near this house. So we decided to investigate. We saw the ghost; we saw it go to ground in what appeared to be a grave. And having waited a bit we proceeded to explore out of curiosity."

"Do you usually go on a hiking tour armed with revolvers?" asked the other with a sneer.

"Not usually," answered Drummond. "But we had them with us, and decided to bring them tonight."

"Most convincing. And how far did you get in your exploration?"

"Down to the bottom of a tunnel. Then it seemed to be getting so wet that we only went a short way along the level..."

"When the lights were switched on?"

"Exactly."

"And you cut the wire?"

"I did."

"And now supposing you tell me the truth. It will perhaps assist you if I tell you what you did. You continued along the level and climbed the shaft on the other side. There you entered a large cave, which unfortunately for you has its entrance guarded by that burglar-proof light ray of which you may have heard, and which rang the alarm in my room. You remained in the cave some ten minutes, and then left. You again sounded the alarm, by which time I had taken the necessary precautions to prevent you escaping. Am I right?"

Drummond shrugged his shoulders; denial was stupid.

"I see that I am. Now then – who are you?"

"My name is Hillman; this is Mr Singer, and the man you've wounded is Morris."

"Names are notoriously difficult to invent on the spur of the moment, I agree. But if you must go to the car industry why not Mr Rolls, Mr Royce, and Mr Bentley? Still the point is immaterial."

He lit a cigarette.

"My name is Stangerton," he continued. "Will you smoke? Unlash them. I think," he went on as the ropes were cast off, "that you have sufficient sense to realise that any attempt to throw your weight about will merely precipitate your inevitable end."

"Which is?" asked Drummond politely.

"Very simple. The only difficulty lies in the fact that Mr – er – Morris has been wounded. Otherwise by now you would all have – ah – fallen over the cliff in your pursuit of that elusive ghost, which the whole village will be sure to know you came to look for. Very dangerous cliffs here."

"I appreciate your quandary," said Drummond pleasantly. "Even the most warlike of ghosts is unlikely to plug a man through the arm. So what do we do?"

"The programme still remains the same for you and Mr Singer. You see the currents in this part of the coast are notoriously treacherous. So if two of the bodies are ultimately washed up that will be sufficient. The third need not be discovered, and won't be. So Mr Morris will be buried on the island tomorrow night."

Drummond blew out a cloud of smoke.

"So you intend to murder us in cold blood," he remarked.

"I am sorry about it," said Stangerton quietly, "but I have no alternative. You must put yourselves in my place. You are not fools; you must realise that something is going on here which I require kept secret. How dare I let you go? You are bound to talk of what you have seen. If, on the other hand, I keep you all as prisoners – what then? The villagers will talk. Hooting Carn will become a centre of publicity – the very thing I wish to avoid. And so – though believe me, I have no personal animosity against you – you must be killed... And killed in such a way that the manner of your death will arouse no suspicion. Another cigarette? And then I fear we must get on with it."

"Thanks," drawled Drummond.

His hand was as steady as a rock as he helped himself from the tin, though for the life of him he could see no way out. What Stangerton had said was plain, horse-sense; from his point of view there was no other way of looking at it. He could neither afford to let them go nor keep them as prisoners. But one more effort could do no harm.

"Look here, Mr Stangerton," he said quietly, "aren't you being a little drastic? I admit we were trespassing, and that we went where we had no right to go. But surely our curiosity was understandable."

"Perfectly. But your revolvers were not... In short, Mr Hillman, I do not believe that you are three genuine hikers."

"Really! What do you think we are?"

"Journalists."

Drummond raised his eyebrows.

"Under these circumstances aren't you afraid that our papers may become inquisitive?"

"I am sure they will. Hence the necessity of your accidental death. I anticipate that quite a number of people will follow you up, but they will discover nothing. For one thing, the ghost has walked for the last time: his utility is exhausted. As a matter of fact it was, I think, a mistake on my part not to have stopped him after that young fisherman's death... However, that cannot be helped now. Tell me" – he stared suddenly at Drummond – "what was it that brought you here? Was it the fact that the man was burned?"

"That certainly has given rise to comment," answered Drummond.

"You were a fool, Freystadt, a damned fool," said Stangerton angrily. "I told you so at the time."

A heavy-jowled German looked up sullenly.

"It vos a great opportunity the gaz to test," he muttered. "I did not of other things think."

"Gas," remarked Drummond languidly. "Is that what you're making in the chamber of horrors?"

"Amongst other things, Mr Hillman; amongst other things."

Drummond's brain was racing: this was something new. Gas had so far not entered into their calculations: it was a completely fresh development and one which, at the moment, he could not fit in. And then with a bitter sense of futility came the realisation that it did not much matter whether he could or could not.

"And now I think we must conclude our talk." Stangerton was speaking again. "I am genuinely sorry that I have to take this course. I bear you no animosity whatever personally; to me you are just three individuals who have found out more than it is good for you to know. And so you must be removed. Bind their arms again."

It was then that Drummond went berserk. With one glorious upper-cut he broke the jaw of the man behind him and the fight began. Once, twice, and yet again he threw them off him as they waded in, his fists smashing into every face lie could see. The table overturned: two chairs were splintered to matchwood. And it was not until one man got him by the ankles that like a falling oak he finally crashed to the ground, with ten of them on top of him. He felt his arms lashed behind his back as he lay there panting. He heard, as balm to his soul, the groans and curses of the men he had hit. Then came a boot in his ribs, and he was hauled to his feet...

He stood there swaying drunkenly, with the blood streaming down his face. On the floor lay Peter unconscious. His guard had hit him on the base of the skull with a piece of gas-piping before he had had time to join in. And Algy, helpless with his shattered shoulder, stood against the wall watching.

"A good one, old Algy," laughed Drummond. "A good one for the last."

His eyes roved round the ring of men: paused on Stangerton's plum-coloured eye: paused on the gas expert pulling out some teeth in a corner. And once again he laughed, a great laugh that rang through the room, and rang and rang again as a challenge to the last grim Visitor he had diced with so often in the past.

"Come on, you spawn," he roared. "Or are you still afraid?"

"Lay him out, Pete," snarled Stangerton, to the wielder of the gas-piping. "Lay the devil out and sling 'em both over the cliff."

Three men sprang on Drummond and held him, and he grinned at Algy.

"So long, old man, so long."

He braced himself for the blow; then gradually he relaxed. For a sudden silence had fallen on the room; the grip of the men who held him had loosened. And glancing up he saw that a man was standing at the top of the stairs – a man whose face was in the shadow.

"What an appalling noise," came a quiet voice, and Algy gave a start of surprise. "What on earth is happening, Mr Stangerton?"

The newcomer came down into the room; it was Menalin.

"Dear me!" he remarked staring at Algy. "If it isn't our friend Mr Longworth – the village idiot. And what may I ask are you doing here?"

"Having a look at the bridal suite in the new Madeira," drawled Algy.

"And you?" Menalin paused in front of Drummond. "Who are you?"

His eyes narrowed; he leaned forward.

"Surely I cannot be mistaken even though I have only seen you once. Remove the beard; remove the blood... It is... Well, Captain Drummond we meet at last."

"The honour," remarked Drummond, "is entirely yours."

"You know these men, sir?" Stangerton had found his voice.

"Not the one on the floor – but the other two."

"They are journalists who have been spying."

"Journalists!" Menalin smiled. "Well, it's as good a profession as any other when pushed to it."

He lit a cigarette, and stared at Drummond.

"What do you mean, sir?" cried Stangerton.

"They're no more journalists than you are," answered Menalin. "They're in the British Secret Service, and I pay this gentleman, at any rate, the compliment of saying that he's one of the very few really dangerous men I've ever met in my life."

CHAPTER 16

Challenge Accepted

An angry murmur ran round the room, and Menalin held up his hand.

"I do not think we want all these people here, Stangerton," he remarked. "The room is insufferably hot, and Captain Drummond has not improved their appearance."

With a gesture Stangerton dismissed them, keeping only those who had acted as guards.

"Lash their legs," ordered Menalin, "and then you three can go also. Remain within call. I fear, Captain Drummond, that you will have to sit on the floor, since you appear to have broken all the chairs except this one."

"But surely, sir," said Stangerton nervously, "if these men are in the Secret Service it is all the more important to dispose of them at once."

"And have every policeman in England on the spot when their bodies are washed ashore? Don't be a fool, Stangerton. The one place they must not be disposed of is here."

"But it would appear accidental," persisted the other.

"What does it signify how it appears?" snapped Menalin. "All that would matter is that they were in this locality – not that they were dead."

He sat down and lit another cigarette.

"But supposing that it is known that they came here?" cried Stangerton.

"The supposition had already occurred to me," said Menalin calmly. "And if it is correct, nothing that we can do will alter the fact. Our one aim must be to create the impression that, although they came here, they left again, having found nothing of interest. And our only method of doing that is to have their bodies found as soon as possible and as far away as possible. So will you get through to Mr Burton at once. It will probably take you a considerable time at this hour of the night, but that can't be helped. And, when you've got him, ask him to start at once, bringing his cure for asthma."

"For what?" cried Stangerton.

"Asthma. He will understand. You might add that a mutual friend has arrived from the Continent who needs it badly. And now," he continued as Stangerton left the cellar, "I feel that I should enjoy a chat with you, Captain Drummond."

Drummond looked at him thoughtfully.

"What is the programme?" he asked.

"So far as you are concerned, a perfectly painless death as soon as Burton arrives. One, moreover, which has the advantage of appearing natural. I can assure you that when he first told me that he could do it, I didn't believe him. I thought it was the figment of a novelist's imagination. But there is no doubt about it; his claim is justified. It appears that if a large injection of a drug called adrenalin is made into a vein, death occurs in about five minutes. And since the drug is destroyed very quickly by the blood, no trace remains. I was so taken by the idea that I asked a Harley Street man at dinner the other night, and he confirmed it. Apparently, so he told me, pituitrin has the same effect. But, as adrenalin is used for hay fever and asthma, and pituitrin only in childbirth, I suppose Burton, dear fellow, thought the former more suitable."

"Do you mean to tell me that Burton jabbed a needle into Jimmy Latimer without waking him?" cried Drummond.

"I fear there was a little lying on that occasion, Captain Drummond," smiled Menalin. "The barman's assistant had his orders before the boat sailed. Had Latimer not had a drink – well, there were other methods available. But since he did – it was easy."

"It was doped, you mean."

"Precisely. Enough to produce a very sound sleep. And a whiff of chloroform did the rest. But that is all *vieux jeu*. Tell me about yourself. I little thought when I arrived here yesterday that I should have the pleasure of meeting you."

In spite of himself Drummond smiled: there was no trace of sarcasm in the words.

"Under slightly different conditions, I would have said the same," he remarked.

"Conditions which no one regrets more than I do," said Menalin. "But when one enters a game of this sort, one knows the risks."

"Are you prepared to put your cards on the table?" Drummond looked at him questioningly. "I know something: I may say I know a good deal. But there are still many gaps. And since I am in your power…"

"You would like your curiosity gratified? Certainly, Captain Drummond. I will pay you the compliment of saying you deserve it. And perhaps you, too, will gratify mine over one or two points that are not quite clear to me.

"We must go back nearly two years," he began, "if we are to get the matter in its true perspective. It was then becoming evident to everyone who knew anything that the situation in Europe could not remain as it was. I am not going to bore you with a dissertation on international politics, but it was obvious that, within the next few years, matters must come to a head. Every big power was arming feverishly, with the exception of

England, who seemed fundamentally incapable of appreciating the situation. Strange, too, for she must have known…

"It was at this stage of the proceedings that I was called in and given *carte blanche*. England – or rather her Empire – was the prize, and the problem that I had to solve was the simplest method of obtaining it. There was no urgency: the time was not then ripe. But, as you can imagine, a matter of such magnitude could not be solved in a few weeks.

"To start with I dismissed at once any idea of a war *à outrance* like 1914. Not only was it a clumsy proceeding, but because that war had proved almost, if not quite, as damaging to the victors as to the vanquished. Besides, in anything of the nature of drawn-out proceedings, your country has always shown an amazing power of recovery. And so I concentrated on something in the nature of a *coup d'état*, where a smashing blow could be delivered before the war began. In fact, I still hope that we shall avert war altogether, which will be most satisfactory financially."

Menalin lit another cigarette.

"I regret I cannot offer you one?" he said, "but, from what I saw of your fighting capabilities, I fear your arms must remain bound. To continue, however: I happened to be staying with a friend of mine in Milan, when an act of sabotage took place in a factory in which he was interested. A discontented workman had managed to get hold of some explosive, and with it had wrecked a large and costly piece of machinery. And though there was nothing novel in that, it gave me the germ of an idea. For the thing that struck me was the very small amount of explosive that was required to do almost irreparable damage, *if it was applied at the right spot in the machine.*

"As I say – there was the germ: from it grew my present scheme, which you have by now, doubtless, grasped in its main outline. If so much damage could be done in one factory, what would be the result if it occurred simultaneously all over the country?

"There were, of course, difficulties – serious difficulties. The first was to devise some method by which explosive could be delivered to a large number of different places in safety. The second was to get it introduced into the factories without it being spotted. The third was to ensure that it would be fired successfully. And it was at once obvious that something in the nature of a time bomb was the only solution.

"It was the second of these points that decided us in our choice. Any form of tin would have been good enough for one and three, but, in order to comply with two, we decided to use a tin that apparently contained food. No one would then say anything to a man taking it in for his dinner. In addition it gave us a standard size, a point of value which you have also, doubtless, appreciated. We could now decentralise our work. By the way, do you like Burton?"

"I do not," said Drummond grimly.

"No more do I. But he has been very useful to me. I met him first some years ago, and he is efficient. He will do anything for money, and in addition, for some reason, he dislikes this country intensely. And so I installed him in England to do the preliminary spadework at this end. I must say I have no fault to find with the way he has done it.

"It was he who first hit on Maier – the Swiss. Incidentally, was it you that night, Captain Drummond?

"It was," said Drummond.

"Dear me! It seems to me that you must know much more than is good for you."

"I admit," remarked Drummond calmly, "that up to date you have told me very little that I hadn't guessed. Why did your men kill Maier?"

"He was foolish enough to try blackmail."

"I thought it was something like that. However, please go on."

"Or perhaps you would like to continue for me?"

"If you prefer it," said Drummond calmly. "The machine made by Maier was some form of time fuse which fits into the top of a Petworth fruit tin. These tins, having been emptied of fruit, are filled with explosive and resealed in that island. In due course they will be despatched all over the country, and at a previously arranged time they will be exploded in different works."

"Capital," cried Menalin. "Capital. And perfectly correct. One refinement, however, I would like to point out to you, which was Maier's pride and joy. According to the distance which the opener travels round the tin depends the time it takes for the bomb to explode."

"And what of those tins that are not fitted for a fuse?"

"You note everything. In many cases more explosive – ammonal incidentally – than can be contained in one tin, is necessary. So there are some tins full of plain explosive. One of these lashed to a fused tin increases the charge."

"A pretty plot," said Drummond slowly. "And you really believe that that will bring this country to her knees?"

"Good God! No!" laughed Menalin. "That is only half the entertainment. The other half I made myself personally responsible for. And upon that side of the scheme I doubt if you are quite so well informed. No mention of it was contained in the papers that blew into Major Latimer's possession. And that is another thing I have often wondered. How much did he tell that woman, Madame Pélain."

Drummond smiled.

"We will leave the ladies' names out of it, Mr Menalin, if you don't mind."

"As you will. Though I can assure you no harm will come to her. I know he got the map of the bomb distribution, and one sheet of the general instructions. To refer, however, to the second half of the programme.

"You, of course, fought in the last war, when doubtless you sampled from time to time the unpleasant effects of gas. Starting in its rudimentary method with chlorine, various products such as phosgene, mustard gas or yperite and others were involved. But the war came to an end before some of the more advanced compounds were used. And it was to them that I naturally turned in my researches.

"There was one invented by an American chemist, to which was given the name of Lewisite. It is a pale yellow liquid, which smells faintly of geraniums, and is made, if it interests you, from acetylene, arsenious oxide, and sulphur chloride. It is extremely poisonous and, under good conditions, sixteen hundredweight of the stuff would be sufficient to give a blanket of lethal gas twenty feet high, over an area of one square mile. Or to take another calculation, a hundred bombers, each carrying five thousand pounds of Lewisite could poison an area of three hundred square miles. No wonder it is generally known as 'The Dew of Death'.

"Starting with this as a foundation Freystadt, whom you have seen, tells me that he has evolved a formula which is fifty per cent more powerful. But, even if he is optimistic, the figures I have given you should be good enough for my purpose – which is the simultaneous knock-out of certain strategical spots, of which, naturally, London is the first. The liquid will be dropped in hundreds of thin containers which will burst on hitting the ground. Then the gas is given off, and, since it is heavier than air, there is no escape in the streets of a city. And, if a few machines are hit, it does not matter in the slightest. The gas will be disseminated just the same when the plane hits the ground. Even in an open district, such as Aldershot, the effect should be considerable, though not so deadly as in a confined space."

Drummond was gazing at him speechlessly, and Menalin smiled.

"You may think," he continued, "that I am trying to harrow your imagination; possibly that I am exaggerating. My dear sir – why should I? In a few hours you will be dead, so what could be my object?"

"But what *is* your object in such a devilish scheme?" shouted Drummond.

"The finish of England as a world power," said Menalin, and though he spoke calmly his eyes were gleaming. "For centuries you have taken what you want, and done what you want; for centuries you have ridden roughshod over anyone who crossed your path. And now you have been so amazingly foolish as to cut down your fighting forces, when the countries who loathe and detest you have increased theirs. True you are thinking of increasing them again; but, my friend, it is too late. And I can imagine nothing more dreadful and humiliating to an erstwhile great power than the position you have recently found yourselves in. Egged on by wild theorists, both lay and clerical, your government has brandished a stick which, when its bluff was called, turned out to be a paper wand. And the utterly incomprehensible thing, to me, is that you must have known what the result was going to be before you started."

"Let's cut that out," said Drummond harshly. "Who are flying these planes?"

* "The...of course."

"And are they doing this bomb business also?" continued Drummond.

"Not entirely. One might almost say that that is cosmopolitan, though many of your own countrymen are involved in it. You must surely be aware, Captain Drummond, of the immense number of people who in the old days were called Anarchists, and now disguise themselves as Communists or

---

* Author's Note – In view of the tension that still exists in the European situation today, it has been considered advisable to suppress Menalin's reply. But it should not be difficult for the reader to fill the gap.

Workers of the World. But a rose by any other name… And when it comes down to brass tacks the main plank of their creed is destruction of the capitalist. You'll find a cell of them in every big works, and all we have done is to harness their activities to our own ends.

"Naturally," he went on, "great care has been necessary in dealing with them. Even now the vast majority of them will only receive their orders at the last moment when they are actually issued with the tins. So that, if mistakes have been made, and some of them communicate with the police, it will be too late for the authorities to do anything."

Drummond sat staring at him dully, and it was Algy who suddenly spoke.

"What do you get out of it, you bloody swine?" he said.

Menalin swung round and stared at him.

"I'd quite forgotten the village idiot," he remarked. "Though I must really congratulate you on the way you played the role. Tell me – how did you hear of the island of Varda?"

"It gave you a bit of a jolt didn't it, hog hound? Why – everybody knows of it, you poor fish."

Drummond gave him a quick glance; Algy was no fool and it was a possible line to take up.

"That," said Menalin calmly, "is a lie. But evidently somebody does."

"And so," continued Algy, "it has really been most entertaining listening to your ridiculous scheme. We realise that you can kill us with some ease, but I don't think murder will make it any better for you when you're caught."

"Please don't relapse to the idiot level, Mr Longworth," begged Menalin. "It hurts me when you do. Can you really imagine that we have not guarded against the possibility of the island being discovered?"

He lit another cigarette, and Drummond made an urgent sign to Algy to signal him out of action. The man's overweening conceit might make him speak.

"Every good general," continued Menalin, "has a line of retreat. And this old house with its marvellous facilities for our purpose, was not quite safe enough as it stood. There is, of course, nothing incriminating in this house at all; everything is in the island. But it was obvious that we might come under suspicion, in which case we had to allow for the possibility of the police doing what you gentlemen have done tonight. And so, to obviate that risk, we mined the part of the tunnel that goes under the sea. Fire that mine – and it is fired electrically from here – and a seal of water, eighty yards long, forms between the island and the mainland…"

"Jolly for the birds on the island," drawled Drummond. "And for all the pretty fruit tins which would seem to lose some of their efficacy."

"I said a line of retreat, Captain Drummond. There is another exit from the island on the side looking out to sea. Impracticable, it is true, when it is rough, but feasible when calm. It would be a nuisance to have to use it, as it entails boats and a ship, instead of transport by lorry. But it is there just in case of necessity."

The door flung open and Stangerton returned.

"It's taken me all this time to get through," he cried. "However – it's all right. Mr Burton is starting at once."

Menalin glanced at his watch.

"So he should be here about nine tomorrow – or rather this morning. Well," he continued, getting up and stretching himself. "I think I shall retire to bed again. I have enjoyed our chat immensely, Captain Drummond, and I shall doubtless see you once again. You had better leave a couple of armed men on guard, Stangerton. I have a wholesome respect for these young men."

He yawned, and went up the steps.

"Good night to you all: good night."

The door closed behind him and Stangerton went to the entrance of the tunnel.

"Come in here," he called out, and the men who had lashed them up in the first instance entered. "I leave them in your charge," he continued. "And don't let there be any error."

"Trust us," said the man with the broken jaw, kicking Drummond in the ribs. "There ain't going to be no perishing error."

Stangerton followed Menalin, and silence fell on the room. At the table – their guns in front of them – sat the three guards smoking. Peter still sprawled unconscious on the floor: Drummond and Algy, arms and legs lashed, leaned uncomfortably against the wall. Once in a while came an involuntary grunt of pain from Algy, for his arm was hurting abominably: otherwise there was silence.

Nine o'clock in the morning: could nothing be done before that? Ceaselessly the problem went round and round in Drummond's brain. He had tried the lashing behind his back, and given it up. An expert in the art himself, he recognised another expert's handiwork. And even if he did get his arms loose, what was the good? His feet would still be lashed, and he couldn't undo them unseen.

Nine o'clock! Ginger Lawson would not begin to be uneasy until the whole day had gone by without receiving a wire. Under no circumstances could he be there until the following day. And that would be twenty-four hours too late. By that time they would be dead and their bodies dumped two hundred miles away. If there was only some way of getting the information through. Even a clue…

God! What a scheme! Out-Vernes Jules Verne. And Jimmy Latimer had known nothing about the gas! Moreover – and there lay the appalling side of it – the thing was practicable. A few bombs might go wrong: a few aeroplanes might crash – what did it matter? There would be a trail of death and destruction over England beside which the devastated areas of France in the last war would have appeared as smiling fields. And suddenly he gave a short laugh...

"Glad you find it funny," sneered one of the men at the table.

"Frightfully," said Drummond.

He had just visualised the scream of merriment with which the whole story would be greeted at the Golden Boot... Or in his club...

He could hear the remarks.

"My dear fellah – fancy resurrecting that old fable. Why, the damn' thing came out of the ark with Noah."

And yet it was practicable: the more he turned the scheme over in his mind the more did he become convinced of that fact. Even if the results were not all that Menalin expected, the material damage inflicted would be enormous, apart altogether from the ghastly loss of life. Even if they were able to fight on, and the blow was not an absolute knock-out, the dice would be hideously loaded against them.

At length he fell into an uneasy doze. He was utterly exhausted: not even his magnificent constitution could last for ever. The fight on top of the doings of the last few days had temporarily finished him. And when he opened his eyes again a dull grey light was filtering through a grimy, cobwebbed window high up in the wall. Day had dawned, and with it full recollection came flooding back.

The three men still sat at the table: the electric bulbs still shone in the smoke-laden air. And in the distance the thump-thump of the machine proclaimed that work on the island had started again.

He looked across at Algy, who was muttering deliriously to himself: he looked at Peter who still lay unconscious on the floor. And for those two things he gave thanks. They, at any rate, would be spared the hours of waiting for the inevitable end.

Footsteps sounded on the floor above: the house was awake. And he wondered apathetically what the time was. How long was there to go? How long before Burton arrived?

Like most people he had often wondered what were the feelings of a man in the condemned cell when he woke on that last fateful morning. And now he was in the same position himself. Fear? No, he was not afraid. His principal emotion was one of rage at his helplessness. If only he could get free, even for one half-minute… And in a fit of almost childish fury he strained at the rope round his arms; strained till the veins stood out on his forehead…

Suddenly the door opened and Stangerton came down the steps.

"All right?" he asked. "Given no trouble?"

"None at all," said the leader of the guard. "The guy with the wounded arm has gone a bit queer, and the big feller has been asleep."

"Is the other one dead?"

"No. He's breathing. But he hasn't moved since I hit him."

"Well – it's over now. Mr Burton has arrived sooner than I thought he would. Are you ready, Captain Drummond?"

And just for the fraction of a second Hugh Drummond's mouth went dry.

"Delightful of you to ask me," he said after a short pause. "I take it that it doesn't much matter whether I am or not."

"I'm sorry that it is necessary," remarked Stangerton quietly. "Unlash his legs."

So they were going to move him, and for an instant wild hope surged up in his breast. Anyway, it was better than being killed like a trussed pig.

He got stiffly to his feet, and stood swaying slightly. "Up the stairs, please," said Stangerton. "Two of you come with him."

He found himself in the hall. At the foot of the stairs Burton was talking earnestly to Menalin, and Stangerton joined them.

The matter under discussion was evidently important: the words "urgent" and "vital" caught his ear, as he glanced idly round.

He felt a curious sense of detachment – almost of unreality – now that the end had come. On a table by an open window lay a large hypodermic syringe: beside it stood a blue medicine bottle. And even as he stared at them curiously, it happened. Like lightning a hand shot in from outside holding a similar bottle, which it substituted for the first.

Drummond felt his mouth opening: the thing had been so quick that he could hardly believe his eyes. Who did the hand belong to? The men guarding him had seen nothing: the other three were far too engrossed in their conversation to have noticed. Who did the hand belong to? What did it mean? And the wild hope he had felt in the cellar below came surging back again.

"We must get off at once." He heard Burton's voice from across the hall. "Will you tell Dorina? I'll get this done, and then we'll have our inspection. Now Captain Drummond, I'm sorry matters should have come to this, but I understand Mr Menalin has explained the situation to you."

He picked up the bottle and the syringe.

"I can assure you of one thing: it is perfectly painless. You will just fall asleep. Unlash his wrists and roll up that sleeve."

His mind a seething medley of conflicting thoughts, Drummond felt the prick of a needle in his arm. And then his brain grew ice-cold. He must act – act for his hope of life.

"You will just fall asleep."

Burton's words rang in his ears: so be it – he would.

"Lay him on the floor," came Burton's order, and the two guards put him down.

Act – act for his life. And for more than his life: for the possibility of defeating them after all. So he stared at Burton with a sneer on his face, then let his eyes close, only to force them open again with a great effort. Closed again: opened. And then at last they did not open…

"Good," said Burton quietly. "Now the other two."

"How long before he's dead?" asked Stangerton.

"It varies. He's a very powerful man, so that in his case it may be ten minutes. But he'll never wake again. Have you told Dorina?"

"Yes." It was Menalin speaking. "She'll be ready in half an hour. And she doesn't want to come to the island."

"Half an hour will just give us comfortable time," said Burton.

Came the sound of footsteps descending into the cellar, and still Drummond lay motionless, eyes closed, breathing deeply. Of ill effects he felt no trace; whatever it was that was in the second bottle was harmless.

And now there began a period of tension which well-nigh drove him crazy. For there had dawned on him a scheme so utterly gorgeous in its simplicity that he could scarcely lie still in his excitement. If only he could do it…

From the cellar came the sound of voices, but he did not know if they were all down there, or whether someone had been left on guard. He dared not open his eyes, though the temptation to do so was almost overwhelming. He must wait…wait…

Suddenly he felt that someone was bending over him, and a voice whispered "Drummond." He looked up; it was Talbot.

"Got a gun?" he whispered and Talbot shook his head. "Then hide yourself and stand by to help."

He closed his eyes and listened. No time now to wonder how Talbot had got there; no time for anything but his plan…

The minutes dragged on leaden feet; a clock nearby ticked maddeningly. And then came a sentence from the cellar.

"The damned dope doesn't seem to have had any effect on this crazy guy. Go and see how the big stiff is getting on."

Drummond smiled inwardly; Algy, being delirious, would naturally have shown no reaction to a harmless injection. Then he braced himself; the moment had come. Steps were ascending the stairs; one of the guards was stooping over him and he had held his breath.

"This one's a goner," the man sang out, and the words died away in a strangled scream of terror. For the goner had wrenched the gun from his hand, and had him by the throat in a grip of such ferocity that his eyes were starting from his head. And the next instant he was rushed backwards to the top of the cellar stairs.

The two men below were staring in amazement; amazement which turned to terror as they looked up.

"Shoot," howled one. "He's got a gun."

Two shots rang out, and Drummond felt them thud into the back of the man he held. And then two more, and from Drummond's side there came a quick gasp. For Talbot was standing there, and Talbot was no mean shot himself. And Talbot had seen two faces cease to be faces as a bullet crashed home in each. Drummond had shot to kill...

His grip relaxed on the man he held, who toppled over and fell like a sack to the floor below. And for one moment Drummond stood motionless, his head thrown back. Then he gave a bellow of triumph; he had done it. For the shaft was mined, and in front of him was the switch-board.

It was the third key he pressed that did it. From far off there came a dull rumble that seemed to shake the house, followed by a terrific blast of air that swept from the entrance of the tunnel. Then silence – save for Algy's delirious muttering...

"Quick," cried Drummond. "Follow me."

He raced from the house with Talbot behind him, and made for the edge of the cliff. There – the first time he had seen it from the outside – lay the island of Varda, its red cliffs rising sheer from the water. And halfway between it and the mainland there floated a mass of dirt and timber, which still eddied lazily in the oily swell.

"Trapped," said Drummond quietly. "Like rats. I wonder if they'll bolt."

But that they were never destined to see. Suddenly the whole island seemed to split open in front of them. A sheet of flame shot into the sky; rocks, chairs, bedsteads, men and portions of men were hurled upwards and outwards to finish finally in a sea that now boiled angrily as tons of stuff fell into it.

Appalled, yet fascinated they watched, until the last echo had died away; the last traces had vanished beneath the water. From out to sea came the wail of a siren – for the day was misty; above their heads ten thousand gulls screamed discordantly. And over what had once been the Island of Varda there drifted sluggishly a pink cloud...

CHAPTER 17

A Double Toast

And so it ended in failure – that monstrous and diabolical plot. What caused the ammonal in the island cavern to explode must remain for ever uncertain. One man and one man only was saved and his mind was deranged. He was picked up in the sea clinging to a baulk of wood. And sometimes in the night he would wake and shriek – "Don't shoot. For God's sake, don't shoot. You'll kill us all" – till he lay back exhausted and drenched with sweat.

And it may well be that in that dark cave, the lights extinguished, the tunnel blown in, blind panic reigned. Men fought and screamed; guns were drawn. And some chance bullet found its target in the high explosive. But as I say it will never be known.

Of the woman Dorina, no trace was ever seen again. When Drummond and Talbot returned to the house her car had gone; only the one in which Burton had come from Birchington Towers remained – the one in which Talbot had travelled, hidden in the boot.

For he, in accordance with Drummond's orders, had been on the watch when the telephone call from Stangerton came through. And he had overheard it. He had seen Burton's preparations, and had managed to get hold of a similar bottle which he filled with water. Then with a tremendous effort he had squeezed himself into the boot, and thus had he come at the crucial moment to Hooting Carn.

So that there may be some who will say that it is he to whom the principal credit should be given; that save for him Drummond would have died. Others may claim that, save for Ronald Standish's message about the Island of Varda, the scheme would have succeeded. As for me, I prefer Hugh Drummond's own opinion.

It was expressed at a dinner party he gave three weeks later – a party I was privileged to attend. Ronald had returned; Humphrey Gasdon had come over from Paris. Ginger Lawson was there, and Talbot; Algy with his arm in a sling – Peter still very shaky. And two others, who sat, one on each side of their host.

The port had gone round, and suddenly Drummond rapped on the table, and stood up.

"Gentlemen," he said quietly, "there is only one possible toast tonight, and that is a double one. To the girl who walked on the Downs, and to the girl who walked in her sleep."

SAPPER

THE BLACK GANG

Although the First World War is over, it seems that the hostilities are not, and when Captain Hugh 'Bulldog' Drummond discovers that a stint of bribery and blackmail is undermining England's democratic tradition, he forms the Black Gang, bent on tracking down the perpetrators of such plots. They set a trap to lure the criminal mastermind behind these subversive attacks to England, and all is going to plan until Bulldog Drummond accepts an invitation to tea at the Ritz with a charming American clergyman and his dowdy daughter.

BULLDOG DRUMMOND

'Demobilised officer, finding peace incredibly tedious, would welcome diversion. Legitimate, if possible; but crime, if of a comparatively humorous description, no objection. Excitement essential… Reply at once Box X10.'

Hungry for adventure following the First World War, Captain Hugh 'Bulldog' Drummond begins a career as the invincible protectorate of his country. His first reply comes from a beautiful young woman, who sends him racing off to investigate what at first looks like blackmail but turns out to be far more complicated and dangerous. The rescue of a kidnapped millionaire, found with his thumbs horribly mangled, leads Drummond to the discovery of a political conspiracy of awesome scope and villainy, masterminded by the ruthless Carl Peterson.

SAPPER

Bulldog Drummond at Bay

While Hugh 'Bulldog' Drummond is staying in an old cottage for a peaceful few days duck-shooting, he is disturbed one night by the sound of men shouting, followed by a large stone that comes crashing through the window. When he goes outside to investigate, he finds a patch of blood in the road, and is questioned by two men who tell him that they are chasing a lunatic who has escaped from the nearby asylum. Drummond plays dumb, but is determined to investigate in his inimitable style when he discovers a cryptic message.

The Female of the Species

Bulldog Drummond has slain his arch-enemy, Carl Peterson, but Peterson's mistress lives on and is intent on revenge. Drummond's wife vanishes, followed by a series of vicious traps set by a malicious adversary, which lead to a hair-raising chase across England, to a sinister house and a fantastic torture-chamber modelled on Stonehenge, with its legend of human sacrifice.

SAPPER

THE FINAL COUNT

When Robin Gaunt, inventor of a terrifyingly powerful weapon of chemical warfare, goes missing, the police suspect that he has 'sold out' to the other side. But Bulldog Drummond is convinced of his innocence, and can think of only one man brutal enough to use the weapon to hold the world to ransom. Drummond receives an invitation to a sumptuous dinner-dance aboard an airship that is to mark the beginning of his final battle for triumph.

THE RETURN OF BULLDOG DRUMMOND

While staying as a guest at Merridale Hall, Captain Hugh 'Bulldog' Drummond's peaceful repose is disturbed by a frantic young man who comes dashing into the house, trembling and begging for help. When two warders arrive, asking for a man named Morris – a notorious murderer who has escaped from Dartmoor – Drummond assures them that they are chasing the wrong man. In which case, who on earth is this terrified youngster?

Made in the USA

SAPPER

Bulldog Drummond

CHALLENGE

HOUSE OF
STRATUS

This edition published in 2008 by House of Stratus, an imprint of Stratus Books Ltd., 21 Beeching Park, Kelly Bray, Cornwall, PL17 8QS, UK.

www.houseofstratus.com

A catalogue record for this book is available from the British Library and the Library of Congress.

ISBN 07551-167-4-7